Young Georgia Marsh had come to Greece in search of a job—and in search, too, of a way to forget her dead lover. Within hours, she found herself witnessing the murder of her beautiful cousin, being hijacked by Arab guerrillas, and finally arriving at the mountaintop fortress castle that was the home of the powerful multimillionaire, who hired her to teach the children of his wealthy and influential friends.

Joan Aiken, along with Daphne du Maurier, is considered to be one of the finest writers of Gothic-suspense today. Miss Aiken is the author of many best-selling novels, including such excellent Gothics as *The Silence of Herondale* and *The Fortune Hunters* which are also published by POCKET BOOKS.

A CLUSTER OF SEPARATE SPARKS
was originally published by
Doubleday & Company, Inc.

Books by Joan Aiken

A Cluster of Separate Sparks
The Fortune Hunters
The Silence of Herondale

Published by POCKET BOOKS

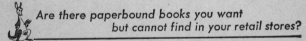

*Are there paperbound books you want
but cannot find in your retail stores?*

You can get any title in print in **POCKET BOOK** editions. Simply send retail price, local sales tax, if any, plus 25¢ to cover mailing and handling costs to:

MAIL SERVICE DEPARTMENT
POCKET BOOKS • A Division of Simon & Schuster, Inc.
1 West 39th Street • New York, New York 10018

Please send check or money order. We cannot be responsible for cash. *Catalogue sent free on request.*

Titles in this series are also available at discounts in quantity lots for industrial or sales-promotional use. For details write our Special Projects Agency: The Benjamin Company, Inc., 485 Madison Avenue, New York, N.Y. 10022.

Joan Aiken

A Cluster
of Separate
Sparks

PUBLISHED BY POCKET BOOKS NEW YORK

A CLUSTER OF SEPARATE SPARKS

Doubleday edition published March, 1972

POCKET BOOK edition published February, 1973

This POCKET BOOK edition includes every word
contained in the original, higher-priced edition. It is printed
from brand-new plates made from completely reset, clear, easy-to-read
type. POCKET BOOK editions are published by POCKET BOOKS, a division
of Simon & Schuster, Inc., 630 Fifth Avenue, New York, N.Y. 10020.
Trademarks registered in the United States and other countries.

Printed in the U.S.A.   Cover art by Jack Thurston.

For
Larry Ashmead

I

It had been a long, hot, and upsetting day, but the violent death of my cousin Sweden was unquestionably the most upsetting occurrence in the course of the twenty-four hours, and that is saying something, for, although blood is thicker than water, I always did have plenty of reservations about Sweden. From an early age I had been irked by her bossy, patronising ways, and the undoubted fact that she bore a strong resemblance to Garbo cut no ice with *me*. But when you have known a person all your life and nursed them through a fairly touch-and-go case of pneumonia, some closeness must be expected to remain, and Sweden had evidently felt this too, which was why, in answer to my low-ebb letter, she rang from Beirut to offer me a job, and why it was a terrible shock for me to see her lying in a pool of her own blood.

I'm not very good at getting things in chronological order; well, really, they didn't *happen* in chronological order. However, I'll start at the beginning of that day, and it began at 4 A.M. when the Olympic Airways plane landed at Dendros airport. If you keep this early start in mind you will be able to make allowances for the fact that I did not always behave with proper British *sang-froid* and presence of mind—after all I had had no sleep to speak of since the night before. And anyway I'm not proper British.

The island of Dendros is supposed to have one of the five most dangerous commercial airports in the world, but, as our plane circled and circled in the blazing hot summer night, while men on the strip below scurried about with flappers and blue lights—not a job I would care for—I felt quite cheerful about the possibility of a crash. At least it would presumably be a quick end, far better than the lingering dismal senility to which we are doomed by the

1

progress of science, and in many ways it would have seemed a simple solution to my own predicament. So I gazed with calm at the encircling mountains outlined by small red warning lights, and the occasional glimpses behind them of a long, sparkling curve which was the Aegean coast. Sea, mountain, or airstrip, it was all one to me, and so of course we made a perfectly safe, though bouncy landing, and presently taxied back over what felt like a series of irrigation channels to the usual airport building in the course of total demolition and reconstruction.

Leaving the air-conditioned plane resembled stepping into an oven; the warm night air smelt of dried-up grass and baked rock, and the cicadas were working overtime, like amplified, audible corkscrews. I'd come from Florence, which had seemed warm enough, but it was a mild spring day in County Durham compared with this eastern Mediterranean heat. Overhead, among stars big as ash trays, the Milky Way was a thick white belt smack across the sky, like a pedestrian crossing.

We straggled over dry, hummocky ground into the shell of the airport building, where dust lay thick and rusty iron rods stuck at perilous angles from unfinished concreting. Black-wrapped Greek mothers were greeting daughters home on vacation with tears and embraces; there were scenes of family reunion all round. I looked about vaguely for Sweden, but I didn't really expect to see her—you don't expect even your nearest and dearest at 4 A.M.—and sure enough, she wasn't there. Sweden, six-foot, blond, and beautiful, is as visible in any crowd as a banana in a coal scuttle.

After an immense delay the baggage truck was loaded up and trundled the ten yards from the plane to the airport building; after another immense delay it was unloaded again and all the baggage cunningly dumped on the far side of a four-foot-six palisade, so as to slow up and complicate the process of passengers finding their own luggage to the maximum extent. No one worried about Customs here, evidently, but by this means some taxi drivers were able to snap up those passengers who were quickest off the mark, whistle them into town, and come back for a second load while the battle over the fence was still being fought.

"Is there a bus?" I asked a man with whom I had fallen

into chat while we waited for the plane to disgorge the luggage.

"No bus at this time of night—taxis," he said.

"How much is the taxi fare to Dendros town?"

"About a hundred drachmae."

Since I had only a hundred left—a little over a pound—I was wondering whether it would be possible to spend the rest of the night at the airport and catch the first bus in the morning, when, maybe divining these calculations from my expression, he said,

"I drive a newspaper truck. Athens papers—you know? You like to wait ten minutes, you can come with me. I go a long way round, you don't mind that?"

"My goodness, no! That's wonderfully kind of you—I don't know how to thank you."

"Please! It's a pleasure."

With a load off my mind I readdressed myself to the scrum at the baggage fence, fought my way to the rail, and saw my rucksack tantalisingly out of reach under a heap of mailbags. It was handed me by a large smiling man whose toe I had just trodden on; people are kind. I rejoined my friend and helped him load stacks of *Le Monde, Die Welt,* and the Continental *Daily Mail* into his Volkswagen truck; then we were off.

"English?" he bawled above the rattle.

My Greek is too grammatical—they always guess. I said yes, rather than launch into the explanation of how I am Greek-Chinese on my father's side and Russian-French on my mother's. Anyway I was born in England.

"Over in Dendros on holiday?"

He rapidly twitched his truck off the main road and shot up a one-in-three incline into a forest; a sudden warm waft of pine resin surrounded us.

I decided that it would be simpler to say yes to that too, though it was far from the case; if Sweden's job did not materialise, and if I could not borrow some cash from her, I did not quite know what I was going to do; go to prison, probably, or become a Distressed British Object.

"I'm meeting my cousin; she has a sailboat; she's come from Beirut."

"Aha, sailing wonderful round here. You will have a fine holiday. You come from England today?"

"No, from Italy; I've had a job there, teaching."

"You are a teacher, eh? You don't look like a teacher."

People always say this, but I don't know what a teacher is supposed to look like.

"I'm not a real teacher, exactly. I tutor backward children."

"They are to be envied," he said gallantly, changing down another notch as he spun the truck round some fearful hairpin bends.

I grinned, thinking of the three untameable children of Count Angelo di Capello, who would hardly agree with him. Still, in spite of our daily and ferocious battles, we had parted with tears, and I would always have a kindly memory of them, if not of their father, whose equally unbridled disposition had finally brought the job to an end.

My benefactor began outlining a festive recreational programme for me and my cousin in Dendros.

"Two days you spend in Dendros town. Fur coats you should buy, they are very fine, also silver jewellery and knee boots. Go to Alexis Diarchos in Aristotle Street, he is my cousin, mention my name, Andreas Stavros, you will get a good bargain. Visit the folk museum, the Sultan's summer palace, walk round the ramparts. Then you must go to Aghia Maria, they have a wine festival this week. Ancient ruins—you like ruins?"

"So so."

"We have plenty. Temple of Apollo, ancient village of Chros, shrine of St. Spondiko—"

"How splendid."

"You like butterflies?"

"Butterflies?"

"There is a valley full of them—most curious, most unusual. This you must certainly visit. You can sail your boat in—there is an anchorage where a stream runs down. Caterpillars there are too—very exceptionally large ones. Such wild life can be seen nowhere else."

In fact I am not all that crazy about butterflies—or caterpillars—but at this moment he halted his truck on the edge of a precipice, said, "Excuse me—back in one moment only," and darted off with a bundle of papers to a large chalet-type building dimly to be glimpsed among pine trees. Day was not far off now—the view down below was of tree-clad hills and lower hills and foothills and olive orchards, all in varying shades of grey and paler grey.

"Now we return to the main road, you do not object that we go down a rather rough track?"

"Rougher than the one we came up?"

"That? That is a fine road—made by Mussolini. The Italians are pigs, but they make good roads."

"They certainly are pigs," I agreed with feeling. During the months I spent in Italy my bottom had been pinched so unremittingly and vigorously that I was permanently bruised, never able to sit in comfort. I *hate* Italians.

We bounded down what seemed to be a watercourse, back to the plain where the tang of pine exchanged for the warm, sweet, dusty scent of fig leaves. Traffic along the fig-bordered main coast road was not quite heavy, and all going our way—bicycle trucks loaded with tomatoes, tiny donkeys nimbling along under immense loads of grapes and melons, all bound for the market in Dendros town.

We made a couple more detours to deliver papers to other hotels, which became bigger and more stylish as we approached the city.

"Where do you stay in Dendros—at a hotel? Pension?"

"On my cousin's boat, I hope. She said she'd moor somewhere in the harbour."

Just supposing she isn't there?

My cousin Sweden is a psychiatrist. The average person tends to think that anybody in the medical and allied professions will be reliable, virtuous, teetotal, infallible, all-knowing, and godlike. If you are related to one of these characters you know that isn't so. Sweden, possibly because she has to take such pains with patients to live up to their high expectations of her, is just about as unreliable as a person can be. The hours I have put in hanging about for her on station platforms, or waiting in vain for her to telephone, if put to practical use would probably have earned me enough to pay my air fare back to England, I thought. If I hadn't been in such a hole I would certainly have been sceptical about a chancy proposition like meeting Sweden off a boat in a Greek harbour.

She simply has to be there, that's all.

We shot up over a shoulder of cliff. The Aegean beat against the coast to our left in great white-crested rollers, and beyond them, only forty or so miles away, loomed the misty and snow-capped mountains of Turkey.

Dendros town lay ahead, white and insubstantial in the pre-dawn light. Suddenly we were running through suburban streets, avenued with acacia and chinaberry trees, flanked by Italian-style villas standing in untidy gardens. We left the sea, but met it again in a moment by crossing from side to side of a narrow point. On this more sheltered side the waves were smaller. In another couple of minutes we had run out onto a wide quay, and the harbour lay ahead of us, palely reflecting the pewter-coloured sky. My friend pulled up.

"You really wish to be left here?" he said doubtfully. "I have to deliver these papers or I could help you find your cousin."

"Oh, thank you, but she may not even have arrived yet; please don't trouble."

"You like to come with me while I deliver the papers, we could go back to my house afterwards, my wife would give you coffee?"

I imagined the feelings of his wife, roused at 5 A.M. to give coffee to a strange young female. I remembered the Contessa di Capello.

"Truly, it's *very* kind of you—I don't know how to thank you—but I'll be fine here. I'll wander round the harbour—maybe her boat is over there."

A long stone-built harbour bar ran out, parallel with the quay, ending in a round castellated stone tower with a lighthouse on top. Inside this bar dozens of small craft were moored, indistinguishably close together.

"Well, if you are sure—"

"Sure. Thank you.. Thank you! *Efharistó!*"

"Parakaló." With a final wave and beaming grin he spun his truck on its way.

The sun was just rising over the harbour bar; three little windmills, which stood in an absurd, decorative row along it, had their white triangular sails suddenly dyed bright red and threw long shadows across the placid water.

I set off to look for Sweden's boat. My long, hot day was under way.

The boat is called *L'Aiglon;* I know it well, from school holidays running schnapps out of Holland, holidays ferry-

ing distraught or sulky patients across the Channel, holidays stuck in the mud off Whitstable or Southend. Since
the drastic disruption in my life three years ago, Sweden
knew that she could always call on me as a crew. I was
quite glad of the distraction. But I was quite glad, too,
when she presently removed herself and *L'Aiglon* to a job
at the eastern end of the Mediterranean—I am not really
all that fond of sailing. *L'Aiglon* is a twenty-foot clinker-
built sloop, absolutely reliable, unsinkably built with flota-
tion tanks, and quite hideously uncomfortable. Even I, not
large, found the cabin a torture chamber of the neither-sit-
stand-nor-lie variety, how Sweden and her patients en-
dured it for as much as half a day, heaven knows.

I walked slowly and carefully all round the harbour,
and out as far as the tower. No Sweden. But on my way
round I had noticed with gloom that there was a second
harbour beyond the town, which was all surrounded by
massive ramparts and ran out to a point. How like Sweden
to say, "I'll be in the harbour somewhere," without speci-
fying which harbour.

The second one, when I got to it, however, proved to be
on a much larger scale and full of cruise liners, freighters,
and oil tankers—there were no small yachts. So I went
back to the first one again.

By now it was about six. The sun was up and hot, traffic, mostly donkey and pedestrian, was flowing in and out
through the arched gateway that led to the old town, and
around a colonnaded building that faced the quay. I
strolled over to this and, looking through one of the
arches, found that it contained the market. Stalls all round
the interior were piled with fish, vegetables, fruit, meat,
earthenware pots, cage birds, and cheap clothes.

I fingered the coins in my pocket. A hundred drachmae.
A hundred drachmae wasn't going to get me back to
England, whatever happened, and in the meantime I was
ravenous; I hadn't had anything to eat since breakfast yesterday. A snack consisting of fruitcake and orange squash
or Nescafé—who *does* think up these plane collations?—
had been served on the flight shortly after we left Athens,
but I hadn't felt inclined for it.

I walked through into the market area and saw that several pavement cafés were thronged with elderly men sit-

ting over tiny cups of Turkish coffee and large glasses of water. Evidently you supplied your own bread; a stall by the gate sold sesame rolls or slender two-foot bread sticks.

Suddenly realising that I wasn't far, in fact, from total collapse, I bought a handful of bread sticks, swung my rucksack down on to the cobbles, and sank gratefully onto one of the hard little metal chairs, which was already hot from the sun.

The coffee took a long time in preparation, but when it did come it was wonderful—thick as pea soup, strong as dynamite, sweet as a liquorice allsort. I spun it out with sips of water, dunking my bread in a way that Mother would not have approved.

Mother died when I was seven. We loved each other very much—I was a late child, the long-hoped-for girl after six boys—but she was really not up to coping with me after raising my brothers and I daresay I would soon have become a great trial to her, because we were not at all alike. Anyway she was just tired out, really, and died of a thrombosis; my father didn't care for life without her, he caught a bad cold which turned to pneumonia and finished him off a year later. They were both biologists—that is, my mother was when she had time. After they died I was brought up mainly by my elder brothers, which is why I get on comfortably with men. My brothers—who have all become highly dedicated scientists of one kind or another —brought me up on a basis of rational indulgence, and this state of affairs was disrupted only by the occasional incursions of Sweden, tough, unsentimental, with a feminist chip you could knock sparks off. She was about seven years older than I, and her parents had been killed in a plane crash; occasionally she found it convenient to spend holidays with us. None of my brothers liked her much but they tolerated her because of her undoubted intelligence; in age she came somewhere in the middle of them, but she treated them all with lofty superiority.

The café proprietor stopped without being beckoned and asked me if I'd like a second cup of coffee. I thanked him, but didn't dare. Reckoning it was time to move on I paid, shouldered my rucksack again, and walked back onto the quay, looking left across the harbour entrance to see if a small red-sailed boat was coming in from the east. Not a sail in sight.

The August sun was blazing down now, burning through my cotton shirt, making my jeans cling to me uncomfortably. I longed for a bath, for a shady room, for a bed on which I could throw myself down and sleep for hours. This once, when *L'Aiglon* came in, I'd be glad to curl up on one of her narrow, uncomfortable slatted bunks.

There were two or three benches on the quayside, but they all stood in the full sun. Across, on the other side of the wide road that flanked the harbour, were big shady trees with little chairs and tables clustered under them, but these all pertained to one café or another—if I sat there it would cost me the price of another coffee. Beyond the market, under the honey-gold ramparts of the old town, stretched a kind of public garden; I walked along and explored this, hoping for a patch of grass, but it is useless hoping for grass in August in those latitudes; all I found were cobbled paths and gritty flower beds. No benches; only rows of more little metal seats in the full sun, waiting for some *Son-et-Lumière* occasion. I tried perching in the shade on the edge of a terraced flower bed, but was bitten quick as lightning in about sixteen very sensitive places by the largest ants I have ever seen outside the insect house at the zoo. I moved back to the quayside. Still no red sail but I made the trip—rather slowly now—out along the harbour bar to the round lighthouse, checking all the small craft along the way, in case *L'Aiglon* had slipped in while I was drinking my coffee. She had not.

There was a little fresh breeze out here, though, and a small patch of shade on the rocks below the lighthouse on the landward side. I climbed down very gingerly and carefully, wedged myself and rucksack into a sharp and angular cranny, leaned my head against the pack, and slipped into an uncomfortable doze.

It was punctuated by dreams, half memories. The nasty scene with the Count and his wife: "I assure you, Contessa, I haven't the least wish to go to bed with your husband; may I speak candidly? If he were to enter into a contest with a Gila monster, in winning ways, handsome looks, and general eligibility, the Gila monster would have

it over him, hands down, in every respect." I can think of
cutting retorts like this when asleep; awake I am too kind-
hearted to let rip. "Take your money and go, Miss Georgia Marsh; we wish never to see your face again." Staying
at the Pensione Walter Pater with rapidly dwindling cash,
hoping for another job, beginning to realise that the Contessa's enmity hàd prevented any chance of one. My letter
to Sweden, care of Beirut University, wondering if it had
any chance of finding her. Why not appeal to my brothers? Well, I never had, they would think it very poor-
spirited; also, two were in the Antarctic, one in Chile, one
at Berkeley, California, one in Tasmania exploring hori-
zontal vegetation, and I wasn't quite sure where the sixth
had got to. And then there had been Sweden's telephone
call—what it must have *cost:*

"Miss Georgia Marsh—hallo, George? Look, I can
offer you a job; I'd been thinking of getting in touch but
didn't know your address. You still have your gift with difficult children? Well, listen—did I ever tell you that in between my university jobs I'd become psychiatric adviser to
this place—it's a kind of special school, run by a private
philanthropist—"

"In Beirut?"

"No, no, in Dendros—where? *Dendros,* it's one of the
Dodecanese, your Greek will come in handy. Can you fly
out here right away? Someone's fallen ill, there's a vacan-
cy."

"Not sure if I've got the fare."

"Good God," she said impatiently, "you must get paid
quite well, what do you *do* with your cash?"

I might have told her. I might have said, I squandered it
on going to the funeral, in Boston, Massachusetts, last
June, of a woman I never met or wished to meet, paying
for the transatlantic trip on credit; I didn't say so.

"I'll get a banana boat or something," I said.

"Well, make it here somehow. No, if you can't raise it,
let me know and I'll wire you the money. Meet me on
Wednesday, in Dendros harbour; I've got a bit of leave
and I'm sailing across in *L'Aiglon* tomorrow or the next
day."

Instead of asking all the practical questions that would

have occurred to anyone with sense, I said, "But supposing I don't land the job?"

"Don't worry about that, you have ideal qualifications. Languages, experience, sense—it's yours already. For once," said Sweden coldly, "it won't matter that you didn't complete your university career. Besides, you're my cousin; no, there won't be the slightest difficulty."

"What is this place?"

"Plenty of time to tell you about it when we meet. We'll sail around the coast in *L'Aiglon* and I'll gen you up. See you on Wednesday."

She rang off.

The phone shrilled again, no, it was a big yacht, impatiently hooting its way into the harbour. I started awake, and found that my patch of shade had shrunk and vanished; I was being grilled like a sardine.

A knot of Greek boys had collected on the causeway above me and were discussing my nationality among themselves.

"She must be German; look at the rucksack."

"The face looks French."

"The legs and the cheekbones aren't French; English or Scandinavian, I bet you fifty drachs."

"Speak to her—go on."

"No, you!"

"You say something, Dimitri—you're the linguist. Go on, say your English word."

Teasingly, they pushed the smallest one to the front. "Miss, miss, this boy wishes to speak to you. Go on, Dimitri, speak, don't be afraid, say it!"

Alarmed at his sudden prominence Dimitri, who, like the rest of them, wore black jeans, espadrilles, and a tiedyed shirt, looked at his feet, blushed, and shuffled. At last—

"Watermelon!" he brought out bashfully. They all patted him on the back.

"Come and have a drink with us, miss? Ice cream? Coffee?"

I thought how much I could do with all those things. I thought how much I liked these boys, how much nicer they were than the Italian youths who hunt purposefully in couples with intentions quite different from this harmless ragging. But I was too tired and anxious to get involved with them; too tired for explanations and conversation. I waved my hand in a friendly but dismissing manner, shook my head, gave them an indulgent, elder-sisterly smile, and said, *"Po, po, po,"* which is the Greek equivalent of the French *"oh la la,"* or the English "tut tut." They grinned acknowledgment and moved off; when they had reached the other end of the pier I struggled to my feet. The short sleep hadn't done me any good; my head ached, my eyeballs stung as if they had been rubbed in salt. I felt hungry and sick, both. Never mind, perhaps *L'Aiglon* had slipped in while I slept, it was now eight-thirty. I made the circuit of the harbour, looking for the familiar red sail. It still wasn't there.

The big yacht, which was called *Phaedra,* had worked her way, with maximum fuss and attention, into a superior berth, and the passengers, elegantly clad and dark-glassed, were now coming ashore, on a shopping or sight-seeing excursion doubtless. One of them was a striking blonde. She wasn't Sweden.

Somebody had put up awnings over the benches on the quayside. I loitered near—they were all occupied—until one of the sitters got up and moved on. Then I pounced on the vacant place. We ought to export shade from England; little do we realise the value of the commodity we have in our midst, all unregarded. I clung to that seat like a limpet as the sun climbed overhead, and meanwhile amused myself by watching the crew on board *Phaedra,* who, as soon as the passengers had disembarked, gave up tidying their craft and lounged on deck playing backgammon.

Presently a man in a peaked cap wandered off the ship and along the quay; there was an empty spot on the bench beside me just then, and he sat down.

I had fished out a paperback copy of *Bleak House* and was trying to forget my anxiety in reading. *Bleak House* is one of my favourite books; usually it has the power to dispel all care, but today the casual charm didn't work; I found Esther Summerson an insufferable, self-centered bore. Usually her "O, poor little me; I do wonder why they all loved me so?" strikes me as funny; today I wondered uneasily if I ever strike people like that? Some critic —I think it was Mrs. Leavis—said Dickens was fully aware what he was doing when he created Esther, that her inverted self-assertiveness was a reflection of her illegitimacy, and that the whole thing, anyway, was a savage portrait of his wife; well, if his wife resembled Esther he had good reason to be savage.

"It's an interesting narrative method, isn't it?" said a voice at my elbow.

I nearly jumped out of my skin. I'd forgotten the man in the cap. I took a cautious sideways survey of him—he was smiling at me tentatively—and decided from his general air of intelligence and authority that he was some fairly high-up officer—maybe the captain. But he was distressingly thin—really like a skeleton, I thought, noticing the skinny hand resting on his white-duck-clad knee—the head poised on a scrawny neck seemed too small, out of proportion to his considerable height. His face was deeply lined, as if he'd seen trouble; one doesn't get furrows like that just from gazing ahead into the Mediterranean gale; he looked as if he'd been in a prison camp. And I guessed that the grey in his thick dark hair and astonishingly bushy eyebrows had come prematurely.

But he seemed friendly enough.

"You mean, the way it keeps swapping to and fro between first-person narrator and third?"

"It was a very advanced thing to do, surely; not all that number of people have done it since, have they?"

"I can think of some."

"Why do you suppose Dickens did it?"

"Because he couldn't sufficiently depict Esther's awfulness unless he gave a whole dollop of her stream of consciousness?" I suggested, and mentioned the Leavis theory. We began having a discussion about other unlovable characters in fiction, and the possibility of their faults having been unsuspected by their creators.

"Pierre Bezukov."

"Cordelia."

"Dora—Dickens is full of them."

"There seem to be more women than men."

"All those are by male writers."

"But Fanny Price is just as bad. And Dickens has plenty of sickening males too—think of the Cheerybles."

"Would you care to come and have some coffee over

there?" he said, nodding towards the café tables under the trees.

I was cagey. "Well—it's very kind of you but I'm really waiting here for my cousin—she ought to be along soon—"

But I was strongly tempted. After all the captain of a cruise ship is here today and gone tomorrow—there'd be no risk of deeper involvement.

"If she's shopping she'll be hours yet, Dendros is so full of temptations."

By now stalls loaded with tourist-bait had been erected all along in front of the public gardens. Worry beads, all shapes, sizes and materials, fake amber as big as walnuts, wood, coral, turquoise or gilt, hung thick as runner beans; there were sponges, embroidered waistcoats, silver jewelry, amazing shell-encrusted articles, leather slippers with curled toes, ikons, and Mars bars, surely deliquescing in the fierce heat, or do they manufacture special unmeltable Mars bars for export to Greece? The thought of Mars bars made me recall again how hungry I still was.

"We can watch out for your cousin from over there—what does she look like?"

On the point of saying, "Well, all right, thanks, I'd love to," I turned to my neighbour.

But he was looking past me. His expression had stiffened.

"What a nuisance," he said. "I'm very sorry, I'll have to withdraw that offer. My employer is coming. Perhaps another time?" He gave me a swift, apologetic smile, stood up—he really was unnaturally tall and thin—made a half-bow, and walked to meet a stocky grey-haired man in faded linen jeans, gaudy shirt, and dark glasses, who was coming along the quay. They conferred, and presently went on board *Phaedra;* my friend turned and gave me a final smile as he walked behind the other man up the gangplank.

Pity; I could have used that coffee.

Some more time went by.

Feeling self-conscious now, glued on my seat hour after hour, under *Phaedra*'s portholes, I decided that, financial crisis or no, an ice was a simple basic necessity. I was not only hungry, but also parched with thirst, and the Greeks, bless them, bring you big, beautiful glasses of ice-cold water with even the smallest order.

Swinging my heavy rucksack by one strap I wandered slowly across the road, slowly selected a seat at a little table in a patch of shade, and reopened *Bleak House,* hoping that the waiter would be slow in coming, so that the whole process might be strung out as long as possible.

Around me, people were finishing their *apéritifs,* their beers and ouzos and piles of opulent, glossy olives and thick slabs of sharp, white nourishing cheese, and were beginning to order lunch. There were heart-rending smells of lamb grilled on skewers, souvlakia, and all the different forms of mince that the Greeks delight in, presumably because their meat is so tough: stuffed tomatoes, stuffed vine leaves, and moussaka, which is a kind of super shepherd's pie with a cheese omelette on top. Greek food is not *haute cuisine,* but I'd gladly have sold my birthright for a dollop of moussaka right then. Doggedly I applied myself to *Bleak House;* doggedly, when the waiter finally did stop at my table, I ordered an ice ignoring the two-foot-square menu he proffered.

"Just an ice, please. And a glass of water."

He looked reproving. He pulled out a chair and sat down by me, all prepared to argue.

"Young ladies do not eat enough—how about a nice grilled steak—chicken—rosbiff?"

"Just an ice, please."

"Ice cream is not very cold today—weather too hot."

"Still, I'd like one, please.'

"You are slimming," he said mournfully. "Young ladies are all slimming. It is bad for business. And with you, not necessary—you look very nice as you are."

"Thank you. But still, just an ice!"

"Okay," he sighed, and wrote it on his pad.

I returned to *Bleak House* and its mixed narrative method. Another advantage of first-person narrative, it struck me, is that you are spared the boring necessity of describing your hero, or heroine. We never do, from first to last, learn what Esther looks like, except insofar as Mr. Cuppy greatly admires her at the start of the book, and hastily withdraws his offer of marriage after her smallpox. On the other hand there is the disadvantage of the reader's being aware that the narrator, must, presumably, survive all perils in order to finish telling the tale, which does rather detract from the suspense.

Of course you can adopt the P. C. Wren stratagem: "There was a sharp rifle report, I felt a sudden searing, burning pain, and the pen dropped from my nerveless grasp . . ."

Editor's Note: This incomplete manuscript was found lying beside the dead body of Miss Esther Summerson, who is thought to have been attacked by desert Bedouin as she sat writing her journal in her tent at the Wadi-al-Kabir oasis.

Well, you can award yourself ten points for strength of mind if you refrain from looking ahead to see if there is an Editor's Note at the end of *this* narrative.

The waiter came back with my ice and big, beautiful glass of water, all dripping with condensation.

"Reading, reading," he grieved. "English young ladies —you are English are you not? Yes, I thought so—English young ladies are always reading. Charles Dickens, Mary Stewart, *My Brother Michael*—see, I am cultured too! But is there no other thing besides reading to pass the time?"

"Plenty. But I happen to like reading."

"You stay in Dendros? You like to come to a recital of folk music and Dodecanese songs this evening? Very cultural, very nice."

"Why—that's so kind of you," I said, taken aback, "but I hope I shan't be here this evening."

"You hope? What is wrong with our town, you don't find it beautiful?"

"Oh yes, yes—very—" I looked through the trees at the honey-coloured battlements of the old town, glowing above the harbour like a fairy-tale castle, "it's just that I'm not sure of my plans. My cousin is coming to pick me up in a boat—"

Luckily at that moment someone bawled "Janni!" and my waiter was obliged to go off.

I consumed the ice very slowly, in quarter-teaspoonfuls.

It was divine. A kind of custard ice, rather solid, with bits of plain hard chocolate and candied orange peel scattered about its interior. I made it last as long as some people took over their entire lunch; nobody minded. The Greeks expect you to sit a long time over your meals. Plato's *Republic* was all written during lunch.

Presently the waiter drifted back to me again and I paid him.

"What do you do now? You are still waiting for your cousin? Better go and look at our folk museum, a cultured young lady like you would find it very nice."

Well, it would make a change from the quayside. Besides all the gaps on the benches were filled again.

"Is it a long walk to the museum?" I looked doubtfully at my cumbrous and bulging rucksack.

"You like to leave that here? I can put it in the kitchen —it will be quite safe. The boss won't mind—he's my father. Too heavy to carry that about in the hot sun."

"Oh, you are kind. Thank you so much. *Efharistó, efharistó.*"

"Please! It is nothing at all." He swung it up and carried it toward the smell of meat fried in olive oil.

Sweden always says that I am idiotically trusting. Still, there was nothing of value in that rucksack, nothing of value in my whole life really.

I walked off, following the waiter's directions, towards the gateway into the Old Town, and crossed a bridge over a dried-up moat which the thrifty citizens had put to use as a market garden—there were rows of beans, tomato plants, grapevines, thistle artichokes. Over and round the fortress walls hung and trailed and sprouted shrubby creepers with scarlet flowers, hibiscus maybe, and some that were a frightful shade of magenta, perhaps bougainvillea.

The folk museum, not far inside the town gates, was all set about with immense stone cannon balls. Medieval wars were so much more economical than present-day ones; their munitions were so durable; at the end, presumably, both sides merely collected up all the other army's missiles and started again.

I went into the Museum of National Art and Folk Culture, entry fee five drachmae. The first thing I saw was a beautiful carved wooden settle in a dark shady corner. Without looking to right or left, I made for it, swung my feet up, and shut my eyes.

That time I went off fast and deep.

There's something called Korsakoff's syndrome, Sweden told me about it one time. Inside us, did you know, tucked away underground, we carry a whole series of nicely adjusted time clocks, which enable our bodies to bring off, on occasions, all sorts of ingenious tricks. For instance, one of Sweden's patients undergoes a complete personality change from 9 P.M. to twelve midnight every night; during those three hours she's rational, cheerful and approachable, then at midnight, just like Cinderella, bang: catatonic again. Well, if you suffer from this Korsakoff's syndrome, it means that you can remember nothing of the immediate past, that your time-clock operates to shut it off within the limit of a certain definite period; or else that your memory lives all the time at one significant point in your life.

It's that way with me. Like an elastic band released from the tug, as soon as consciousness relaxes, back I snap three years, to one face, to one voice.

However . . . no use talking about it. Or anyway, I'm not going to, just now.

And I wasn't given much time in the museum, which was probably just as well; I wake swimming in tears from these trances.

A gentle hand was shaking me and a firm, though kind, voice was saying in my ear, "I am sorry, *thespinis,* but it is absolutely forbidden to sit or sleep on those seats. I am so sorry, but you must wake up."

Yes, I must. I dragged myself forward three years and sat up, yawning, feeling as if I'd been roused in the middle of a surgical operation, from under a total anaesthetic. The curator was looking at me sympathetically, and so was a tall young character in red espadrilles, white jeans, a pink shirt, dark curly hair, and a very classic cast of features; too classic to be Greek. I thought he might perhaps be an Arab.

"I am sorry but you may not sleep in here," the custodian repeated, firmly.

I nodded, yawning some more, and moved stiffly towards the entrance. The pink-shirted lad followed me out.

"You wish to sleep some more?" he said sympathetically.

"I'll be awake in a minute, thanks; I came over on a night flight, that's all——"

"I and my friends sleep on the beach—we have sleeping bags. You could come there for sleep. We are leaving tonight, we will not disturb you."

"That's so kind of you, but I'm supposed to be meeting my cousin—"

How many times had I said that in the course of the day.

"This evening we give a party because we are leaving," he went on persuasively. "First you have a sleep, then you come to our party? It will be very nice!"

"Really it's sweet of you, but I can't. I have to get back to the harbour."

"Then I come with you. It is on my way to the beach."

I had no wish to be uncivil, and he seemed quite pleasant, so we walked along together, through the cobbled streets, lined with yet more tourist shops, across the moat bridge, and out onto the harbour front, discussing the transmigration of souls, because the street happened to be called Pythagoras Street and it seemed a handy, impersonal topic. My companion thought it a highly plausible theory.

"How many people can you not recall who resemble animals? It is because they were so in a previous life."

"I don't agree. We look like animals because we are animals, at one remove of evolution. And anyway the soul, the ego, whatever you like to call it, is a highly individual thing, formed by circumstances—how could it be separate, like a fish in a tank or the yolk of an egg; how could it be posted on and reappear again and again? We aren't gramophone records."

Of course I'd *like* to believe that it could.

"The reborn soul naturally will continue to change in new circumstances. You are a sceptic. But I shall soon convince you," he began optimistically, but I interrupted him. The harbour now lay extended before us.

"I'm terribly sorry—it's all very interesting and I'd love to argue about it some more, but I'll have to leave you now. I can see the sail of my cousin's boat coming in over there."

Old familiar, patched red sail—never would I have thought I'd be so pleased to see it.

II

"Good-bye!" I said lightheartedly to the pink-shirted boy. "Next time we meet you can have another try at convincing me." And I cut away to the right, in order to circle round onto the harbour bar.

It took longer than I had expected, first because of the swift and constant flow of traffic which made crossing the wide quayside highway a ten-minute operation; then I found that, in preparation for some waterside performance that evening—maybe the waiter's folk-song recital—a large section of harbour front had been roped off and covered with rows of yet more little metal chairs. By the time I had skirted them and gained the harbour bar the red sail had vanished. Then I came to a stop, remembering that I hadn't collected my rucksack from the café. But Sweden, presumably, would not want to set sail again immediately; she would very likely be wanting a meal; we could go back to the café and pick up the rucksack at the same time.

Once more I plodded out along the causeway. Third time lucky. *L'Aiglon* was tied up three boats back from the tower at the far end. I caught hold of the mooring rope, hauled her within reach, stepped aboard, and called:

"Ahoy, Sweden? It's me, George."

No answer. No Sweden to be seen. I jumped down into the well, noticing a child's toy, a red-and-blue-painted camel, on the seat. Sweden must have had passengers, then.

"Sweden?"

But it became clear that she was not on board. I looked into the cabin—it was in the usual state of chaos. Obsessively tidy in her working life, Sweden completely changed her ways when afloat and lived in a state of uncaring squalor that shook even me, and I am fairly untidy myself. The bunks were piled with gear, clothes, charts, and bedding;

dirty plates and cooking utensils and a child's chamber pot occupied most of the scanty floor space; on the table were dozens of sheets of drawing paper covered with a child's scribbles, and also some of Sweden's beautiful, effortless sketches: a ship, a gull, a dolphin, an old man smoking a pipe on a quayside. A portfolio with more drawings lay open on the bunk. Evidently she had fetched out some old work, for purposes of entertainment perhaps: I recognised sketches of London, Tower Bridge, St. Paul's seen from the river, the British Museum, a street of Georgian houses. Suddenly shaken by homesickness, seeing that one, I flipped on through the heap, though I was yawning again, wondering how long Sweden would be gone, whether it would be worth shifting all the things off the other bunk and trying to put in a quick kip before she returned. I imagined she hadn't intended to go far, for she'd left a lamp burning. Outside, dusk was beginning to creep over the harbour; inside, the cabin was drowsy with the smell of warm paraffin. Inert from weariness and relief I went on turning over the drawings, and came to a handful of the playing-card-sized portrait heads that Sweden had had a fancy for doing a few years back: patients, colleagues, friends. One of myself, with long hair as I'd had it three years ago caught my eye; hastily sliding it into the middle of the pile I uncovered another face which dealt me such a blow that I let out a whim of pure pain; it is curious how sometimes one's body can function faster than one's intelligence.

It was a face I knew I'd never see again.

My Darling: By the time you read this letter . . .

But, as I said, I don't intend to go into all that now. This isn't the time or the place for it.

Coming across the sketch like that had a queer effect on me, though. I was really dazed with shock. I looked about for somewhere to sit; there was nowhere. So I squeezed on into the little forward cabin which accommodated the cooker; here there was a child-sized bunk on which oilskins were piled; I pushed some of them onto the floor and sat down, still holding the sketch, still looking at it.

But Sweden never even met Martin.

She could have, though, no reason why not. They both lived in London during the same period, they both had connections with London University. They could have met. But how could Sweden know him and I not be aware of it?

Sheer pain beyond a certain point is soporific; without cognition, I fell into a kind of rigid doze, leaning back against the bulkhead, the little square or card still clenched in my right hand.

If I dreamed, I don't remember it.

When I woke it was because the boat was rocking—someone had jumped on deck. My third short spell of interrupted sleep had left me stupid and slowed-up; it took me a moment to work out where I was, and when and who.

During that moment several things happened which my mind automatically took in and presented to me later in flashback; at the time the sounds were meaningless.

Sweden's voice said: "Here it is. No need for you to come on board."

A man's voice said, "Just the same I want to, for a moment."

L'Aiglon rocked again. Sweden's voice—nearer now, in the main cabin doorway—said irritably, "I'm afraid I've no drink on board and anyway I'm bushed. *Do* go—I want to start clearing up—George may be here any minute."

"Yes, okay, this won't take any time."

"What won't take any time?" she said impatiently. Then I heard her give a faint gulp, as if she had been winded, there was a kind of slither, which ended in a thump, and the boat lurched again, violently, throwing me to my feet. I had a glimpse through into the main cabin and saw Sweden on her back, head down, in a most extraordinary position, jammed between the table and the untidy bunk. Something—not for another moment did I see that it was the handle of a knife—stuck out from the white T shirt she wore, and a dark jagged line, blood I realised later, divided her face from chin to forehead like the mask of comedy and tragedy.

Beyond Sweden's body I could see a pair of legs in pale or white trousers; the upper part of the man was concealed from me by the upper half of the divided cabin door, which must have swung to when the boat rocked.

Now a pair of hands came into sight and began lifting

and thrusting Sweden so as to shove her farther into the cabin.

He's killed her, I said to myself stupidly. She's dead.

It struck me in a vague way that, almost immediately, in the act of moving Sweden's body along the cabin floor, he would be bound to see me. In the same way as when I found the sketch of Martin, my body had acted before my mind reacted to the significance of this. I found myself climbing, quietly and economically as in a dream sequence, up the ladder and out through the little forward hatchway. Here, so long as I crouched low, the cabin roof and a fold of dangling jib sail screened me from the view of the person in the well. Mechanically I slid the sketch into my plastic shoulder bag and zipped it up, so as to leave my hands free. Obviously it was not advisable to go along to the stern and get ashore that way; but the next yacht was moored only six feet or so away; I might be able to jump across.

A boat hook lay among the tangle of stuff by the mast. I slipped it gently from under and fished for the shrouds of the next-door boat, which lay tidy and silent and protected by canvas covers; obviously unoccupied at present.

The hook caught. Inch by inch, slowly and carefully, I eased the two boats together.

L'Aiglon's cabin door creaked, and she rocked again.

Hastily I gave a last tug with the hook, let go of it, and stepped across the narrowing gap.

My foot slipped and I fell into the harbour water with a loud splash. I thought I heard a shout from behind me— then I was under water, out of my depth, and going down. I kicked out, swam a few strokes, and banged my head on the hull of the next boat. In a way that was a help—still under water and with my lungs feeling like a scooped-out melon, I felt my way round to the far side of the boat and then came up, out of sight, I hoped, for a gulp of air.

No sound, now, from *L'Aiglon*. Perhaps Sweden's murderer had realised that it was stupid to draw attention to his presence. Perhaps he had decided that my splash was just a large fish rising—were there fish in Dendros harbour?

Or perhaps he was sneaking along the quay, just waiting

for me to surface so that he could deal with me as he had dealt with Sweden.

He can't have had more than one knife though, unless he reckons to stab two or three girls every afternoon. He'll have to find some other weapon to use on me, unless he goes back and pulls it out of her. But of course in this line of shipping there must be plenty of things that would do as well—mauls, gaffs, pump handles, marlinspikes . . . What is a marlinspike, anyway? Something you spike marlin with. Marlin are a kind of large fish. No, they are a kind of small hawk.

While speeding through these not very relevant lucubrations, I found time to push the strap of my bag over my head, so as to free my arm, and was quietly dogpaddling round the next boat; and the next, and the next, until I had put a hundred yards or so between myself and *L'Aiglon*. Still no sound from the quay. I swam on. And my harassed mind now presented me with two propositions, bracketed together like an equation.

Something has caught up with Sweden at last, and
What the hell am *I* going to do?

It was queer; up to then I had never consciously thought, or let myself think, that Sweden's way of life was at all out of the ordinary. Perhaps because I didn't entirely like her, I had inhibited myself from criticising her. She was just Sweden, offhand, arrogant, beautiful, given to going on odd trips with odd patients, maintaining a reserve bordering on secretiveness about her private affairs. If I didn't entirely trust her, that was just due to natural jealousy, I had always told myself.

Now all these subterranean opinions came leaping up to the surface, like worms when you dig, and I realised that I had been expecting this catastrophe for a long time.

But what was *I* going to do?

Having swum within sight of some steps on the harbour wall I reckoned that anyway it was time to go ashore. Although the water was warm, reckoned by English standards, I was not. I slipped between a dinghy and a fishing boat, hauled myself onto the bottom step, and knelt there, listening, dripping, shivering, squeezing my trouser legs. Lucky I had left my rucksack with the waiter, I thought; loaded with books, it would have sunk me like a flatiron round a kitten's neck. I took off my shirt and squeezed it; put it back on.

Now came the delicate part. The steps, unfortunately, were under a streetlamp: If Sweden's murderer was watching, back there along the causeway, he was going to be able to see me coming up, not exactly like Venus from the waves. Suppose he carried a gun as well as a knife, or was a medium-fast runner, my chances were not good, because that swim, after a long hot day's waiting, had left me feeling about as athletic as a spoonful of melting consommé.

I had a bit of luck, however. Along the quay from the shore end wandered a group of boys and girls, talking, laughing, and singing. Some of them carried guitars and plunked on them. Others, like me, had been swimming in their jeans. Unobtrusively, as they passed, I nipped up, through the middle of the group, and sped away in the opposite direction, thinking with satisfaction that their arrival would confuse my trail nicely.

I skirted the quay as fast as I could, crossed the harbour road, cut through the market, empty now, stalls tidied and closed for the night, and arrived at a largish sloping square, with a big tree in the middle, where five streets converged.

There were plenty of people about here; it seemed a safe place to pause. Cafés were crowded; even a few shops, furriers and jewellers, were still open. A traffic cop was ignoring a clump of frustrated pedestrians at a crossing while he fiddled with his string of worry beads and chatted to an elderly man in glasses. I approached the cop, but the impatient glance he gave me—and he did not look an intelligent man—dispelled any intention I'd entertained of telling him about Sweden. Instead, I asked where the police station was.

"I am going there myself," said the spectacled man. "I will show you. No trouble at all; a pleasure. It is not far."

As he led me down a diagonal street, going back in the direction of the harbour he said, giving me a doubtful, cautiously assessing glance:

"You are an English young lady? I hope you have nothing to complain of in our town? I hope you have not been robbed?"

"No—no, I haven't, thank you. I mean—it's nothing like that. But something very bad—my cousin has been hurt, killed perhaps, on her boat in the harbour—"

I could not be certain whether he understood me. He gave me another anxious look, muttered a stronger version of "Po po po," under his breath, stuck a hand beneath my arm, and led me at a rattling pace out into another wide, open square, with formal beds of shrubs and Greek flags stuck about, enclosed by a number of plainly municipal buildings. Into one of these, with an imposing flight of steps approaching its porticoed entrance from either side, he led me, across a large tiled vestibule, up some stairs, and into a tiny room with a table, two chairs, a typewriter, and a map of the Aegean Sea.

"Now," he said, "here you wait and rest while I find my friend Captain Plastiras. He is a very sympathetic man; he will look after you."

The door closed behind him but opened again almost at once and he reappeared with a cup of Turkish coffee. "Drink this while you wait; it will do you good."

"Oh, thank you so much; how sweet of you—"

He was gone again; his kind, furrowed face registering anxiety and goodwill.

An awful lot of time then went by. Apparently my friend was having trouble finding *his* friend—perhaps Captain Plastiras had not yet come on duty, or was interrogating someone, or off somewhere detecting; or on the telephone . . .

I drank the coffee. First feelings of thankfulness at my good fortune melted into impatience, despair, resignation, impatience again. Meanwhile my clothes dried off, more or less, in the hot night air. I unzipped my thick plastic shoulder bag, discovered with relief that the harbour water had not penetrated inside it, found a comb and unsnarled my hair, put on a bit of eye shadow, stood up, sat down again.

Then it occurred to me that Sweden's body might already have been found; perhaps the police were out there now, making measurements, taking photographs, or whatever they did; probably that was why no one had time to spare for me. But surely in that case I ought to be out there, too, telling them what I knew; I stood up again.

At that moment Captain Plastiras came in. He was a large, smiling man, looked like a very nice gnome, and had the trimmest uniform and the highest polish on his bald head that I have ever seen. Two big brown eyes like horse chestnuts gave me a careful, kindly scrutiny. I took an instant liking to him.

"You are the young English lady who has had a fright, my friend Dr. Stavrakis tells me. Now, you sit down again and tell us all about it, eh?"

His friend the paternal Dr. Stavrakis followed him in and stood solicitously by, both of them scrutinising me with concern and sympathy.

I was impressed again by my luck. One hears such tales of tough, thin-lipped foreign police and their sinister habits of third degree, browbeating, bureaucracy, and general xenophobia; nothing could be more of a contrast to the treatment I was getting. Still, there seemed no way to tell my tale but flatly and baldly.

"I saw somebody murdered."

The change in the room's atmosphere was almost comic. They had been prepared, I imagined, to condole, soothe, listening commiseratingly to a tale of assault, to exclaim and lament and assure me that it wouldn't happen again.

Now their eyes met with a click like magnet and bread knife joining.

"Indeed? That is very terrible," said Captain Plastiras. "Where did this occur?"

"Down at the harbour. In a boat—*L'Aiglon*—my cousin's boat."

"And the person you say you saw murdered was—?"

"My cousin."

"Your cousin. A man or a lady?"

"A lady—girl—woman. A bit older than me. Her name's Sweden—Dr. Sweden Hannfelder."

"I see." He wasn't writing anything down, though I felt he ought to be; this unnerved me.

"And who committed this murder?"

"I don't know. It was a man. I didn't see his face. He stuck a knife in her."

Again I felt their eyes meet and lock over my head.

"He stuck a knife in her. And this happened on a boat in the harbour. Where were you then?"

"I was on the boat too."

"But were not attacked by this man?"

"I—I managed to get away. Jumped overboard." *Fell* sounded too ignominious.

"She was wet when I first encountered her," Dr. Stavrakis murmured aside to the captain.

"Your name is Miss—?"

"Georgia Marsh." I proffered my passport, thanking heaven for the impermeability of my handbag. Plastiras went through it carefully as if looking for bloodstains.

"You arrive in Dendros today? You are staying where?"

"Nowhere. I mean—I had planned to stay on my cousin's boat."

"And she arrived—?"

"Also today. From Beirut."

This time he did stick his head out of the door and gave a quick low-voiced order to someone just outside. Then he came back, sat down, and went on in his pleasant, easy, conversational tone.

"You arrived this morning by which plane?"

I told him, and, prompted by more questions, patient, unhurried, painstaking, took him through every single event of my long, hot day.

"You have had a very unpleasant time," he said. "Waiting, waiting, all the day, in the heat. English young ladies are not accustomed to our heat."

I realised then what, in spite of the kindly atmosphere, had been bothering me about this interview.

They weren't taking my story seriously.

"I'm not suffering from sunstroke, if that is what you are thinking."

"Of course not. Of course not," he said patiently. "Did you hear me suggest such a thing?"

"Look—hadn't we better go down to the harbour, so that I can show you the boat—Sweden's body?" I half stood up.

"Do not trouble yourself," he said without moving. "I have already sent my men down. You will not wish to see such an unpleasant sight twice over. Now—you say that when you jumped overboard you hit your head on the next boat?"

"Yes—but it was nothing much of a bang." I put my hand up to the spot on my forehead. There was a smallish lump. Dr. Stavrakis moved forward, said, "You excuse me?" with a kindly smile, and felt it too. He nodded at the captain.

"And you have had no food all day except for an ice cream—nothing to eat since yesterday morning?"

"I am not lightheaded!"

"Of course not, of course not. Did I imply it?"

He asked me about my job in Italy, why I had left, what I proposed doing now.

"My cousin said she knew of a job for which I would be suitable."

"And what was that?"

"Teaching in some school that she's connected with—a private school."

"Its name?"

"She didn't tell me."

"But you know where it is. In Dendros?"

"I'm afraid I don't know. If she told me over the phone —I don't think she did—I failed to take it in."

There was a knock at the door. Captain Plastiras stepped outside and conducted a short, low-voiced conversation. Then he came back and sat down, still with the same benevolent expression.

"Can you describe the boats alongside that of your cousin's?"

"Certainly I can! One was about the same size—eighteen to twenty feet—painted blue, with canvas covers over the cockpit and hatch and sails. The other was a good deal bigger, white, with two masts . . . it had some name like *Electra* or *Euphrosyne*. I didn't see anybody on board either of them."

"Yes. Now, my dear Miss Marsh, I do not wish to distress you, but I really think you have been a little hallucinated. You see, my men have been down to the harbour, they have found no *L'Aiglon* and no body—indeed the harbour master tells us that no boat of that name has registered with him today—and in between the two boats you mention there is quite a different craft, a local fishing boat called *Aghia Maria*."

"The third from the lighthouse?"

"The third from the lighthouse."

I stared at him in silence for a moment, assimilating this.

"Somebody—the murderer, I suppose—sailed off in *L'Aiglon*. Of course, that was why he didn't follow me. He just cast off and took her out to sea."

"Possibly so." But there was considerable reservation in his tone.

"What can you do—coast guards—Interpol—foreign ports?"

"You do see, Miss Marsh," he said gently, "we have only your word that this boat was here at all."

"And you yourself have admitted," Dr. Stavrakis took on, "that you have had no sleep, virtually nothing to eat for thirty-six hours. You have been sitting and walking about in the hot sun, you have been suffering from great anxiety about money and your future and your cousin's whereabouts. So here is what probably happened: You go along the quay, you see a boat with a red sail, the *Aghia Maria*—because you so much want it to be your cousin's boat you persuade yourself, weak, tired, hungry, and anxious as you are, that the boat *is* your cousin's—you start to climb on board but you slip and fall into the water; you bang your head and have this hallucination about murder and stabbing."

"You just don't want to believe me because it is simpler not to—" I began impotently.

"Of course we would like to believe you. We think you are a very nice young lady but just a little upset at present."

Upset! The sheer pressure of the exasperation I felt forced me to my feet.

"*Please* can we go down—"

To the harbour, I was going to have besought them, to look for what, if any, clues might remain, but instead of finishing my sentence I fainted, which was the very worst thing to do from the point of view of convincing them as to my general coolness and rationality.

I wasn't out for long. I could hear them tutting and po-

po-ing above me, then Dr. Stavrakis picked me up, most tenderly and solicitously, and I was given a glass of ouzo —aniseed so strong that it raises the hair on your head right up.

"Now she must have something to eat—a good dinner," said Dr. Stavrakis authoritatively.

"That will be my pleasure." Captain Plastiras shouted a command out of the door.

Evidently it was for a car, because the two men then tenderly helped me down the stairs, out through the main entrance, and a car was waiting, with a saluting chauffeur.

"I am coming too," said the doctor, as Captain Plastiras helped me in. "What will your wife say, Oreste, when she hears you have been seen dining with a pretty young lady? But if I come too, her suspicions will be set at rest."

"But what about your wife, my friend? What about *her* suspicions?" While the two men ribbed each other in this pleasant way, our car sped back towards the café district. I decided to let events take their course for the time being. I really didn't know what else to do; and at least I was going to come out of this excursion a meal to the good, and that was solid gain as far as I was concerned. By now I was so hungry that even Sweden's murder seemed a problem that must be deferred until I felt in better case to tackle it.

"Have you any especial preference for a café?" Plastiras inquired courteously.

"I don't know any—yes, I do, though; could we go to the one where I left my pack? Then I can pick it up. Besides, the waiter was very nice to me."

"You have never been in Dendros before?"

"Not really. Once, when I was about five, I just stepped ashore from a Hellenic cruise with my mother. I don't really remember it."

Dr. Stavrakis was interested in this trivial piece of family history to a degree that seemed to me out of all proportion, and continued to question me about my parents, brothers, cousin and past, while Captain Plastiras—who was plainly well known here and treated with considerable deference led me through my friend's café to a table which was expeditiously found for us, indoors this time, near the bar.

"The young lady had better have some brandy," said Dr. Stavrakis, so brandy was brought for me and I sipped at it. It was weakish and tasted powerfully of vanilla, but did have a fine warming effect. Meanwhile the two men drank ouzo. Great plates of salad were brought—olives, cheese, cauliflower, gherkins, green peppers and tomatoes —the best tomatoes I ever tasted, I thought, luxuriously rubbing a crust of bread in my olive oil. The two men were talking; when I had leisure from that wonderful salad I realised that they were talking about me.

"The cousin, of course, is a mother figure to her, so she comes here full of expectation, remembering this childhood trip; the cousin's boat with the red sail, very symbolic without doubt—"

"Dr. Stavrakis," I said accusingly, "you are a psychiatrist."

"No, no!" He beamed shyly, turning pink. "Psychology is my hobby, only; really I am just a police doctor."

We were all relaxing. Plastiras unbuttoned his uniform jacket, revealing an unsuspected pink vest and an elaborate triple crucifix on a chain.

He went on with his theories. Two bottles of unresinated white wine presently arrived—Dendros Blanc Sec it was called on the menu—and I listened through a pleasant detached mist of alcohol. My lonely day, Sweden's face with the trickle of blood from chin to brow, seemed a long way in the rear. In due course an enormous fish was put down before me and I concentrated on getting it off its bones. It was, like the salad, the best I had ever tasted, grilled over charcoal with oil and tomatoes.

"Barbouni," said Captain Plastiras. "Very good, red mullet I think?"

My friend from lunchtime recognised me, waved, and presently came across to say,

"Aha, you have made friends, I see! She won't come to the folk concert with *me,* but a captain of police is another matter."

"You mind your tongue, Janni my boy," said Plastiras in great good humor, "or I'll tell your Aunt Anastasia."

"And your cousin? You found her? You liked the folk museum? I have your bag for you when you want it."

"Janni!" bawled the proprietor.

A large party was arriving, evidently expected, for three tables had been placed together and quite elaborately set with elegantly folded napkins and three glasses to a place. The waiter bolted off.

Through a warmth of brandy, Dendros Blanc Sec, and food I watched the party take their seats, and speculated about them. The little man at the head of the table must be the host. Where had I seen him before? His face was vaguely familiar. Grey hair, rather scanty, brushed back, a hooked nose, a mouthful of stained, protruding, battered teeth. He wore a gaudy shirt and laughed a great deal; he drank a lot of champagne but ate nothing; he seemed much amused by his guests. But not amused in a very sympathetic way, I thought; he was laughing at rather than with them. There were three other men, three women. All three women were young and dazzling; a dark-eyed blonde with her hair piled in a terrific chignon, a black-haired sulky beauty, a redhead whose restless eyes, at odds with her hair, were a dark toffee brown. The little host appeared to find all the girls exceptionally funny; he kept patting the arm of the dark one, who sat beside him, as if to reassure her that things *could* not be so bad as she supposed.

Of the three men, one was a colourless-looking, neat character, with brown-fair hair and horn-rims; give him a hat and briefcase, he'd be a civil servant or minor diplomat. The second was pure Playboy: blond, six-foot, tanned, he looked as if he'd just stepped off his water skis. And the third was my friend of the harbour bench who had chatted about unlovable characters in fiction; although he sat with his back to me, the height and skeletal thinness was unmistakable. It seemed likely that the rest of the party were the owner and guests from the *Phaedra*. And looking back at the host, I remembered him; he had been the man who came along the quay and had been referred to by my neighbour as his employer.

They were all very gay; but just too far off for me to hear in what language they conducted their gaiety.

"What now?" said Stavrakis, noticing that I had finished my red mullet.

"Nothing more."

"You are underweight. You should have an ice."

"No," contradicted Plastiras. "Baclava. Bring the young lady some baclava. And we will all have Turkish coffee. Ah, you are looking at our neighbours over there; that is the wickedest man in this island."

"He does look wicked," I agreed dreamily. "But in quite a nice way. Like the bad fairy who turns up at the christening. What's his line in wickedness?"

"Oh, he has many. He is a millionaire. He lives in a fortified palace on the coast with his own anchorage and airstrip. He travels a great deal. Without doubt he evades all the customs regulations, without doubt he fiddles his taxes, breaks all our laws, and probably holds orgies as well; famous and beautiful women come to stay with him from all over the world. But he also gives huge sums to charity and government funds, and helps over the preservation of local antiquities, so nobody is allowed to put a finger on him."

"How did he make his pile?"

My baclava was brought: layers of paper-thin pastry baked brittle with nuts in between, the whole thing smothered with extravagantly sweet honey; it was paradisial.

"Oh, oil, and selling arms to the winning sides in wars."

"Clever fellow to know which are going to be the winning sides," I said, stifling a yawn. Sweden, Sweden, what am I going to do about you? I simply don't know.

"And now it is time to put you on your plane," said Plastiras affectionately, hoisting me to my feet after I had drunk a beakerful of rather sickly banana liqueur, courtesy of the house apparently.

"Plane?"

He nodded to Stavrakis, who received my rucksack from the friendly waiter.

"I have got you a seat on the night plane to Athens."

"But I haven't any money to pay for it! And what the dickens am I supposed to do when I get to Athens?"

"You have a connection on to London; that also is arranged. As for the fare: my pleasure. You can pay me back by and by; it is of no importance when."

"Oh, you are so kind. You really are kind."

We were in the car by this time, speeding out past the mimosas and the Italian villas. It felt like a conveyor belt shooting me off the void. I started to cry.

"You see, to tell you the truth, I don't in the least want to go back to England."

"You will be best there," said Dr. Stavrakis magisterially. "You have family?"

"Six brothers. But——"

"Well, then! Things will sort themselves out. And if your cousin should arrive here and inquire for you, why, we will be sure to hear of it, and we will tell her where you are. Home is the best place for you."

"I haven't got a——"

"Now, my dear young lady, please do not cry. Captain Plastiras is a very tenderhearted man, he will probably begin to weep also and how shall I possibly explain this when we arrive at the airport?"

The airport had not changed since I saw it last, eighteen hours ago; hollow, dusty, echoing, and chaotic. A mass of hopeful passengers was engaged in a battle to stand nearest to a pair of glass doors leading out to the airstrip; these were being held shut by a massive airport policeman.

One nod from Plastiras and I was whistled through the formalities.

"Now: some wine, some coffee? There is a bar upstairs."

"For heaven's sake! No, truly, I shall sleep like a trout all the way to Athens as it is. You've been so kind; please don't wait any longer."

But they obviously intended to wait; doubtless in order to make sure that I didn't sneak off and hitch a ride back to Dendros town as soon as they had left.

Lights began flashing outside; by now the passengers were mauling each other like tigers in front of the exit; but at this moment there was an interruption. A procession of black-robed men in the tall, flat-topped hats like black chefs' caps that orthodox priests wear came streaming across from the ticket desk. More police appeared and shoved back the crowd, the priests were ushered through a second pair of glass doors, and we saw them pick their way over the building works to the airstrip and climb the steps of the plane.

"Well, well," said Dr. Stavrakis, "who would have guessed that Dendros held so many priests? There must be some religious conference taking place in Athens. You are in excellent company, my dear young lady; God will certainly never allow such a saintly planeload to encounter any mishap."

He beamed at me as if he had organised the whole thing himself.

"The only question is, will there be room for anybody else?"

Plainly there was not going to be room for many more; the tourist-class crowd was being pushed away into some limbo of cement mixers and sandbags; fighting was even more frenzied and despairing. My status as the protégée of Plastiras, however, stood me in good stead; a section of crowd was shovelled to one side and the cop held open the door for me, just enough to slip through.

"Good-bye, dear Miss Marsh. I hope we meet again sometime in happier circumstances," the doctor said kindly.

"Enjoy your trip!" Plastiras shook my hand affectionately and passed over my rucksack.

There seemed nothing to do but go.

On the blue-carpeted plane I slipped into the first empty seat, wedging my pack as best I could under the seat in front. Beside me was a priest; taking a sideways glance I saw black robes, about a yard of bushy grey beard, and some brown wooden beads. Well, at least *he* wouldn't want to chat with a female.

Fastening my safety belt I sank back in mindless exhaustion, resolved simply to let events take their course.

Now we were taxiing, twirling this way and that on the airstrip, like a bowler about to make his run-in. Take-off in a plane is a wonderful sensation, I'd place it among the three best in life. I never think about crashing, I simply relax and wait for the lift.

Something that had vaguely bothered at the back of my mind since stowing my rucksack now came to the front. Wasn't it rather odd that my priest-neighbour should be wearing red espadrilles?

Where had I seen red espadrilles before, today?

"So we meet again!" said a pleased voice in my left ear. "And now I hope I shall have time to convince you on the subject of the transmigration of souls."

My neighbour had removed his beard and gave me a sunny smile of welcome. He was the young pink-shirted Arab from the Museum of National Art and Folk Culture.

III

I looked up and down the narrow aisle. Several other priests had taken their beards off and appeared to be relaxing.

"This is some kind of fancy-dress excursion?" I inquired.

"You could say so. Yussuf is in with the pilot right now, encouraging him to turn east."

He spoke with a slight American accent, I remembered from the afternoon.

"East, where to?"

"The middle of the Jordan desert. We've got a place there."

"Oh, no!"

"What's wrong with that?" He was affronted. "You'll love it. We guerrillas aren't savages; don't think it. We're all educated. I did sociology at Berkeley; Yussuf did economics at Leeds. People who come and stay with us practically never wish to go back to their old lives—we have very high ideals, we are happy, we love each other, we are all brothers together in a happy community with everything shared. You don't like the sound of that?"

"No, I don't! I don't like the transmigration of souls, when I die I want to stay peacefully dead. And just now the *last* thing I want, the very *last* thing, is to be hijacked off to the middle of the Jordan desert with a lot of idealistic Palestinian liberators, if that's what you are. Your cause may be good or bad, I'm not making any judgments, I daresay there's plenty to be said on both sides, I'm not interested! I've had just about enough go wrong on me today; I would like the rest of this flight to proceed according to plan. Will you please tell the chap with the pilot to just let him go straight and uninterrupted to Athens *this once?*"

My voice came out rather wavery and hysterical; taking a hasty breath I gripped the arms of my seat and counted twenty.

My companion looked at me worriedly.

"This I can't very well do. Yussuf would never agree."

"Well then, just put me down somewhere along the way. Anywhere!"

"Honey, there just isn't anywhere along the way. We cut straight across from here to Jaffa. And we can hardly land in Israel, you do see that?"

"I don't want to go to Israel either."

"Really you are very hard to please," he said reproachfully.

"Can't you just turn back and drop me at Dendros again?"

"Well," he said in a doubtful tone, "I'll go and tell Yussuf how you feel; I'll see what he thinks. But I'm not very hopeful, I'm afraid. Honestly, you'll just love the desert when you get there."

He shed his thick black cassock, revealing the pink shirt and white jeans I remembered, climbed over me with neat agility, and departed towards the pilot's cabin.

I stared out of the window, full of foreboding. There were the huge stars, happily blazing away in the peaceful sky. There, down below, was the coast line of Dendros, traced in a curving line of lights. Out at sea, one or two sparks for small boats, and an illuminated V for a larger one, making its way south. The *Phaedra,* perhaps, with its wicked millionaire, haggard captain, and bunch of well-fed but ill-assorted passengers. I had not envied them before, but I envied them now; at least they, presumably, were going where they intended to go. And I, where was I going? I seemed to be slipping farther and farther off course. What would kindly Captain Plastiras and Dr. Stavrakis say when they heard where their well-intentioned meddling had landed me, in a guerrilla base in the middle of the Jordan desert, to be swapped for some political prisoner or sent sky-high with the plane? I felt sure they would be highly scandalised. Or—here a very unnerving possibility occurred to me—could they perhaps have known what was going to happen? Could this be their notion of a joke, a speedy and trouble-free means of dispatching potential troublemakers from their green and photogenic isle?

But they both seemed such nice men. I dismissed the suspicion. My thoughts reverted to Sweden. Death is a hard thing to assimilate; you can only take it in by degrees. Who had killed Sweden, and why? Had the murderer travelled with her from Beirut, or had he met her the minute she tied up in Dendros harbour? And what had happened to the child? For it was plain there had been a child on board—the toy, the scribbled drawings, the plastic pot all bore witness to that. The child must have been handed over before the murder to some third party. Had the child, too, come from Beirut?

Beirut. Why hadn't I suggested to Plastiras that he might check with the Beirut port authorities? They would know whether a small boat called *L'Aiglon* had left, and when.

She might have put in at a Cyprus port on her way across, was almost bound to have. Beirut to Dendros must be all of three hundred miles, farther than Penzance to Dover. I studied the map on the back of the Olympic Airways brochure and hoped that, if we did fly to the middle of the Jordan desert, we had enough petrol for the trip; the distance was about three times as far as from Dendros to Athens.

After an interval of numb stupidity, my obstinate mind was beginning slowly to tick over again. I thought of Sweden's sketches. What a fool I had been; why hadn't I thought of showing the one I had taken away with me to Captain Plastiras?

But he would have said it proved nothing; it didn't constitute evidence that I had been on the boat. She could have given it to me at any time.

I took it out and looked at it. Pain surged back. Pain is atavistic; a useless function, like precognition. You can't rely on it as a warning, it merely hampers action.

A shadow came between me and the overhead light; my pink-shirted seatmate was returning.

His eye seized on the drawing at once. I suppose guerrillas, whether at Berkeley, Leeds, or in the desert, are
trained to be lightning-quick in their reactions.

"The scientist who defected," he said with assurance. "I
never forget a face."

"He didn't defect. That was the whole point."

"Oh, well, I was only fifteen then. And it wasn't our
quarrel. He was a German, wasn't he? But now, I have
happy news for you; you have cause to be grateful to me. I
persuaded Yussuf to allow the plane to make a quick
landing at the south end of the island; there is an old air
force landing strip there, now privately owned. So are you
not lucky? There is a village not far away; you might even
be able to get a bus back into Dendros."

"I very much doubt it. But I am extremely grateful to
you just the same."

"Well, even if no bus, I am sure some kind person will
turn up to help you," he said, and grinned, which made
him look even younger than his eighteen years. He
climbed nimbly over my knees and back to his seat. "I think
people always like to help you; I wonder why that is so?
Perhaps because all the time you look rather sad? 'Ali,'
Yussuf said to me, 'what has got into you? What a fuss
you make about this girl. She would have had a fine time
in the desert.' 'I am not so sure about that,' I said, so in
the end I was able to persuade him. Now you must tell everyone that we guerrillas are most reasonable and approachable."

"Some of you! But this was extremely kind; I really do
appreciate it. How soon shall we get there?"

"In about five minutes, I imagine."

Sliding Martin's portrait back into my wallet I noticed
another sketch on the back, in a different style; more re-
cent work of Sweden's this, done in felt-tip not charcoal,
with less detail, but quite recognisable: the captain of the
Phaedra.

"You should fasten your belt again, we are starting to
descend. We had better hope," said Ali cheerfully, "that
the pilot is not nervous about landing on an unlighted
strip. What a lot of trouble you give us!"

I looked past him, out of the window. There were no
lights or buildings to be seen at this end of the island,

which was very sparsely populated. I took a little comfort in remembering that it was a good deal less mountainous than the northern end; the range that divided Dendros diagonally ran off into the sea before it reached the southern tip, which was flattish agricultural land.

"But you had better put up a prayer to St. George."

"Why him?"

"Do you see that cluster of lights up there on the left?"

I did, and let out a gasp. They were high above us.

"I thought we had crossed the mountains?"

"So we have. That is the last spur, right on the coast. The light on top of that pinnacle is the Abbey of Aghios Georgios."

"Oh well, St. George is my patron saint. And I suppose if the village is too far away, I can at least climb up to the abbey and ask to be taken in."

"I would not depend on it."

A white, serrated swatch of rocky, tree-covered ground suddenly opened up before and below us; then vanished again as the plane did a steep turn.

"Why not?" I unloosed the clutch I had taken on my handbag.

"Firstly that little hill is about four hundred feet up from sea level; quite a stiff climb in the dark. Secondly, I understand there are no monks now. Some private eccentric owns the place."

"The same person who owns the landing strip? How do you come to know so much about it?"

"I and my friends have been in Dendros a week, waiting for a suitable plane. Naturally we chat to the locals. But the village, Imandra, is somewhere quite near."

"Oh well, somebody there will have to put me up."

Another stretch of landscape swept up towards us, this time a fraction flatter; we hit it, bounced, hit again, braked, scraped round in a bumpy curve, then came to a jerky and shuddering stop.

I dragged my pack from under the seat.

"Out through the emergency exit will be best," Ali said, and undid it. Of course there was a nine-foot drop; no handy little trucks or airport staff to wheel up a flight of steps.

"I fear you will have to jump for it." He didn't sound

entirely regretful; I guessed he felt this was no more than my just desert for being so intransigent about the trip to Jordan.

"What a nuisance it will be for you if I smash a leg."

I levered myself out through the narrow doorway and dropped down on to exceptionally hard, gritty concrete. My feet and hands stung, my teeth jarred in their gums like stones in a loose setting.

"Okay!" I called up to Ali. "No broken bones."

"Congratulations! You must be a high-jump expert."

He tossed my rucksack down to me, then stuck his head out of the hatch to call, "Good luck! I am really sorry you did not come with us to the desert. What is your name? I will send you a postcard."

"Georgia Marsh. But where will you send it?"

"Wherever you wish!"

"*Poste Restante,* Dendros," I suggested, and he chuckled, and slammed the hatch. The plane revved up, I grabbed my pack and made a hasty dash sideways—which proved a rash act, for the air strip was not wide and almost at once I tripped and fell full length into a whole wilderness of prickles. Behind me, as I cursed and dragged myself upright, the roar and light of the plane receded, approached again frighteningly, and suddenly diminished upwards. I waved, in case anyone was looking out into the blackness, waited until the plane was well away and my sight had grown accustomed, then looked around, trying to make a survey of this piece of nowhere into which I had been decanted.

There was an awful lot of dark.

But by degrees I began to distinguish a faint light off to my left; after a bit of thought, and hunting among the mass of stars for the Great Bear, I reckoned that this must be southeast and therefore the village of Imandra, at the foot of the isolated pinnacle which had the Abbey of Aghios Georgios on its summit.

I set off walking in that direction.

At first it was hard and most unpleasant going: bare, gritty ground, with tussocks of dry grass put there, it seemed, expressly to trip a nighttime walker, and some kind of low-growing prickly furzelike scrub, very painful on the ankles and even more so when one fell into it. There were trees, olives I guessed, at fairly wide-spaced intervals, but these were easy enough to dodge, since they showed up against the star-packed sky. Presently I struck a rutted track, which at least gave me a feeling of direction as it ran towards the distant light, but wasn't significantly easier walking.

I was really very tired by now. I had serious thoughts of just lying down by the side of the track and hoping for death, but the ground was *so* hard, and *so* gritty; furthermore it smelt of goat, or donkey, or both. I walked on, lifting first one foot, then the other, with a conscious effort.

After what felt like an hour, but might have been about twenty minutes, the light was perceptibly nearer and had divided itself into a cluster of separate sparks. Then smells of fried onions, and coffee, and grilled meat, and herbs, and night-scented flowers began wafting out on the warm dark air to meet me like an extended hand from civilisation. I hobbled on a bit faster—blisters on both heels now —crossed a bridge over what appeared to be a dried-up watercourse, and found myself suddenly in a narrow, cobbled, walled street.

I knocked at the first door I came to. It was set in a wall and had a number on it: 37.

Voices which had been talking and laughing inside fell silent at my knock and in a moment the door opened.

"Please," I said to the youngish woman who stood there, "could you tell me where there is a telephone I could use?"

She did not answer; she seemed at a loss. Possibly my accent had her baffled. Instead she turned and said over her shoulder to somebody behind: "It's a stranger: a woman."

She was elbowed aside—kindly but briskly—by a man who said,

"Please, kyría? What can we do for you?"

Behind him I could see a vine-covered courtyard, lit only by what gleams filtered through from the sixty-watt streetlamp on the wall of the house opposite. About a dozen people were in the court, some sitting piled together on a camp bed, some on deck chairs, some on the ground. All the faces—elderly, wrinkled, middle-aged, young, babies—gazed at me attentively.

"Is there by any chance a telephone I might use?" I asked again.

Heads were shaken; they all looked at one another and shrugged.

"There! What did I say!" exclaimed a tiny, bright-eyed old lady who sat bundled up in dark swathings in the centre of the group on the camp bed. "Haven't I always said that if Stephanos Vassiliaides took the key home with him to Makanos, sooner or later it would be a nuisance, and you see I am right. Here is the poor young lady, had an accident with her car, no doubt—"

"Have you had an accident with your car?" the man asked me politely.

"Well, no, as a matter of fact I was dropped by a plane."

"Spondiko have mercy on us—a *plane?*" chorused the females.

"Didn't I say that must be some guest of Kyrie Capranis landing on the airstrip?" said an old boy with Crimean War moustaches.

"A plane? You came off a plane? Where from?"

I had to explain the whole affair, and it took a long time, even though I omitted any mention of Sweden and her death. Before I had got into my tale very far I was provided with a seat on the camp bed and a drink—neat scotch in a teacup; and several old ladies clustered round, patting me commiseratingly and giving me an occasional hug.

"Being taken off to the desert—fancy!"

"What an escape!"

"Ah, they're a wild lot, those Palestinians; not a bit like us Greeks."

This reception was wonderfully comforting; my only problem now was keeping awake.

"So you see," I finished, swallowing a huge yawn with an effort that made my eardrums crackle, "I ought to ring up Captain Plastiras in Dendros and tell him what has happened. He won't be a bit pleased, I'm afraid."

"In that case," said the man who had let me in, "would it not be better to wait till the morning? Captain Plastiras has probably gone to bed by now. He'll be even less pleased to be woken up again. Besides, he can't run after the plane and fetch it back, can he?"

This seemed a reasonable viewpoint.

"Besides," he said clinchingly, "the only telephone is in the post office, and that is locked up for the night, and Stephanos Vassiliaides is the postmaster, and he has taken the key home with him and it would take an hour to get to Makanos and an hour to return——"

"Oh, please don't trouble then——" I said hastily.

"Pavlo," said the little old lady on the bed, "you are keeping the thespinis talking while anybody can see she is as tired as a dog. Give her your bed—you can go and sleep with Eleni and Vassily."

"Yes, Mother," he said meekly. Everybody began to bustle about. A lot of the family—they all seemed to be brothers, sisters, in-laws, nephews, great-aunts, grandchildren, related in one way or another—departed, bestowing pats, hugs, and good wishes on me as they passed. A plump youngish woman, who smiled at me but did not venture to speak, fetched out rosemary-scented clean sheets from one of the various doors opening into the courtyard and vanished into another; in a moment she came back to say that a bed was ready for me.

I stammered a few words of thanks; my Greek was flowing away on a tide of sleep. The room prepared for me was two-thirds bed—a raised platform with a balustrade was approached by three steps; a mattress on it had been smoothly spread with the clean sheets.

The door shut gently behind me. I undid my rucksack, rummaged for nightwear, and in three minutes had flung myself down on the hard, flat mattress; in three seconds more I was gone, leagues deep in black oblivion.

Sometime, before daybreak, I vaguely heard a tremendous ruckus of motorbikes; presumably the male population of Imandra taking off for work in Dendros town. Then I slept again, and didn't wake until the sun was almost overhead, filtering down through the crisscross of the vines over the courtyard outside my window.

I clambered, stiff and yawning, to my feet, and down the steps of my platform bed onto a stone, cobbled floor, very hard on my bare blistered feet.

Apart from the platform, with its carved wooden balustrade, and a kitchen chair, the room was unfurnished, unless you counted some rather pre-Raphaelite religious prints on the wall, and half a dozen coloured photographs of Queen Frederika.

I opened the door and put my head out into hot sun.

Seen by daylight the courtyard was delightful. The floor out here was also cobbled, in a black-and-white design with a galley in the middle and flowing waves round the perimeter. The walls were whitewashed and against them a variety of red-painted receptacles—Snowcem tins, catering-size Nescafé tins, petrol cans and bomb cases—burgeoned with all kinds of flowering plants and sweet herbs, roses, geraniums, phlox, basil, marjoram, thyme, sage, mint, and southernwood. A dazzling blue morningglory trailed down over my bedroom window. From a clothesline among the grapes hung some cheerful cotton dresses and some snow-white sheets; a smell of lamb stew came from a tiny kitchen which contained a calor gas stove, a large refrigerator, and not much else.

When I stepped out, the bright-eyed old lady, who had been sitting on the threshold of the street doorway hemming a length of handwoven material, exclaimed, "Aha!" jumped briskly to her feet, shut the street door, gave me a hug, and led me to another door which, on being opened, revealed a useful room with two holes in the floor. One of the holes had a waterpipe with tap poised over it; both had a rushing torrent going past beneath.

The water in this primitive shower was warm; naturally; it had probably travelled for miles through 90° centigrade rock.

Emerging, feeling fine, I found that the old lady had breakfast waiting for me. Turkish coffee in a tiny aluminum pot shaped like two pyramids meeting in the middle; melon; small yellow figs; and a bunch of the red grapes which she reached and picked from the arbour overhead.

"Kyría you are too good."

"A happiness," she said cheerfully. "It is not every day that God sends us a young lady dropped from an aeroplane."

She placed me in a chair, first tipping off it the thinnest white-and-tortoise-shell cat I had ever seen. It was like a heraldic animal, with every sinew showing under the scanty coat that was nearer to a lion's pelt than a cat's fur, but it seemed healthy and amiable. Having given me my breakfast the old lady plumped herself down on the camp bed to gossip, and the cat immediately jumped onto her lap with a loud, self-welcoming chirrup.

"What's his name?" I asked.

"Gata, gata," she said, rubbing the animal's narrow, intelligent head. He rose to the caress with a beautiful flowing movement, like a performing seal.

"Gato, surely?" There was no doubt as to his maleness.

But she repeated, "Gata," pulling the long, stringlike tail. "Now, tell me your story again, because this afternoon I shall go to see my sister at Mandriki, and she will want to hear all about it."

So I told my story again, the expurgated version, merely saying that I had hoped to meet my cousin in Dendros and had failed to do so.

"And now, if you will be so kind as to tell me where it is, kyría, I will go along to the post office and telephone Captain Plastiras."

Unfortunately it seemed that the post office was open only from ten-thirty to ten forty-five in the morning, and from six to seven in the afternoon; Stephanos Vassiliaides had once again departed to his home village with the key.

"But I have a good idea," said the old lady, who had told me her name was Mrs. Elektra Panas. "You say your cousin had spoken of a position as teacher in a school on this island?"

"Well, yes," I said hesitantly, "I think it was on this island—"

"Then without doubt it is up there in the house of Kyrie Capranis."

"Where is his house?"

"Why, up on the mountain. He lives in the old abbey. Look—"

She led me to the end of the little walled yard, where there was a gap in the overhead vine, and pointed upwards: craning my neck back I could see a steep pinnacle of hill above us, crowned with dogtoothed walls. It really was like a crown: a ring of wall surrounding the hilltop.

"Good gracious. Is that Aghios Georgios?"

"Yes it is. That is where Mr. Capranis lives. And part

of the abbey—it is very large, as you can see—he has turned into a school for his own son and the children of his friends. Is it not likely that your cousin did her work there?"

It seemed not only likely but obvious; everything fell into place.

"Maybe you'd have seen her in the village?" I said, and described Sweden.

Mrs. Panas shook her head.

"He has so many friends—English, French, Italian. But they don't come down into our village much. What is there for them here? When they want to go shopping, Captain Cruikshank takes them up to Dendros in the *Phaedra*."

"Captain Cruikshank? A very tall, very thin man?"

"Ne! Ne!" she said, nodding vigorously. "Thin as a shark's skeleton. And sad-faced: he looks as if his whole world had fallen off a cliff."

If Captain Cruikshank had known Sweden, if he had known she was expecting a cousin, I thought vaguely, mightn't the fact have come up during our brief talk? Well, no, not necessarily; and anyway, perhaps he hadn't known her.

"So you should certainly go up to the house of Kyrie Capranis. Maybe you will find your cousin there, or news of her. Anyway," ended Mrs. Panas practically, *"they* have a telephone, or even two, so you can call Captain Plastiras from there."

This seemed a good notion. I was not entirely certain what line to pursue when I got there, but an assault on the Abbey of Aghios Georgios was plainly the next step.

"Can you tell me the way?"

"My granddaughter Maria works up there, cleaning; every day at this time she comes down with a bundle of washing. She can show you the way. Now, thespinis," said the old lady briskly, "if you are going to have a job up there as a teacher, you will be needing somewhere to live. Doubtless they will offer you a handsome room up in the castle, but I do not recommend it—myself I'd as soon stay in a prison as up there on that bare crag, inside those thick walls. We can let you have a room and breakfast every day here; what do you say? My son Pavlos is a decent fellow, the best fisherman in the village, and if my daughter-in-law is a bit dim, at least she is very well-meaning, poor soul."

"I think that is probably an excellent plan," I said slowly. "I agree with you—I'd much rather be down here than live perched up there. But it is far from certain that they will offer me a job, or that I'd want it. But may I leave my bag down here for the moment, while I go up there?"

"Of course! And now, here is my granddaughter."

A round-faced, pretty girl came in with a huge bundle of sheets. There was a pink granite sink at the end of the courtyard; she dumped the bundle in this and kissed her grandmother, who told her that her skirt was disgracefully short; what in the world must they think of her up in the mansion of Kyrie Capranis?

"All the skirts of the ladies up there are much shorter, Grandmother. In fact, most of them go round in bikinis."

"Really I expect it is a den of iniquity," muttered the old lady. "Still, I must say, it is always interesting to hear about those people. Now, Maria, here is this lady who wishes to be taken to speak to Kyrie Capranis; she is going to be a teacher in his school, very likely. So you must show her the way up the hill."

"It is terribly steep and the young lady looks tired," said Maria. "Hadn't she better ride?"

Before I could protest that I was quite capable of walking they had fetched a donkey from a shed across the alley and strapped on it an elaborately pommelled saddle and a headpiece decorated with red and blue enamel beads.

I *was* quite tired still, in fact, and glad enough to ride, particularly in view of my blisters and the fact that the way to the Capranis residence lay up a flight of about a hundred cobbled steps, set in a long zigzag through the village, which skirted the lower slope of the hill.

Imandra's inhabitants—most of whom seemed to be sitting on their doorsteps, waiting to chat to us as we passed by—had a gay taste in house decoration. Red ochre, white, apple green, viridian, powder blue, magenta—each frontage was more dazzling than the last. But the paintwork of doors and windows never varied; they were all the same shade of dark dung brown. Someone must have sold a thousand gallons of the stuff to the parish council.

Finally we had run the gauntlet of smiling and inquisitive faces; the donkey trundled on, fetlock deep in dust, up an almost vertical path.

"In the spring," said Maria, striding easily alongside and encouraging the donkey, not that he seemed to need it, with frequent cries and thumps, "in spring this hillside is all covered with flowers—rockroses, anemones, hyacinths—it is beautiful then."

Even now it smelt sweet from small, hardy, dusty plants —rosemary, lavender, wild thyme. Here and there a huge, ghostly-looking asphodel thrust up from the bare earth.

Scorching sun beat on us from above and below; on either side of the promontory, could be seen the sea, clearest aquamarine. As we climbed higher it became plain that the Abbey of St. George—which seemed less like an abbey than a fortified castle, built of the local marmalade-coloured rock—was actually perched on a fearsome overhang. Down below it, sheer cliff dropped four hundred feet or so to a little enclosed bay.

"There's Papa," said Maria.

Down in the bay a tiny blue rowing boat hung suspended over the almost black deeps of the water close under the cliff; and I could also see the white stern of a bigger boat.

"It that the *Phaedra*?"

"That's right, thespinis. Oh, she's a beautiful ship! Kyrie Capranis let everyone in our village go on board her last summer, for a treat, on St. George's day—carpets in every room, just like a hotel! And a swimming pool! Imagine it—who'd think it necessary to have such a thing on a boat?"

"Mr. Capranis and his visitors must have a stiffish climb up and down to the harbour when they want to go on board."

"Oh, no, thespinis, there's a lift, it goes right from top to bottom."

"Good gracious, he *must* be rich."

"Indeed he is. Just wait till you see the inside of his house. And then, to have a whole school of his own, just so that his little boy can get some company. As well as the children of his friends, they say he fetched over some poor boys and girls from America, children of people who had emigrated."

"Why did he do that?"

"They were homesick; or their parents had died; I am not sure. He is a very good man. Of course he has plenty of room for his school."

I could see that he had.

The Abbey of St. George had plainly served various different purposes during the course of history. The massive surrounding walls, built so as to take advantage of natural rock formations, now towered above us, and the spiky grillwork along the top suggested that at one time it had been a Turkish fortress; so did rows of turban-shaped arrow holes in the stonework.

Maria led us between a double row of cypresses, which gave exceedingly welcome shade, and up another flight of steps, carved from the rock. When we reached a pair of no-nonsense wooden gates, fourteen feet high, she said,

"I think we had better send Agamemnon home here; I do not like to take him inside."

"Will he go home by himself?"

"Oh, bless you, yes. And he knows he had better not loiter, or Granny will give him such a thumping! She's waiting to go and see Great-aunt Aspasia."

So Agamemnon was turned loose and went clattering away down the mountain on his neat little hoofs.

Inside the great gate we seemed to be in a market garden: beds of tomatoes, sugar cane, cucumbers, okras, aubergines, and neatly terraced vineyards rose above us, flanking more flights of steps leading ever up.

"Are there many children at this school?" I asked, gazing at all the veg.

"Yes indeed, and little devils some of them are! The things that get broken, the mess they make! Clearing up after them is no joke. As for the way some of them scream and carry on sometimes . . . When I told Granny she said they all sounded shockingly spoilt."

An echo came back to me—Sweden saying "Do you still have your gift with difficult children?" What sort of brats were these children of the millionaire and his friends?

"Rich people's children," I said vaguely.

"But the ones from America were not rich, I believe they came from a very poor neighbourhood."

"Maybe they feel shut in here." The massive walls now encircled us, cutting out the view of the Aegean.

"I wouldn't blame them," agreed Maria. "I can tell you, I'm glad to get out of the place at nighttime."

We were now climbing across a bare piece of rocky ground scattered with bits of stone and sections of ruin, part of the old abbey, no doubt. High to the right, at the very tip of the hill, rose a tremendous flight of steps topped with half a dozen orange Doric columns.

"What's that?"

"Oh, some old temple." Maria shrugged. "No one uses it now. But there's a little church down below it—there, to the right; once a year our priest from the village comes and holds a service there, it's the Church of St. George. Now"—we had come round an inner, buttressed wall and ascended yet another flight of steps—"that's the dwelling house, up there on the left, and that, beyond, is the separate school building. Do you want to go straight to the school, or shall I take you to Mr. Capranis?"

"Oh, I'd better see him first, I think. After all, the whole thing may be a mistake, and nothing to do with my cousin. Or even if it is the place where my cousin worked, he may not want *me*."

Not if he wants to keep clear of trouble, I thought, but Maria said,

"I expect he will. After all, you must be very clever to speak Greek so well, and then quite recently a lady teacher fell over the cliff, so I daresay they are quite anxious to replace her."

"Indeed! Was she killed?" The death rate among assistants in this school seemed unusually high, but of course the situation had more hazards than the average school location.

"Not *quite,* but I think she is still at a hospital in Athens till her bones mend. My uncle Elias looks after this garden. Isn't it beautiful?"

"Very." There were more cypresses; a fountain; and a wealth of plants all sprouting from stone urns, roses, hibiscus, geraniums, sweet-scented shrubs. An old boy was doddering about, watering with a hose; Maria waved to him gaily and he gave her an avuncular scowl.

"Is there a spring up here, then?"

"Several. One of them was sacred to some old goddess called Athene. But there isn't much earth; Mr. Capranis has to have it fetched from miles away."

Somewhere ahead I could hear children's voices. We walked through a grove of potted bay trees and looked down into a vine-hung circular enclosure with a lily pool in the middle. There was a hammock seat with an awning, and a table with drinks. Two smallish children, a dark boy and a fair girl, bickered by the pool, and on the seat a man lolled, swinging, watching them.

"That's Mr. Capranis," muttered Maria. She seemed nervous and hesitant all of a sudden. "I—I'm not really supposed to come up here—but I had to, to bring you, didn't I? So I daresay it will be all right."

"Is he a bad-tempered man?"

Maria gave me a cautious glance.

"Well," she was beginning, when my question was answered by Mr. Capranis himself, who suddenly sprang from his swing seat and gave the small girl a terrific clip on the ear; not surprisingly, she burst into ear-splitting howls.

Leaving Maria by the bay trees I darted down the pink marble steps that led to the pool and grabbed the man's arm.

"What the blazes do you think you're doing, giving that poor child such a slap? Don't you know that you should *never* hit a child on the head—you might damage her for life."

"Oh, po, po, po!" he said laughing. "What a commotion to make about one small slap! Anyway, Suzanne's head is harder than a bullet; I doubt if anything softer than a nuclear missile would do much damage. And, pray, what right have you to question my actions, may I ask, miss? I was not aware that you had been invited here?"

He glanced up the steps behind me. "Maria Panas. Who is this aggressive young lady?"

Maria looked frightened to death, so I said, "It's all right, Maria, I'll explain. Don't worry." With a relieved nod she disappeared between the bay trees and I went on, "Maria kindly showed me the way here from the village because I wanted to come and see you. I believe you know —knew my cousin, Dr. Sweden Hannfelder. My name's Georgia Marsh."

"Oh *indeed?*" he said slowly. His derisive expression faded and gave way to one of concentrated thought. He subjected me to a long up-and-down scrutiny, which I did my best to return in a cool and haughty manner, while absently patting the head of Suzanne, whose sobs were dying down to self-pitying snuffles.

Mr. Capranis was stocky, grey-headed, and deeply tanned. Today he wore a magenta tussore shirt—open to reveal a good deal of grizzled furry chest—burnt-orange shorts, and local-made thong sandals. He had a hook nose, battered teeth, and an air of well-founded confidence.

He was of course Captain Cruikshank's boss, the host at last night's table for seven, the person who had been referred to by Plastiras as the wickedest man on the island.

IV

"Paul, my treasure," said Capranis, "I think you had better run along back to Dr. Tatula while I sort things out with this young lady. But come here and give me a hug first."

"Okay, Papa."

Paul, who might have been five, did not resemble his papa. He had a thick thatch of soft, lustreless black hair, a pale little wary face, a pair of dark, watchful eyes. He did not radiate any of his father's easy assurance that people would do what he wanted. But he did seem to have a complete trust in his father, and obviously there was deep affection between them. Capranis kept the boy in his arm for a moment, stroking the dark soft hair, then said, "Run along, chicken. And take that hellion with you."

Paul looked doubtfully at the square, blond, freckled Suzanne but she, scowling at Capranis, said, "You don't think I'd want to stay with *you,* do you?" in a Brooklyn accent you could cut with a hacksaw, thrust out her tongue at him, snatched up a couple of toys that Paul had been about to collect, and departed with a swagger.

"Good-bye, Papa. See you after supper?"

"Yes, my treasure."

The little boy went slowly up the pink marble steps, and Capranis looked after him as long as he was in sight.

"Now, Miss Georgia Marsh. Sit down. Have a drink."

"Thank you. Some orange juice, if I may."

There was a vacuum jug of it, with ice cubes. He poured me a glassful. After the four-hundred foot climb it was welcome. He then poured himself a tot of ouzo, mixed it with water till it turned cloudy, and raised it formally. He was still giving me that poker-player's survey, as if wondering how much he would be obliged to tell me. But evidently he did not intend to be the one to start.

"So, what can I do for you, Miss Marsh? Have you come here to see your cousin?"

"Mr. Capranis," I said slowly, "I think you know that my cousin is dead."

He did not blink, but set his ouzo down carefully on the paving. We were seated side by side on the hammock seat, slewed round diagonally, eyeing one another like gladiators.

"Oh?" he said with deliberation. "I wonder what makes you think that?"

"I shouldn't be a bit surprised if Captain Plastiras had told you."

He rubbed his chin thoughtfully.

"And how come *you* to be so sure she is dead?"

"I saw her dead body. And then her boat, with the body on board, was handily spirited away—before the police could be put to the awkwardness of an investigation. And I was bundled on to a plane, before I could make a fuss."

"Only somehow you bundled yourself off the plane again. You are a strong-minded young lady, are you not?"

"The plane was hijacked by a set of characters rigged up as priests. But I persuaded the hijackers to put me down on your air strip before continuing to the Jordan desert."

"That was most resourceful," he said genially. I felt I was affording him the same kind of malicious entertainment that his dinner guests had on the previous evening; it was annoying.

"Mr. Capranis, I want to find out why my cousin was murdered."

"My dear young lady! Why in the world should I know?"

"She was employed by you here."

"Allow me, that is not exactly so," he said politely. "Dr. Hannfelder had a position at Beirut University and a private practice there. But she used to come over here at regular intervals to advise me about children in my care—we have some disturbed children, you know—"

"Oh? No, I didn't."

But his statement tied in with what Maria had said about screams and tantrums.

"And sometimes Dr. Hannfelder would also bring over patients of her own, so that they might relax in my little oasis. But I must inform you that I do not have the habit of murdering my employees."

He suddenly beamed at me. His smile was about as trustworthy as that of a crocodile but, despite the Punchinello nose, the disreputable teeth and piratical black fringe of grey hair below the bald dome, the effect was one of immense charm. However I withstood it, and returned him a scowl worthy of Suzanne, at which he grinned more widely still. His eyes were brown, opaque as conkers.

"That was how matters went this time, you see," he went on confidingly. "Dr. Hannfelder had brought over a poor little child whose parents had been killed by a bomb —ah, these Middle East troubles, what untold human suffering they cause. So, the orphan is delivered on board my yacht, and what then? Next I hear from the police that Dr. Hannfelder is reported murdered. If only for the child's sake, we do not want the tale spread about; should this poor waif learn that the *one* person she knows in the world, the person who brought her to safety, has been killed—what a disaster."

"Surely she's bound to learn sooner or later?"

"I can see you are strong-minded, Miss Marsh. Well, we will hope that it is later. In the meantime, the staff here have not been told this tale of Dr. Hannfelder's assassination. They believe her to be off on one of her frequent sailing excursions.

"And I shall be pleased, Miss Georgia Marsh, if you will also maintain discretion on this matter."

Suddenly his tone had an edge to it which, despite his nondescript appearance, made me realise that here was a powerful man as well as a rich one.

"Not unless you give me a good reason," I said coldly.

He took a cigar from a wooden box and lit it, then, apparently recalling his manners, mutely offered me one, which I mutely declined; all the time he was considering me through half-closed eyes. The half-closure gave him a decidedly non-European and even more saurian appearance, for pouched lower lids came halfway up across his eyes.

"You are very unlike Dr. Hannfelder," he said at length.

"None the less we were first cousins; our mothers were sisters."

"And they came from?"

"Batum."

"I see; hence the name Georgia."

"My mother was homesick." Then I said rather crossly, wondering how we had strayed so far from the point, "You were about to give me a reason why I should not broadcast the news of my cousin's murder."

"No I was not, my dear Miss Georgia," he said affably. "I am still considering the matter. Now: for instance here we are talking as if your cousin is dead. But are you so certain that she is not, perhaps, just badly hurt?"

Again I had that feeling of contained power. He was offering me a way of retreat.

"No, she's dead. I'm certain of it. And something ought to be done about it."

"You mean," he said, regarding me through the slit eyes, "that her murderer should be brought to justice?"

"Yes, I do! And I'm not going to be put off by you pretending that I'm only being melodramatic and silly and—and feminine."

"My dear Miss Georgia! Why should you not be feminine if you wish?"

We seemed to have got sidetracked again.

"Mr. Capranis," I said, "I understand you have a telephone here."

"Every luxury of civilisation, my dear young lady. Even that!"

"Well then, would you be so kind as to let me call Captain Plastiras on it?"

"To discuss the murder with him?"

"Yes! And also to tell him about the hijacked plane, and how I'm still here."

"A perfectly sensible scheme. Then, if somebody pushes you down the oubliette while you are here, at least police suspicion will be directed to the proper quarter." He gave me the wicked grin again and added, "We really do have an oubliette, you know; I believe the Turks installed it. Nowadays it would be called a garbage-disposal chute. It's in the kitchen. Remind me to show you."

"Mr. Capranis—"

"Yes, yes! Come to my study, and you shall have a chat with the good Captain Plastiras directly. He is, incidentally, a very old friend of mine; we play backgammon every Friday night. Perhaps he did not tell you that he comes from Imandra?"

My heart sank, but I followed him. He led the way out of the arbour, along an alley, between espaliered fig trees trained against massive walls.

"This part is medieval," he said, nodding towards the high, forbidding structure that we were approaching. "The Grand Masters of the Templars used it for a weekend stopover when travelling to and from Acre. It looks a little rugged from the outside, I agree, but within I trust you will find it more like home."

He turned aside from what appeared to be a main entrance and led me round a buttress to a highly incongruous french window.

"This is my study; here you may telephone without fear of interruption."

The window stood open; he ushered me in with a wave of the hand.

Mr. Capranis's study was the size of a modest ballroom. The chairs—Kensington colonial—were upholstered in shocking-pink leather with rows of knobs which looked like brass but were probably gold. The chandeliers certainly were. Something like a periscope ploughed its way to us through the orange ostrich-plume carpet; emerging, it proved to be the tail of an Abyssinian cat, which rubbed its massive head against Capranis's ankle.

"*Kalispero,* Mog," he said. The cat jumped onto his shoulder.

"The phone is over here," he said, and pressed a button. Twelve yards of fake leather-and-gold bindings glided back to reveal various aids to elaborate living—video recorders, closed-circuit TV, an electric typewriter, photocopier, dictaphone, tape recorder, and one of those things that massage your feet while you wait. There was a gold telephone too.

"No dentist's chair?" I said.

"In the study? Please! We have the dentist's chair *upstairs*—very necessary for some of the children, I can tell you! An excellent dentist flies over from Nicosia once a month. But now—allow me."

He picked up the phone, said, "Niko, please get me Captain Plastiras immediately," and waved me to one of the pink-leather chairs. Without intending to, I sat. The chair was vilely uncomfortable. Its gold knobs hit most of the places that the Dendros ants had assaulted yesterday and the seat was too low; once down, how to get up again?

"Captain Plastiras? Ah, my dear Mike! Are you well— how is the gout? Really? I am so glad. That is splendid news. And Stella? She is well? Excellent! Listen—here I have a charming young lady whom, it seems, you put on a plane last night. Imagine it! Her plane was hijacked by some of those scandalous Palestinians disguised as Orthodox priests—it was really careless of you, my dear fellow, to send her on such a wild-goose chase, you must be slipping, you are certainly due for that holiday! But never mind, this dauntless young lady persuaded them to set her down—at gun point, without doubt—on my air strip, and here she is, demanding information about her cousin." He raised his brows, listening. "Yes, yes. Yes I see. *Indeed* I will make it clear. Naturally, my dear Mike." He nodded thoughtfully once or twice to the telephone. "Right. Yes. I had thought of that myself. Now I will hand you over to Miss Georgia Marsh."

The thick grey brows raised again, at me this time, and

I struggled grumpily out of the safari chair and took the receiver from him.

"Hallo, Captain Plastiras."

"My dear Miss Marsh." *Was* it Plastiras? The line crackled and faded; I could have been speaking to Mars. "I am so sorry to hear that you have had this further unfortunate experience with the hijackers—what a regrettable mishap! But how lucky that you were able to persuade them to put you down on Mr. Capranis's air strip; that was indeed a most happy coincidence. And so now he is to offer you a position in his school?"

"Oh? Is he?"

"An excellent arrangement. I will see that your *permis de séjour* is extended for three months."

"That's very obliging of you," I said, hoping that my tone of deep sarcasm was penetrating through the atmospherics. "Seeing that last night you couldn't wait to put me on the first plane out."

"Circumstances have changed since then, my dear young lady."

"Oh? How?"

"That I am not at liberty to reveal. And I must beg you, too, to exercise the utmost discretion. Do you understand me? The *utmost* discretion. Mr. Capranis will explain. So now—enjoy your stay on beautiful Aghios Georgios."

"Captain Plastiras—"

At this moment the most tremendous rumpus of thumps, shrieks, crashes, children's voices quarrelling, suddenly broke out not far off, somewhere outside the open french window. With an angry exclamation Capranis, who had been standing by me, turned on his heel and strode out. I could hear his voice upraised furiously in the distance.

"So I will say good-bye for the present," said Plastiras, and rang off.

"Hey—Captain Plastiras!" I joggled the receiver. It was dead. But in a moment a much nearer voice inquired,

"Kyría? You wish to phone again?"

"I got cut off. Could you get me Dendros police station again, please?"

"Certainly, kyría."

This time it took much longer to get through than it had for Capranis. At length an official voice barked, "Police!"

"I wish to speak to Captain Plastiras."

"Who is speaking?"

"Miss Georgia Marsh."

Pause. Gabble-gabble-gabble.

"I am sorry, Captain Plastiras is not available."

"But I was speaking to him just now."

"Captain Plastiras has gone on holiday."

"That's ridiculous! I've just been talking to him. *When* did he go on holiday?"

This time there was a long pause, and the sound of voices consulting urgently in the background. At length my informant came back to report:

"Captain Plastiras went on holiday ten minutes ago."

The line clicked and died again. Automatically I replaced the golden receiver on its rest. In doing so I must inadvertently have started off some other control, for the shelf swung into the wall and the panel silently slid back into place, leaving me confronted by the complete works of Lord Lytton bound in morocco.

Damn! I should have asked to speak to Dr. Stavrakis. But had I in fact been through to the police station at all? Anyway, there was no harm in trying again, while Capranis was out of the way. I hunted for the control to move back the panel—could find nothing anywhere, though I scrabbled all over the wall like a climber doing the north face of the Eiger for BBC-2.

"Please! My dear Miss Georgia! Lord Lytton is not an *absolutely* first-class writer, I agree, but, in fact, those backs are mere camouflage—it is pointless to vent your critical feelings on them."

I spun around. Capranis was regarding me with his most malicious grin.

"Now tell me, did you have a satisfactory chat with the good captain? I am so pleased! After that, I expect you would like a cup of tea. I think it is about the time of day when one should offer an English lady a cup of tea."

A cathedral-sized bellpull, spangled all over with silver and turquoise beads, hung by the Parian chimney piece; he gave it a tug.

There was a metallic buzz, and a voice spoke from a grille concealed somewhere among Lord Lytton.

"Kyrie?"

"A pot of English tea, please, Ariadne. Boiling water, milk, sugar. And something to eat with it—what does one serve with English tea? Biscuits! Tea and biscuits, all within two minutes, please."

He turned to me again and said, "After you have had tea I will show you over the school. And, when you have seen it, I am hoping that, as your cousin had suggested, you may feel inclined to accept a position as special tutor with us."

"Oh? My cousin had suggested it, had she?"

"Of course! When Miss Quindrell fell over the cliff. And in view of your special qualifications I am still happy to ask you to join us, in spite of the somewhat sad and complicated circumstances."

"Sweden had spoken of my special qualifications?"

"Naturally, my dear Miss Georgia. She had spoken of you in the highest terms!"

"She didn't mention that I failed to finish my university course or take my degree?"

He gave me his blandest smile, with half-closed eyes.

"She told me of your great gift with children."

"How did the other teacher—Miss Quindtrell?"

"Quindrell."

"How did she come to fall over the cliff?"

"Alas! She was a lady with an enthusiasm for photography. Stepping back to get a long shot of Athene's temple at sunrise she missed her footing. I do hope, Miss Georgia, that you do not indulge in this expensive and dangerous hobby?"

"I should have thought almost any hobby might have its dangers on Aghios Georgios?"

He gave me a narrow-eyed glance; at that moment Ariadne came in with a gold tray of tea. Upended among the gold pot, sugar bowl, pink-flowered Turkish coffee cups, and common-glass milk bottle was a packet of Huntley & Palmer's biscuits.

"Thank you, Ariadne. That is excellent."

Ariadne, who was a toothless crone with a white shawl draped round her head and shoulders, beamed at me and said, "I was not sure how many spoonfuls of the tea so I put in six, was that right?"

"Exactly," said Capranis. She curtseyed to me and left. He poured out the tea; they must have been table-spoonfuls.

"Is this tea how you like it?"

"It's terrific. You could trot a mouse on it."

"Parakaló?" Capranis seemed at a loss; for the first time I felt I had scored an advantage.

"Tell me about your school?" I said kindly, dipping a biscuit. It went black.

"Well." He looked bashfully down his bent nose. "A great many of my friends are people of talent—actors, musicians, opera singers—"

"*That's* who she was." Suddenly enlightened, I let the words out before I thought.

"Who was?"

"Almina Radici. At your table last night."

"Oh. Yes. You have a talent for observation." He gave me another sharp look. "Yes, I am proud to claim Almina Radici as a friend, and she is making use of our services at present. Opera singers, you see—actors, film directors, people who lead such international lives—they have a great problem over the education of their children."

"The children are gifted? Difficult?"

"Not that alone—though they usually are. But the parents have such migratory habits. Oslo today, Rome to-morrow, San Francisco the day after; naturally they wish to see their children whenever possible. Now, remote though it may seem, this island hermitage is in the middle of most of the main air routes, has its own landing field, and, what is more, the parents know they will always be welcome, whenever they care to drop in. Some schools, you see, discourage parental visits, but that is not the case here."

"I see. Little Suzanne, whose child is she?"

"Oh, some Hollywood meteor who is making a film in Italy—Mixie Koolidge, is that right?"

"And the company of these children is nice for your son?"

"Paul enjoys it very much. It would be lonely for him here, otherwise."

When he spoke of Paul his face and manner changed totally—an anxious, protective abstraction came over him which made me for a brief period, feel more friendly.

"But these children have special difficulties, so you need a psychiatrist handy?"

"Indeed yes. Some of them have been indulged all their lives and are quite out of hand. Others, dragged from Hilton to Hilton since they were born, are lacking in any sense of security. A few, in fact, we have to keep in a separate wing after they arrive, until they are adjusted. And, since I will not pretend that the wealthier of my friends do not pay handsomely towards the upkeep of their cherished ones, we can also afford to take sadder cases—orphans, refugees, friendless children whose plight is brought to my attention—such as the one I mentioned." He looked modest and benevolent, like Belial organising a Sunday school treat.

"Why *did* you give that wretched Suzanne such a slap?" I asked.

"My dear Miss Georgia! For the last half-hour she had been subtly persecuting my poor Paul who has not a shred of aggression in his nature. My patience was exhausted."

It could have been the truth. Anyway I wasn't in a position to question it.

"A little more tea?" He raised the gold lid.

"Thank you, no. That was very stimulating."

"Then I will show you the school."

We left the study and walked through a drawing room which seemed to have been designed from a vague memory of Liberty's ground floor. There were alcoves, and Moorish arches, and great swatches of brocade, and massive leather pouffes, and stained-glass windows, and things elaborately made from tusks, and a lot of inlaid cabinets and occasional tables. Mr. Capranis and the Prince Regent evidently had several tastes in common. Here, too, the colours orange and pink predominated, but they could make the place cheerful, despite a smell of thick leather and prosperity.

"I find this a gloomy room," Capranis muttered, striding past a four-foot model elephant made of leather. "I think I must change it. Paul does not like it in here."

"Perhaps he'd prefer the kind of furniture that you blow up?"

"A good idea. I will consider it. Now, this is my organ room."

We had left Liberty's and entered a bare, high-ceilinged hall which seemed to have no furniture in it at all. The floor was Roman mosaic, which gave it the air of a food hall or public lavatory, as Roman paving all too often does.

"I don't see any organ."

He stamped on the stomach of a gloomy lady with snakes for hair, and more sections of wall sprang open to display an organ bigger than the oné in the Albert Hall. It was like looking into a whale's mouth, or a caveful of stalagmites. A Bach toccata was open on the music stand.

"You play?" I asked respectfully.

"Only with one finger."

Even one finger, I reckoned, would fetch quite a quantity of sound from that monster.

"The music belongs to Captain Cruikshank. And you, Miss Georgia? Do you play?"

"Two fingers. Nursery tunes."

"Paul will enjoy that. Perhaps you will play for him to-morrow? You must come and practise whenever you wish —your playing will not disturb me in the least."

A series of vaulted galleries led us on to the kitchen, which was about the same size as Dendros airport, but tidier. Time and motion were not words in common use here, plainly; I wondered if the staff were allowed to wear roller skates, or if these would spoil the black-and-white marble tiles. In any case, the only staff to be seen was the aged Ariadne, who sat listening to the Lovin' Spoonful on a transistor and slicing beans at one of the little pink marble chopping tables that were sparsely distributed in the huge room; I could not imagine *her* on roller skates.

"Your kitchen is very pleasant," I said politely.

"This used to be the entrance hall when the Quirini family owned the place in the thirteenth century; but I thought it would make a nice kitchen. The oubliette is in here, as I said. Presumably so that unwelcome visitors could not penetrate too far."

"Isn't it a little risky to have it in the kitchen?"

"We keep a table over it, so that no one shall step on it by mistake. But of course it is quite safe, unless anyone presses the release spring."

I wondered where the release spring was to be found, and which little table covered the trap, and steered a course round by the wall.

We left the coolness of high stone rooms and came out into the ovenlike heat of late afternoon. The building which Maria had pointed out to me as the school lay ahead of us beyond a stretch of rock-studded ground on which a few fig trees and some shrubs with large delicate white-and-purple flowers battled again the drought and heat.

Under the largest fig tree a group of children sat in the shade watching a man.

"What in the name of goodness does he think he's doing, jumping up and down like that in the full sun? He'll give himself apoplexy."

"That is Mr. Sandstrom, our maths teacher."

"What's he demonstrating—the law of diminishing returns?"

"One of the traditions of our little school," Capranis explained blandly as we passed the scarlet, sweating sufferer. "Did your cousin ever speak to you of Ole Södso?"

"The Swedish philosopher? Yes, she was nuts about him."

Ole Södso, a true Scandinavian, had unloosed, in the early twentieth century, a whole new theory of human behaviour on his flock of willing disciples; this was based on what he called the Muddle Principle. His thesis was that, running counter to the rest of the universe, which is clear, well-organised, and governed visibly by mathematical rules, the human race subconsciously prefers a muddle, and will get into one if it possibly can. It is the duty of the scientist and the well-adjusted individual to battle against the Muddle Principle in various ways which Södso laid down at length in a formidable treatise to which he gave the title *Anti-Björnsen*; Björnsen, it seemed, was a muddler *par excellence,* whose rival school of philosophy held that one should live in as high a state of confusion as possible. Myself, I adhere to the Björnsen school, since I always do live in a state of confusion; even tragedy hits me sideways on.

"But what has the Muddle Principle to do with that poor maniac half-killing himself in front of a lot of grinning brats?"

"Before I go into that, perhaps I should mention the salary that I pay my staff," said Capranis. He mentioned it; the figure, even when translated from drachmae into pounds, made me trip over a rock.

"Now, as you may imagine, for this salary I expect a very dedicated attitude from the teachers," Capranis pursued. "They are all expected to be familiar with the writings of Ole Södso, and to adhere to his doctrines."

Blimey, I thought, but said politely enough, "I still don't quite see how the Muddle Principle—"

"I am coming to that."

We were approaching the school building; he broke off to remark: "An Italian commandante ruled this island under Mussolini; he took a fancy to build this villa here and live in it. I suppose we must be thankful he did not put it in the temple of Athene."

In fact the villa was pleasant enough: stuccoed, shuttered, with clematis and morning-glory growing over its soft ochre walls.

"Gymnasium on the right, main classrooms on the left," Capranis gestured as we walked through the open doors. The rooms were beautifully equipped. "Swimming pool at the rear; of course the children have most of their lessons out of doors."

"The Muddle Principle?"

"You are a tenacious young lady, Miss Georgia. Yes. Well, since this principle holds that any failure to achieve one's object must be the result of muddle, we believe that if the children are bored in a lesson, this must be the fault of the teacher. Consequently, in such a case, it is the right of the children to name and exact penalty. I imagine Mr. Sandstrom must have bored his pupils."

This time I said blimey aloud.

"Oriste?"

"How many children are there?"

"Perhaps twenty needing tuition; none of them very old. Another dozen still adjusting in the Athene wing; up there towards the temple. They come under the care of Dr. Tatula, a very able West Indian psychiatrist, and of Professor Firgaard, who was one of Södso's earliest disciples. You will not be having to deal with the children in the Athene wing."

"Mr. Capranis, I'm really not at all sure I—"

"Now upstairs," he went on, ignoring me, "are the children's bedrooms and the studies of the staff—ah, here, coming down the stairs, is Mr. Smith, who, besides being my personal secretary and assistant, manages the financial affairs of the school and keeps us solvent."

He gave his crocodile's grin at Mr. Smith: the neutral, horn-rimmed man that I had classified as a civil servant the evening before.

"John, this delightful young lady is Miss Georgia Marsh, a cousin of our dear Dr. Hannfelder. Miss Marsh is a professor of European languages—she is going to be our special language tutor for the more advanced children in Persephone wing."

I opened my mouth to gasp, to protest, to contradict, but Capranis was going on smoothly, "By the way, John, about those Houston figures, I wanted to ask you, did the *Katina Paxinou* sail on the third or fourth of August—"

The two men instantly plunged into discussion, from which Capranis broke off momentarily to say,

"Your cousin's room is just at the top of the stairs, on the right, Professor Marsh. Perhaps you would care to take a glance at it, to see the kind of accommodation we are able to offer our staff?"

I nodded and went on up the stairs, wondering what his object was; by now I felt certain that not a single one of Capranis's words or actions was accidental.

DR. HANNFELDER said the sticker on the door; I knocked, but jumped when a voice said, "Come in!"

However it was only Maria inside, putting clean sheets on the bed. She grinned at me and said, "Kyrie Capranis thought you might like to use Dr. Hannfelder's room while she is on holiday."

"Kyrie Capranis was wrong. I prefer to stay with your granny."

I glanced round the room; it was austerely neat and tidy as Sweden's shore establishments always were. On the bookshelf lay a portfolio of drawings—was it the same that I had seen yesterday on *L'Aiglon?* The black strings were fastened in neat bows. As I fingered them thoughtfully I heard a step on the stair and Capranis entered; Maria scuttled out.

"A very well-read lady, Dr. Hannfelder," observed Capranis, misinterpreting the focus of my interest. "She has lent me some extremely interesting books at one time and another. She has a varied collection."

"Not all of them hers," I remarked, noticing and taking from the shelf a long-sought and mourned American paperback anthology of verse and identifying it as mine by the name written on the jacket.

"Ah well, we all have our failings," Capranis said philosophically. "And if failing to return borrowed books was the worst, the world wouldn't be such a bad place. Now, come along down and I will introduce you to some of our staff and guests." All smiles and animation, he led me down a different flight of stairs and out onto a broad terrace which might have belonged to any Mediterranean hotel; we were now on an outcrop of rock so high above the defence wall that the terrace commanded a panoramic view of Imandra bay and the opposite headland. Beyond the terrace lay a swimming pool, dug into the rock below the temple of Athene, and, clustered at the other end of the terrace under brilliant umbrellas were some of last night's party and a number of other people, lying on pneumatic lounges, wearing beach clothes, looking carefree and relaxed.

"Now listen," hissed Capranis—his joviality dropped from him as sharply and coldly as it had once before— "Captain Plastiras has given you a warning, and I do too! Say nothing, *nothing at all,* regarding your cousin's death. If you wish to discover anything, and for your own sake, remain silent; do you understand? If you choose to be foolish and indiscreet, I will not be responsible for what happens."

Remembering Miss Quindrell who had fallen from a cliff due to her enthusiasm for photography, I nodded, my mouth suddenly dry, and we went forward to join the group.

"But I think you are a sensible young lady," Capranis

muttered, darting a final keen look at me before we reached the others.

If there is one thing I hate and dread, it is being introduced to a large group of people wearing bikinis and expensive sunglasses and reclining on the edge of a swimming pool. Sweden would say this leads back to some terrible childhood trauma; that what I have is the brocade bikini syndrome. Giving things names doesn't help. And it's no use wondering what Esther Summerson would have done, either; that sweet simperer never had to face a poolside of bikini loungers in her life.

As I neared the group, feeling like Crusoe invited to take potluck with a bevy of cannibals, two or three faces began to waver into focus: the haggard, anxiety-laden one of Captain Cruikshank; the sharp-eyed brunette whom I now knew to be Almina Radici, world-renowned soprano; last night's tall Nordic-looking playboy who appeared even taller and more Nordic this afternoon as he chatted to a tiny, gazelle-like West Indian girl whose skin was an exquisite pale oak colour like the best soft brown sugar. There too was the red-headed beauty fanning herself and talking to the blonde whose upswept hairdo, I was ready to bet, had never been under a swimming pool in its life; maybe it was a wig. There was a sensible flowered cotton dress, pair of sensible white canvas shoes, sensible grey perm, embellishing, if that is the word, a lady who could only be a member of English country society; there was a tall, thin, white-haired man who looked like the link between Bertrand Russell and an avocet. There were other faces, too many to take in all at once; their eyes swivelled and trained on me like Turkish howitzers as I approached. Teachers, parents, or friends? Capranis gave no clue; he had fallen two or three paces behind and was fishing in the pocket of his gaudy shirt for a pair of pitch-black sunglasses which he proceeded to put on and from behind which he surveyed the group with his usual derisive expression.

"Now, here's a treat for you all to dispel the monotony of Monday afternoon," he said. "Guess who has come to join us?"

If his remark had been meant to stir up excitement and enthusiasm, it signally failed. A long, flat pause followed;

the blond girl yawned; Almina Radici finally said, "How can we possibly guess, Cappy. Who is she?"

"Why, she's our dear Sweden's cousin from England, Miss Georgia Marsh."

Again, if the announcement had been intended as a bombshell, it failed to detonate. There were a few polite mutters of "Indeed?" "Really?" and "Well, now." Interest could hardly have been less if he had announced the arrival of his great-aunt Emily from Prittlewell. And yet, somewhere, from someone in the group, I did feel as if I picked up some kind of telepathic vibration—alarm? hostility? sheer surprise? It was no use scanning their faces for reactions; all, behind the dark glasses and suntan were bored, schooled to blandness, or just wary. Capranis, I guessed, could be quite a little old joker when he chose; they might be still unsure whether he had told them the truth.

He stood still smiling lazily down at the group and received smiles in return, but it seemed to me that behind the smiles lay tension; that they were all waiting on his favour.

"Where is darling Sweden now? When is she coming over again?" drawled the red-headed girl in a flat antipodean voice. "Oh, I'd better introduce myself, as Cappy never will; I'm Poppy Vanbrough; I teach the kids PT and ballet."

"I'm not quite sure when my cousin's expected next," I said, hoping I sounded sufficiently disengaged. "Mr. Capranis may know more than I do—I've been out of touch with Sweden."

Capranis shrugged. "Three weeks, a month, who knows? Our beloved Sweden is like that person in the Bible—'When you look for me least I shall be with you.'"

Again, from someone in the group, I picked up a cold tremor of disquiet. But Capranis, bland as a sea elephant, had turned to ask Almina Radici whether the air of Dendros agreed with her vocal cords, and she was giving him a long, voluble, and detailed description of how the rock's vibrations upset her top C. It sounded like a lot of hogwash to me, but Capranis sat down by her and lavished on her his full, beaming attention.

I caught the eye of Captain Cruikshank and he gave me a difficult, half-inch smile; I had the impression that it was all his tight-stretched facial muscles could achieve. But his eyes were friendly enough, unlike those of the blonde; from her I received a stare of 90-per-cent-proof hostility that summed up and satisfactorily disparaged my unpressed sleeveless cotton, my upset hair, my generally travel-ravaged and untended appearance.

And I hope one of your contact lenses falls into the moussaka, I thought, giving her back what I hoped was a tolerant nod. Her eyes were black—or very dark brown; exotically tilted in a round small-featured face. She turned, and started talking to Cruikshank; American accent; I guessed she might be Mixie Koolidge.

"Miss Georgia is going to be a contender for your position as chief organist of Aghios Georgios," Capranis broke off to tell Cruikshank. "She has played on all the great European organs and tells me mine is far superior to St. Bravo in Haarlem; she has agreed to give Paul some lessons."

Beginning to get the measure of his little ways I neither gasped nor denied, but gave him a calm and pitying smile; catching Cruikshank's eye as I did so I thought he looked faintly amused.

"I wonder if you'd care to come and meet some of the children?" said a soft voice at my elbow. I turned; it was the West Indian girl who had stood up and was folding a soft blue sari around her swimsuit with a pleasing economy of movement.

"I'd like that very much," I said truthfully. However mixed-up the children might be, they could not be more so than this watchful, uneasy, competitive group of adults. Besides, I like children. If Capranis was prepared to pay me, for reasons best known to himself, a salary five times larger than I'd ever received in my life before, simply to hang around Aghios Georgios for a few weeks, I was fully prepared to try and earn it.

"I am Phyllora Tatula," the girl said, leading the way back to the school building. "I look after the children's health and try to get their problems sorted out. They have their evening meal now and I generally eat with them." She gave me a grin. "I find it more restful than eating with the adults." I nodded in heartfelt agreement. "Also it is a time of day when the children are tired and tense and all their problems tend to come to the surface; one can learn a lot from them then."

"I daresay that goes for the adults too."

"Oh, no doubt! But *their* problems, I am glad to say, are not my concern!"

Lucky you, I thought, wishing I could say the same. I liked this calm, capable-looking girl, who seemed concentrated on her own work and not on the febrile network of relationships that we had left behind at the poolside. Her company was peaceful.

"You are Dr. Hannfelder's cousin?" she repeated, turning and giving me a clear, not unfriendly scrutiny. "You do not resemble her much. She is a fine doctor; I have a great respect for her techniques with the children."

I nodded. Mixed-up, hung-up, self-oriented, disingenuous, Sweden might be, but all this gave her a natural understanding of children's mixed-up and hung-upness; she could sort out the problems of a frantic ten-year-old quicker than a bank cashier sifting copper from silver.

"Excuse me just a moment; before we go in I should like to fetch something from the pottery room. Perhaps you would care to see the children's work?"

Dr. Tatula turned off the path and walked round the side of the schoolhouse. I followed her along a narrow cobbled alley which led into a kind of stableyard. Dusk was beginning to fall now; I found it hard to believe that twenty-four hours had passed since Sweden's death.

"The children do some beautiful work," Dr. Tatula said. "It is one of the things they enjoy most. Hallo, Fernand, don't you want your supper?"

A tow-haired seven-year-old turned from his occupation of chalking the words MERDE ALORS in two-foot letters on the yard wall and scowled up at us.

"I'm not going in to supper. I'm going to starve myself to death."

"Oh, why is that?" Dr. Tatula critically surveyed his inscription and said, "I believe it would look better if the words were outlined in red, what do you think? Would you like to borrow my lipstick?"

Fernand received the lipstick ungraciously, but the 3D effect it gave his message as he laboriously outlined the letters, squashing the pigment right down to the gold tube, restored his spirits and he grunted—he spoke French with a strong Marseilles accent—"That Suzanne squashed grapes all over my picture of Elias's donkey. It was the best I'd ever done. I'm going to knock her head off when I've finished this."

"First, do you want to see how your tile turned out? I was just going to get it from the kiln, so you could have a look at it before you went to bed."

"Okay," said Fernand, very offhand. He passed back the ruined lipstick, which Dr. Tatula carefully returned to her handbag. Taking out a key she unlocked a door and led the way into a big, bare dusty room that held various pottery equipment: moulds, a wheel, dollops of clay wrapped in wet sacking, and a couple of massive wooden worktables. Ranged on shelves were some of the children's artifacts: pots and figures of every size and shape.

"It is nearly too dark to see; wait," and she went over to a bank of switches and turned on a couple of top lights. I looked at the pots. Some of them were beautiful. Some were so strange that they were almost frightening—plainly the products of disturbed minds. But nearly all were made with some technical skill; it seemed that Dr. Tatula was a gifted teacher.

"Where's my tile?" said Fernand suspiciously. "I don't see it."

"In the kiln, of course. Don't you remember, we put it to bake last night?"

She moved to the back of the room, taking yet another key from her bag.

All the rear part of the room was cut off by a mesh of thick, ceiling-high wire like that used round tennis courts. Behind this was a massive brick structure, the size and shape of a village bake oven. The door of this, too, had to be unlocked. It was fastened as well by a pair of heavy bars held in place by large wing nuts which Dr. Tatula proceeded to unscrew.

"We take no chances," she explained. "With the temperature inside rising as high as six thousand degrees, it just would not do to run the risk of anybody getting in when they ought not."

"No indeed. Isn't there a safety switch inside any-where?"

"There's an alarm buzzer in the ceiling; rings in Mr. Capranis's study."

That seemed as well, but I wondered what happened if
he was elsewhere.

Now I understood the suffocating heat in the
workroom. As she opened the oven door a blast of torrid
air came out, lifting my hair and causing me to step back.
Fernand and Dr. Tatula were accustomed; neither of them
took any notice.

"Wait; get your gloves," she warned him though, as he
was about to dart in.

Both of them put on heavy gloves, then Fernand disappeared purposefully through the kiln door and she followed him. I looked in and saw that the walls of the kiln
were covered with rows of flanges like large concrete teeth
sticking out at intervals. Ranged across these at different
levels were removable shelves with the pots and figures
disposed on them, well spaced out.

"Look at mine! Look at mine!" chanted Fernand tri-
umphantly. "It's come out just the way I meant; look at it,
look at it, Dr. Tatula!"

"It is really good, Fernand, you have a right to be
proud."

I wondered if she was being diplomatic but she said,
"Show Miss Marsh," and Fernand came out carrying the
tile which was over two foot square, and thick. I was startled because it must have weighed well over fifteen pounds
and yet he bore it with no apparent trouble; in spite of his
scrawny appearance he must be remarkably strong.

"You can hold it if you like," he said kindly. "Oh, no,
you haven't got gloves on, it might burn you. Here, I'll put
it on the table."

He stood by me in satisfied silence while I praised the
tile, which varied in colour from indigo to pale gold-green,
and had a fine free-flowing design of birds and leaves; it
was really lovely. Then he dashed back to help Dr. Tatula,
who was taking out the rest of the pots and tiles, putting
them on the shelves in the outer room, with various com-
ments, praise, and criticism.

"Paul's statue of Mog isn't bad," Fernand said in a tone
of cool appraisal. "Shall I take it to him when I take my
tile?"

"No. Let him fetch it himself; it's always better."

"Suzanne's teapot is a mess; the spout's come off. Serves her right," said Fernand with malevolent satisfaction.

"It was an ambitious attempt."

"Horrible little show-off," muttered Fernand. The pots were all out now; Dr. Tatula removed the shelves and stacked them outside the kiln. "It cools down faster without them in," she explained.

Fernand picked up his tile and left; she looked after him attentively.

"He is making such a wonderful improvement. Did you notice that he *returned me the lipstick?* A month ago he would have thrown it to the ground and trodden on it, after he had used it. I am so happy about him."

At that moment there was a crash, from round the corner, and a scream of rage from Fernand.

Dr. Tatula rushed out. "If he's broken his tile—" she cried anxiously.

I could hear angry voices—Fernand, stammering with fury, Suzanne's whine, Mixie Koolidge's drawl. A scene not to join, I thought, and turned to retrieve Dr. Tatula's handbag, which had fallen just inside the kiln; what was left of her lipstick would soon melt all over everything else inside the bag if it was not moved without delay.

I stepped inside and stooped to pick it up. As I did so I heard rapid footsteps behind me. The lights went out. Next moment someone gave me a mighty shove, so that I fell sprawling in the dark, scraping my hands and face on the gritty ground. Behind me I heard the kiln door clang to. The sound of its closing was followed by a couple of ominous clinching thuds as the fastening bars fell into place.

V

"Oh dear," I said.

I daresay most people's reaction would be equally lame, on realising that they had been shut inside a pottery kiln. No accident about it, either; there had been nothing absent-minded or indecisive about the purposeful shove that sent me to the ground, or the vigorous clang with which the bolts dropped into place.

One of the mixed-up kids from Capranis's school? Was this the kind of lighthearted prank they normally played on their teachers, or was it special treatment reserved for me? If a kid, it was an uncommonly powerful kid—but then there was the strength of paranoia, wasn't there—every muscle trained in one direction like a laser beam.

And—now for the sixty-four-thousand-dollar question—had whoever pushed me over and slammed the door also switched on the furnace?

It might take a little time to come to any conclusions about this last problem; the temperature inside the kiln was already way over what would be right to make a good creamy rice pudding; I couldn't immediately decide whether it was getting hotter or I was suffering from a hot flush of anxiety. From whichever cause, rivers of sweat were running down between my shoulder blades and my hair was glued against my neck like damp string. I remembered the little verse about horses sweat and men perspire. But ladies only glow. It certainly wasn't so in my case; any glow I achieved would be more in the incandescent line.

While running through these thoughts, chaotic and not very cheerful, I was picking myself up and taking the obvious and immediate steps of banging on the inside of the furnace door and yelling lustily.

"Hey! Hey there! Let me out! I'm inside here! Let me out!"

I read somewhere that civilisation has made some people so ashamed of shouting aloud that they would sooner be raped or garrotted than raise their voices. I am not one of them.

Anyway, whatever unbalanced tot or ill-disposed stranger had incarcerated me, in about two minutes' time, *surely*, Dr. Tatula would be returning to retrieve her handbag, lock the furnace, make all secure, and take me to meet the children at their supper? People don't just abandon an orderly programme like that; obviously dependable characters such as Dr. Tatula don't suddenly take off, leaving a lot of expensive and dangerous equipment exposed and at the mercy of a bunch of maladjusted children.

Or if they do, they must have a mighty good reason.

Unable to postulate any such reason, I went on banging and shouting.

Nothing happened.

If, of course, the person who had shut the kiln door had also taken the precaution of shutting and locking the outer door as well, it was quite conceivable that my voice would not carry as far as the yard outside. Suppose that person had also returned the keys to Dr. Tatula and told her that I'd decided to take the next bus into Dendros? But anyway, wouldn't she come back for her bag? But suppose— as seemed all too likely—that my ill-wisher had gone off with the keys? Surely, though, Capranis or someone would have a spare set?

I was getting a bit hoarse by now; I gave my voice a rest, and listened instead. No sound from outside. Another verse came into my head:

> Ann, Ann, come quick as you can
> There's a fish that *talks* in the frying pan.

That one didn't cheer me either. Although, as I mentioned earlier, I didn't value my life above an expired season ticket because the whole central core of it had been blown out three years before, still, there are many ways of

ending one's joyless existence preferable to being baked
alive at six thousand degrees.

I stopped banging on the door and began thinking. All
the exertion was making me hot; I mean, hotter. Also, it
seemed to me that I had caught a very disconcerting and
unnerving sound coming from the black darkness at the
rear of the kiln. I waited a minute, and heard it again; a
kind of click, or tick, similar to that of an off-peak night-
storage electric heater when it begins warming up.

It seemed likely that my assailant *had* switched on the
oven.

Spurred by this incentive to prompt, practical measures,
I then remembered what I should have done right away:
Dr. Tatula had told me there was an alarm buzzer in the
ceiling.

"Just as well," I had said vaguely at the time, but I
hadn't looked up to see where the buzzer was sited. Anyway, what a damn-fool place to put a buzzer! How were
people expected to reach it up there, for heaven's sake?
Then I realised that normally shelves were laid across the
kiln at different levels; maybe it would be possible to climb
up them. But Dr. Tatula had tidily removed all the shelves
just before Fernand let out his yell; the interior of the kiln
was quite bare.

Click. Click. There it went again.

I found no comfort in remembering that pottery is
baked for a long time, hours and hours; that the oven
probably wouldn't reach its maximum till about midnight.
Much less than its maximum would cook *my* goose.

In an effort to avoid contemplating the effects of even a
temperature far less than its maximum, say about 400°,
on my feeble frame, I turned my mind resolutely to the
task of locating the safety buzzer.

Well, no shelves to climb on, but there were still the
flanges on which the shelves rested; the thing would be to
climb up the wall by means of the flanges, and then grope
around, as far as I could reach, across the ceiling.

Suppose the buzzer is right in the middle of the ceiling?
It will then be out of reach from either side.

Don't let's suppose anything so discouraging.

I had vaguely assumed that after a while my eyes would
get accustomed to the dark and begin to see a little. I sup-

pose they did get accustomed; they didn't complain; but the dark didn't get any less dark; that kiln was really light-proof. It also occurred to me at this juncture that it was probably airtight too; not a comforting thought.

The flanges were made of concrete or firebrick—something roughish and sharpish. They were arranged in pairs, alternating like the bricks in a normal set of courses: two to the left below, two to the right above. Not difficult to climb up except for one disadvantage: they were getting perceptibly hotter.

The kiln definitely was switched on.

My feet, wearing sandals, were all right, but gripping the flanges with my hands was just too painful. What I needed was gloves—thick asbestos gloves, like those Dr. Tatula and the boy had put on to handle the pots.

Unfortunately all the gloves were outside.

It's quite true about necessity being the mother of invention. My mind, working really fast now, reminded me that when Dr. Tatula had opened her handbag to get out keys and lipstick, I had noticed among its miscellany of contents a pair of blunt-tipped surgical scissors.

I'd put the bag down by the door. I found it again, rummaged with sweat-sticky fingers among the letters, handkerchief, lipstick, purse; found the scissors.

My cotton dress was one of the sleeveless button-front kind. I had it undone in two seconds flat, found the centre back, snipped with the scissors, took a shoulder in each hand, tore it apart with one decisive rip. Then I wrapped a strip of dress round each hand—not much insulation but better than none—and, thus protected, climbed up the right-hand set of flanges until my head hit the ceiling.

It was hot up there; hotter than down below, and that is quite an emphatic statement. I told myself that if I were lying on a Mediterranean beach with blue sea lapping half a dozen yards away, I'd love this heat and think it worth a hundred pounds a kilowatt; thus encouraged, and clinging unsteadily with one bandaged hand, I began sweeping the hot ceiling with the other like a windscreen wiper.

I didn't find the buzzer.

So presently I climbed down again and tried the next lot of flanges; rather hotter now. The buzzer wasn't in that section of ceiling either.

I then went back to the door and took the left-hand front set of flanges, and there, bless it, up at the top just inside the door, I found a wire hanging down from a metal rose in the ceiling.

I gave it a good tug.

It came away in my hand.

Oh dear, I thought, for the second time; possibly the third or fourth; the heat of the air inside that oven was really very bad indeed for concentration. In fact I was so weakened by dejection that the jerk of the breaking wire shook me from my precarious balance and I fell awkwardly to the floor, scraping an elbow and a knee rather painfully against the rough-edged flanges on my way down.

Well, I remember realising as I lay in a gloomy frame of mind on the hot floor, at least there's no need for any more climbing up and down; I've located the bell, that's something; it's just a pity if the person who shut me in also cut the wire and that's why it came out. But let's try not to think these doleful thoughts, let's just lie here quietly till the floor gets too hot for comfort, then we'll wind bits of dress round the feet and stand up, then we'll wind *both* bits of dress round *one* foot and stand on that; then what? Keep jumping up in the air? I believe that is what you are supposed to do when a lift cable gives way. But that would use more oxygen than if I just kept still; sometimes it's hard to know *what* to do for the best.

No doubt, if these were to be the last moments of my life, I should have been repenting my crimes, or at least recalling my happiest time, but the mind is a hopelessly uncontrollable piece of mechanism; or mine certainly is. Anyway, fortunately, after five minutes or so devoted to these not very practical plans for the future, I heard a crash outside, the jar of bolts being undone, the rattle of a key in the lock, and, suddenly, blinding light burst in, together with Mr. Capranis, who picked me up bodily like a bit of wilted lettuce, carried me out, and dumped me on the nearest article of furniture—one of the modelling tables.

He was in a furious passion I could see at once; white and sweating with it; his eyes blazed at me and he shook me savagely as he thumped me down. For two pins, it wasn't hard to guess, he would have given me a slap such as he had administered to Suzanne Koolidge.

"What the *devil* do you think you were doing, you *stupid* little fool, walking in there and letting yourself get shut up like a joint of mutton?" he hissed at me. His eyebrows and grey fringe of hair stood on end with rage; his bouillon-coloured eyes were bloodshot, his hands shook.

"Lamb, not mutton," I said weakly. "And I didn't walk, I was pushed."

"Of course you were pushed, idiot! And I suppose it's too much to expect that you saw who pushed you? I thought so. I can tell you, it's going to be pointless having you here if you can't look after yourself better than that!"

I swung my legs down, sat up on the table, and we glared at one another.

"Mr. Capranis. Do you mean to say that you expected something like that to happen?"

"Naturally I did, dolt!" He glanced behind him; I noticed that he had not been in too much of a hurry to shut and lock the outer door. "What do you expect? You tell the police you saw your cousin murdered; you think the murderer will just sit back and wait for you to announce his name?"

"But I *didn't* see the murderer; I told them so. Anyway," I said slowly, "how come you know so much about it? Does everyone? Do the police round here make a habit of publishing all the information they receive?"

"Of course, if it is likely to lead to the apprehension of a criminal. Also there are bound to be leakages; everybody has a cousin or brother-in-law in the police."

"So I'm just bait?" I said sourly.

Capranis burst out laughing; his usual malicious humour seemed to be returning.

"Very nice bait too! You look most pink and appetising, Miss Georgia Marsh, though in point of strict scientific fact I have to inform you that removing your dress would *not* have helped to keep you cool; it would have been better to keep it on."

For the first time I remembered that I was wearing only two bits of underwear; still, they were no more revealing than a bikini and just as cheerfully coloured. I must look terrible, though; baked salmon-pink and draggled with perspiration.

"I was obliged to use my dress to protect my hands while I climbed up the wall," I said coldly, unwinding the strips of cloth which I still had on. "Perhaps one of your elegant guests would be so kind as to lend me her last-year's Balenciaga till I can get back to Mrs. Panas's house where I left my luggage? And then I think, Mr. Capranis, that I won't, after all, accept the very flattering offer of a post in your school but will catch the next plane home and get the hell out of here."

He suddenly gave me half a dozen little quick pats on the cheek.

"No, no, no, no, my darling! You are a girl of more spirit than that, I am sure! Don't be such a faint heart. You want to find out who killed your cousin, come now!"

"Not if it means being baked like a bit of baclava," I said sulkily, finding a comb in Dr. Tatula's bag and tugging it through my sodden hair.

"Well, well, we will keep a better lookout from now on," Capranis said with what was probably meant to be a reassuring smile; the effect was like Mr. Punch planning some particularly cold-blooded act of mayhem. "Now: I know what you need, you need a cold drink and a cold shower, and for Dr. Tatula to put something soothing on those burns and grazes. It has to be admitted that you are a resourceful young lady after all."

"Wait," I said, as he turned towards the outer door. "Dr. Tatula—what *happened* to her? Why didn't she come back?"

"One of the boys, Fernand Labouchere, got knocked over by that pestilent Suzanne and cut himself so badly on a bit of broken pottery that she had to rush him to our first-aid room and stitch him up right away. I think I hear her now," he said, going to the outer door and unlocking it.

He let in Dr. Tatula, who looked nearly as anxious and flustered as it was possible to imagine her. "Six stitches in his chin—and I had to give him an anti-tetanus shot. And his precious tile broken—I thought I'd never get him calmed down. Good heavens," she said, suddenly taking in my state of disrepair, "what has been happening here?"

"Nothing disastrous," Capranis said soothingly. "I haven't been assaulting Miss Marsh, as you might naturally conclude; merely one of our fun-loving pupils shut her in the oven. No harm done, none at all! If you, my dear Phyllora, could lend her a little calamine and perhaps something to wear to dinner—why, then it is all over and no more need be said."

Dr. Tatula opened her lips to reply, as if she felt that plenty need be said, but his uplifted hand checked her, and she closed them again, glanced slowly round the empty room, inspected the oven, locked it, and then checked over my various abrasions.

"Nothing too bad; a bit of suntan cream will be best. Come up to my room and I'll put it on for you. Why don't you put on one of these overalls for now; I'll find you a dress upstairs."

Cotton smocks of various sizes hung on a row of pegs; she fished me down a blue one.

"Charming!" said Capranis gallantly. "Well, ladies, I will leave you now. Oh, Phyllora—bring Miss Marsh directly to my study, will you, when you have doctored her?"

Dr. Tatula's room was cool and pleasant, furnished in a minimal, Japanese style with rush matting and not much else. A big bathroom adjoined it; I took a warm shower, gradually cooling the water, as she recommended, until my skin had adjusted and was its normal colour once more. Then she rubbed me all over with some soothing and nongreasy liniment. Her apparent fragility was deceptive; like most doctors she had considerable muscular development in her slender arms and wrists.

"Now, I think you will be quite okay, but here is a tube of the stuff to put on when you go to bed. Can you wear one of my dresses, I think we are much the same size? This Chinese one would suit you?"

It was a sleeveless, wrap-around garment in a soft, gold-coloured material, deliciously comfortable on my anxious and wary epidermis.

"It's beautiful; this is so kind of you."

"I cannot *think* how such an accident could have occurred," she said, suddenly letting part of her anxiety burst out. "I am almost certain that none of the children would have done such a thing—but I can see Mr. Capranis does not wish it discussed and I expect he has good reasons; you may be sure he will get to the bottom of it. But I cannot help feeling responsible! I am really distressed about it."

"Please don't worry," I said soothingly. "It was careless of me to let it happen. But anyway, no harm was done." I tried to match his tone of tolerant amusement at my laughable mishap.

Dr. Tatula continued to look troubled and unconvinced.

It was dark by the time we walked back to the main building. Huge stars flashed just above, as if one could reach up off the crag of Aghios Georgios and pick them like the grapes on Kyría Elektra's trellis.

When you have narrowly avoided being done in, it is rather like the abatement of the symptoms of some dread disease; you don't dwell on the possibly temporary nature of the respite, you make haste to put the whole business out of your mind. So when, with Dr. Tatula, I walked in through the french windows of Mr. Capranis's study for the second time that day, I did not stop to reflect on the incongruity of the train of events that, fifteen minutes after escaping a horrible death, I should be dropping in on a millionaire for a sociable evening visit.

Capranis came wading through the orange carpet to welcome us with the cat, Mog, perched on his shoulder and a great big V-for-victory smile on his face.

"Wonderful!" he said, surveying me. "Phyllora, I congratulate you. Now you both need a drink without doubt."

But her glance had gone past him to the massive brocade-covered settee at the far end of the room. In front of it, on a gilt leather table, stood a chessboard with pink and black marble chessmen; the rooks and queens must have been ten inches high. The game was unfinished; on the sofa, curled up with his head on a cushion, lay little Paul, fast asleep.

"I had better rouse him and send him off to bed?" she said. "If he sleeps too long here, he will never go off again, and he has been sleeping so much better."

"It seems such a pity to disturb him." The father's eyes rested with such a warmth of undisguised, unadulterated adoration on his sleeping son that I felt a pang of envy like physical pain; so must light seem to the darkness that comprehendeth it not.

However the sound of our voices had already reached Paul; he shivered all over, as a sleeping dog sometimes will, hit out with one hand and muttered a few words of gibberish; his eyes opened, wide and scared; then he saw his father and smiled.

"Bedtime, my chicken," said Capranis, fondling the rumpled dark hair.

"But I only just woke up!"

"You were so tired that you fell asleep while we were playing chess."

"Because of all that swimming this afternoon. He swam three lengths, did he tell you?" said Dr. Tatula.

"Did you, my treasure? That was wonderful."

"Next week I shall do four lengths," said Paul, climbing off the sofa. "And the week after, five, five, five!" He began to skip up and down.

"What happens then?" I asked. "Something special?"

"This is Miss Georgia Marsh," Capranis told Paul. "She is going to teach you all sorts of languages—English and French and Russian and Italian."

Paul eyed me sidelong, assessing my potential. Then he said seriously, "When I have swum five lengths, Papa will take me to see Finnegan."

"What's Finnegan?" I asked, with vague thoughts of James Joyce. "A film?"

"No, *the* Finnegan. The gorilla. He lives in London," Paul explained, obviously taking a low view of my ignorance.

"It is a series of books," Capranis amplified. *"Finnegan Goes Up the Post Office Tower, Finnegan on the Victoria Line, Finnegan at the Festival Hall.* Illustrated with real photographs; he is a real gorilla, and lives with the writer of these books. Paul is crazy about them so I promised that when he had learned to swim I would take him to London to see Finnegan."

Capranis sounded as if he now regretted the promise.

"Come, then, Paul," said Dr. Tatula. "I told Fernand that I'd bring you to see him; he's cut himself and is in the infirmary."

Capranis gave his son a loving embrace and the boy

went out with Dr. Tatula, demanding to be told how Fernand had cut himself; I heard her calm voice giving him a clear and detailed explanation as they passed the window.

"She is wonderful with the children," Capranis said, fishing a bottle from a gold bucket. "Never impatient, always serene, never unfair. We are so lucky to have her. Now, Miss Georgia, here is a restorative; I am sure you can do with it."

He handed me a glass of champagne and raised one himself with the usual gnomic grin.

"To our future co-operation."

"Mr. Capranis. The more I think about it, the less inclined I feel to stay here and pry into the cause of my cousin's death. For all I know she richly deserved to be murdered—"

"Oh, nothing more probable," he agreed, swigging champagne. "Dr. Hannfelder was a devious and self-seeking woman, without doubt. Her great gifts concealed a personality that was not always lovable."

You can say that again, I thought. "—So, if you would be so extremely kind as to let me have some kind of transport to get into Dendros—"

He shook his head. Kindly but firmly. His prune-coloured eyes were inscrutable.

"No, my dear Miss Georgia. You are not so pusillanimous! It will be far better for all concerned if you stay here for a couple of weeks at least. You will enjoy life in Aghios Georgios, that I can certify."

"Oh, sure. With some well-wisher just waiting to shove me down the oubliette—"

"Drink your champagne." He refilled my glass.

"Why two weeks? What are they supposed to solve?" I asked crossly, taking a gulp. It was very good champagne. "Paul learns to swim five lengths, then what?"

For a moment he seemed disconcerted. When not smiling his mouth was a smallish slit, rather cruel in outline, reminding one that he had not, presumably, made his million by benevolence and charity to the under dog. The charity came *after* the million.

"Oh, in two weeks the police will have everything sorted out," he said airily. "My friend Captain Plastiras asks me to keep an eye on you meanwhile. Then you, I, and

Paul can all travel to London together. What could be nicer? Paul has never been there and I not often; you might be kind enough to show us the sights—the Old National, the Grand Vic, the Severn Tournament, the Royal Bore—"

John Smith, the secretary, came in, and checked at the sight of me.

"Oh, I'm sorry, Mr. Capranis—I didn't know you had anyone with you. I came to bring you these papers but I won't interrupt—"

"No interruption. Have a drink, my dear John!"

Smith declined, however, saying that dinner was served on the terrace and he wanted to have it and get away quickly, as there was a lot of work waiting for him.

"If dinner is served we will come with you," said the smiling Capranis, shepherding me towards the french window. Smith followed us.

All of a sudden I felt singularly lighthearted; the thought of sitting down to dinner with that somewhat uncongenial group of strangers did not daunt me in the least. Was it the effect of Capranis's excellent champagne? Or had he taken the opportunity to slip a pep pill into mine?

I vaguely divined that his plan was to see which of the group displayed surprise or chagrin at finding me alive and unimpaired instead of baked to a rusk in the pottery kiln. Well, if he wanted to play Sherlock, he could go ahead and do it on his own; I was in too euphoric a state to be assessing the facial reactions of people I had met only once before.

Anyway, when we reached the long table, laid out with a white cloth and silver and glasses, illuminated by candles, nobody gave themselves away by a conscience-stricken shriek. They were all there, standing, sitting, smoking, chatting, drinking ouzo. But you can't gauge the baffled rage of a foiled murderer when he is sitting in the dark, three feet from the nearest candle. And gasps of guilt, if any, were drowned by the cicadas, who had come on night shift and were making as much noise as a gang of gas fitters with pneumatic drills in the Pentonville Road.

So if the murderer was baffled, Capranis was baffled too. We were all baffled.

In due course we ate salad and iced lemon soup and

charcoal-broiled fish, and grapes and figs. It was all very delicious, but just the same my euphoria began to die down. For one thing I noticed that Capranis, at the head of the table, touched nothing but dry oatcakes out of a tin, though he continued to drink champagne. That made me uneasy; he seemed so like the death's head at the feast. Another contributory factor of my disquiet was the gloomy presence, across the narrow table, of Captain Cruikshank, who spoke neither to his neighbours nor to me, but remained wrapped in some miserable reverie of his own.

All the others appeared to be in the highest spirits. By sitting quiet, munching my salad, and listening to the repartee, I managed by degrees to attach names to faces. The blonde was certainly Mixie Koolidge. The white-haired man was, predictably, Professor Firgaard, Ole Södso's earliest disciple. The tall fair man, conventionally handsome as a plastic toy, was Robert Newhouse, who taught history; it seemed a routine sort of name and profession for someone with his looks; his clothes, too, appeared more suited to Dendros casino than Capranis's back garden. Among the other men, nobody had done more than put on a shirt as a gesture towards dressing for dinner but most of the women had taken the chance to dress up a bit.

Almina Radici was wearing silver lamé; must be very hot and tickly, I thought.

The floral British lady, who had changed into a floral British evening dress, turned out to be a real Lady: Lady Lurgashall. Surely she was too old to have a child at the school? Listening to conversation I gathered that she had escorted some orphan here on behalf of the Sun for Underprivileged Kids Fund. She had a loud, incisive voice and a stand-no-nonsense manner which made me feel that it must have been a pretty bleak trip for the orphan; I would not have wished to be left in Lady Lurgashall's charge.

Almina Radici was being alternately haughty and coy with Newhouse who could be heard pressing her to sing after supper.

"I have no voice; the salt water takes it all away."

"Whales," suddenly pronounced Capranis from his end

of the table, "whales have voices of a sonorous resonance unparalleled in nature. Whales, my dear Almina, are not affected by the salt water; why should you be?"

"I am not a whale," she replied peevishly, "nor do I see why I should be compared with one. And the salt water *does* affect my voice; I cannot sing tonight."

"Then Poppy will delight us," said Capranis, without showing much sign of regret.

"Me?" cried the redhead, who appeared to be Australian. "Not on your Melba! Besides, Jimmy Sandstrom and I are going in to Dendros; there's a new film at the Athene."

Ha! I thought I can hitch a ride in with them. I had not argued with Capranis about his veto; I know a brick wall when I see one and there is no use running into it head on but I felt signally lacking in any wish to co-operate with him.

I resolved to buttonhole Poppy quietly after the meal; she seemed quite approachable. After all, I still had the air ticket that Plastiras had kindly bought me. No one had taken my ticket when I boarded the plane. At the time this had not struck me as odd.

"How are you getting on with *Bleak House?*" asked Captain Cruikshank.

His voice made me jump; it sounded like that of M. Valdemar, the Poe character who had been dead for six months. Looking up I found his dark melancholy eyes fixed on me inquiringly.

"Not very fast. There hasn't been much time for reading in the last twenty-four hours."

"So you never met up with your cousin?" he pursued—still in that low, dry voice that sounded as if it had been kept too long in store.

"No." I answered calmly. "What a pity that I didn't realise you knew her when we talked before; such a lot of trouble would have been saved."

"I suppose so. Still, you would have missed being hijacked, which you will now be able to talk about for the rest of your life."

"True." I'd have missed being shut in the oven too; even more of a fun topic.

"Anyway you got here in the end. Shall you like it, do you think?"

"I'm not proposing to stay. I want to ask for a ride into Dendros with those two. If you'll excuse me, I'll go and speak to them now."

The diners were standing up and strolling off. I noticed a quick flash of interest break Captain Cruikshank's gloom —was it relief?—as I left him.

Moving towards Poppy I overheard a scrap of conversation between the blond Mixie Koolidge and Capranis.

"Cappy-pie, how's about us slipping away from the rest and going for a spin up the coast in *Aurora?* I haven't had you all to myself in God knows how long!"

"I am so sorry, Mixie dear, I have business affairs to attend to this evening. Why do you not get Newhouse to accompany you?"

Capranis spoke without visible signs of regret. But I saw a scowl of chagrin cloud the brow of Miss Koolidge; scanning the group, for Newhouse presumably, she noticed me and the scowl intensified.

I edged my way on to Poppy Vanbrugh.

"Excuse me, but I heard you say you were going into Dendros—could I possibly beg a ride with you as far as the airport?"

"Sure—" she was beginning, when I felt a presence at my elbow like the dwarf Alberich, and turned to find Capranis regarding us both with a malign grin. His methods of unspoken communication must have been potent, for she floundered and corrected herself. "Actually—I'm terribly sorry, I've just remembered that Jimmy's taking his two-seater so there wouldn't be room actually—another time we'd love to—"

With an apologetic lift of her brows she made herself scarce.

"I do not think you would enjoy the film at the Athene," Capranis told me. "The projector breaks down without fail every fifteen minutes. Of course, if one goes with a friend, such intervals of darkness can be whiled away, but to go as a third party—what is the English expression, raspberry—?"

"Gooseberry," I said acidly. "Mr. Capranis—"

"But you will find an excellent hi-fi set in Dr. Hannfelder's room," he went on imperturbably. "Or, if you prefer billiards, I am sure Professor Firgaard would give you a game; he is champion of the North European Table Games League. I'm afraid TV reception here is so poor that it is not worth watching—"

"So kind of you, but as I have a room in the village I think I'll thank you for the delightful hospitality and say good night."

"Your room is where?"

"With Mrs. Panas."

He nodded thoughtfully.

"Very well. Perhaps that is best. Someone shall see you down the hill—Patrice!"

Before I could say that I would far rather be unescorted, he had summoned Captain Cruikshank, who was standing moodily on the edge of the terrace, gazing down at the scanty lights of Imandra below us.

"Patrice, *mon cher,* will you be so kind as to escort Miss Marsh down to the house of Elektra Panas, where she has elected to stay? Guide her carefully on the steep hill, to which she is unaccustomed—for any bone she breaks, I shall hold you personally responsible!"

His threat did not sound entirely playful but Captain Cruikshank took it calmly.

"Certainly I'll escort her; it is no trouble as I'm going down anyway."

"Good night, dear Miss Georgia." Capranis gave me his evil twinkle. "Pleasant dreams! We meet again tomorrow."

That's as may be, I thought, following the skeletal figure of Captain Cruikshank down the path to the main entrance. By the gate I hesitated.

"I ought to say good night to Dr. Tatula. She lent me a dress—"

"Oh, you'd never find her. She may be anywhere—sitting by the bed of some child who has a nightmare." He took my arm in his cold bony hand and led me on, inquiring after a pause, "What do you think of the children in the school?"

"I haven't met any of them yet. And I don't suppose I shall now."

"Oh? Why? You are not staying?"

"Not if I can help it. This was only a trial visit. Is there a bus to Dendros in the morning?"

"No bus till Wednesday. You don't like it here?"

"Not above half."

"Pardon?"

"You're French?" I said, surprised, for he had given the word a Gallic pronunciation.

"Belgian. Various people in the village drive to Dendros daily; if you'd like to come to the taverna with me, I will try and arrange a lift for you."

"That's extremely kind of you," I said gratefully.

Away from the castle, Captain Cruikshank appeared to experience a liberation of spirits.

"You are sensible to decide not to come here. Life on Aghios Georgios is like the books of Joseph Conrad— nothing ever happens *now*. It has happened in the past, or it is going to happen in the future; the present itself does not exist."

I couldn't have disagreed more, but I kept quiet, and he launched into a long disquisition on *Nostromo,* which lasted us down the hill, along Imandra's walled, cobbled main alley, and into a little taverna. It had three tables under a vine outside and six inside. There was an old boy with a moustache like General Smuts behind the bar; Captain Cruikshank instantly started interrogating him about possible cars, but as the juke box was roaring out a ten-times-amplified bouzouki medley just then, I didn't catch what they were saying. However, presently it was all arranged; the proprietor, whose name was Constantine Volonakis, told me that his nephew drove into Dendros every morning and would pick me up at seven tomorrow by the big mulberry tree just across the bridge.

We sat at one of the tables and Captain Cruikshank bought drinks; brandy. I noticed he had what looked like a treble. He drank it as if it were tea, and instantly fetched himself another.

"You come here often?"

Everyone had nodded to him.

"Every night. I prefer it to social life up at the manor." His dark sad eyes already had a glazed expression and he was beginning to sway slightly like a cobra; really I felt I ought to see him up the hill again, but presumably he knew the way very well indeed. He had a third drink and ordered another for me; I had hardly finished my first, which I was sipping, so by and by he absently drank the other one himself.

Our conversation had moved from *Nostromo* to the subject of guilt: a natural enough progression.

"There should be childhood inoculations against guilt, as against smallpox or polio," Captain Cruikshank declared. His articulation was very careful. I found the effect of his cobra-sway, with the small dark eyes always fixed on mine, highly hypnotic. "Most people's lives are crippled by guilt. It is the secret of a successful man like Capranis that he is immune."

"I expect you are right," I said sadly.

"Of course I am! Everybody has their own crime, their hidden torture. Even someone as apparently simple and good as you, Miss Georgia."

"Oh yes," I said, thinking of my three-year burden. "Oh God, yes."

Suddenly I felt a great sympathy for this poor riven, driven fellow. Maybe *he* was the one who had murdered Sweden. If so, doubtless he had good cause. "If we're totting up murders by indirect action, I've committed as many as most. How can we help feeling guilty all the time? Life obliges us to do such terrible things to each other."

"That's it, that is it!" He seized my hand again in his icy bony one.

"What have you done, Captain Cruikshank?"

"Oh, call me Patrice. What have I done? I have been responsible for the deaths of four people—one of them a child."

A frightful pang ran through me. I clutched the hand that held mine. It was so cold, yet imbued with feverish energy—like the hand of Death. I felt its tremor transfer to me.

"What child?"

"My own," he said sombrely. "I was offered a job. My wife begged me not to take it—she was pregnant, not well, she wanted me with her. But the job would pay more money than I had ever earned before—money I could use for my wife, to take her somewhere sunny, away from the fogs of Flanders. So I betrayed her, I took the job, and she died in childbirth while I was at sea. The child died too. I can remember at breakfast—the morning I left—"

His voice dried on him.

Betrayal, I thought. That's it. We betray each other.

My Darling: By the time you read this . . .

"Who were the other two?" I asked hoarsely. Hardly a tactful question; but we seemed to have got past tact, Captain Cruikshank and I.

"People I never met. A scientist and his wife." He spoke inattentively; he was still caught in his own private mangle, his eyes were lost inside him. But I was fixed on him with a painful interest.

"A scientist and his wife?" I prompted presently.

"I never met them," he repeated. "But they died as a result of something I had done."

"What? What had you done?"

He fetched his mind back from whatever distant scene it had been contemplating.

"I helped steal something from them. Nothing I could ever do in the rest of my life would be as deliberately wicked as that," he said dully. "By comparison, everything else is trivial."

Such as murdering Sweden? I wondered. Would one really atrocious crime anaesthetize you from guilt over any smaller peccadillo? Such as pushing me into the pottery kiln, just a practical joke taken to its logical conclusion?

"What was the scientist's name?" I persisted.

He drained what must have been his twelfth brandy and focussed on me.

"Are you trying to help me or to help yourself, Miss Georgia Marsh?"

The little dark eyes pierced mine.

"Nothing can help me, really," I muttered.

"So. Then we let sleeping crimes lie—unless *you* wish to use *me* as a father confessor?"

He smiled his limited, grim smile. No one could have been less a father confessor than this haunted alcoholic seafarer; if I were Capranis, I reflected, I would certainly not employ Captain Cruikshank to sail my yacht. But perhaps he was only addicted to brandy when on shore?

I shook my head.

"Confession doesn't help. But thank you. If I'm to be up at seven I think I should go to bed."

"I will take you to the Panas house."

My lodging was only about three minutes' walk from the taverna, round two acute corners. We traversed it in silence. Overhead I could hear the faint whistling cries of bats. When I opened the courtyard door one of them brushed past me; I felt the wind of its flight against my arm.

"What was that?" Captain Cruikshank checked, and almost overbalanced.

"The cat, after a bat. Look, there he goes."

Gata, or Gato, shot past us, and up a vine stem which was evidently his usual means of access and egress.

Two old ladies and a younger one were chatting and making fish nets in the yard. When Captain Cruikshank saw them he gave me an abrupt good night, nodded to them, and, evidently satisfied that I was sufficiently chaperoned, withdrew. I heard his footsteps turn back towards the taverna.

"Kalinikta, kalinikta," cried the ladies in chorus, jumping up. Madame Elektra stuck her netting shuttle behind her ear and offered me orange juice, coffee, slice of melon, or a nice bunch of grapes, but I explained, with thanks, that I had just come from the taverna.

"Ah, with the captain? That poor fellow! Even the moon doesn't know what he has suffered! Did he tell you about losing his wife? He always does when he has had a few brandies."

It appeared that if the moon didn't know his sad tale, everybody in Imandra did.

"And did you enjoy your day up at the castle?" the ladies asked. "Did you see the gold swimming pool? And the organ that shuts up? And the lavatories that resemble thrones, and the diamond-framed portrait of Mr. Capranis's wife who ran off and married the prime minister of England?"

"Good gracious, when was that?"

"Not the prime minister, idiot!" said the other old lady. "It was the manager of the Bank of England. Or some big bank, anyway. Oh, this was many years ago."

"He divorced her; he is not married any more now. So he has plenty of time for all his good deeds."

"Indeed he has!" came the chorus.

I felt too tired to sit listening to a recital of Capranis's good deeds, so I said good night and retired to my room, leaving the door ajar for air, climbed onto the platform bed, and flung myself down.

Talk about eidetic images! I had enough from that day's impressions to paper the walls of the Inferno; faces, faces, faces, the flanges, like dragons' teeth in the walls of the kiln, the hostility in the eyes of Mixie Koolidge, the love in the face of Capranis as he looked at his sleeping son, the Faustlike expression of Patrice Cruikshank—an odd name for a Belgian—contemplating the devils he had raised.

To settle my thoughts and dispel the flocking images, I pulled from my shoulder bag the paperback verse anthology that I had reclaimed from among Sweden's books, and read a poem by Elizabeth Bishop:

> We'd rather have the iceberg than the ship
> Although it meant the end of travel . . .*

I read it slowly and calmly; decided I could sleep now, and was about to close the book and blow out my candle when a sheet of paper fluttered from between the pages.

It was a photocopy of my own handwriting; an entry from a diary I had kept three years before.

---

* The quote from "The Imaginary Iceberg" from *Selected Poems* by Elizabeth Bishop, Chatto & Windus, © Elizabeth Bishop 1967 (Originally in an American collection, *North & South*).

VI

July 7
Dinner with M. Beautiful fine evening. Instead of Fest.
Hall concert, took picnic and walked on Hindhead.

It had been a mild, balmy night. Big summer moon overhead. Smell of warm earth, hay, honeysuckle, fading wild roses. Ever after, I'd associate those particular scents with the happiness of loving Martin and being with him. And with the absolute agony of knowing to the day when it would all end.

In October he was going back to Harvard, to his wife, Luise, and his little son, Rudi. So we had three months left.

Less than three months, as it turned out. On a Wednesday towards the end of August he had, for his own good reasons, bought a gun and a licence, written some letters, one of them to me, gone back to the flat in Gower Street he'd rented for a year, and shot himself.

Walked on Hindhead. M. talked about his research. Link between protein PN something or other and hereditary tendency to schizophrenia. Says might be possible to produce whole nation of schizos. Frightening thought. But plans to shelve that line and switch to the hormone thing. Lucky he has other lines. Lucky, lucky Martin, to be so dedicated to work. Lucky Catholic undivorcible Luise. No, that's not fair, she's ill and there's Rudi. Would I want to split Martin from sick wife, only son? Stupid question.
Drove back at six a.m. Heavenly summer morning . . .

After Martin's suicide I'd given up keeping a diary. Hadn't the heart for it. It wasn't that I had anything better to do. For weeks, all I seemed able to do was look at my watch. I did that a couple of hundred times a day, thinking: Now he might have been ringing up, or he'd be here or he'd be lecturing, or he'd be at the lab, or we'd be having a meal.

I didn't sleep much at all. Sometimes I'd slide off into a kind of stupor for half an hour and then wake, bang, with my heart racing, deceived that I'd heard the phone ring.

Is that you, *Liebling?*

No, it isn't me, it's a stranger.

Sometimes I wondered how she, Luise, was making out in Cambridge, Massachusetts. I couldn't bear to think of her for long at a time, because it was so much worse for her than it was for me. Husband and son both. And ill, as well. Did being a Catholic help? I hoped so. Sometimes I thought of writing to her; thank God I never actually got to the point. Dear Mrs. Ettlinger, you won't have heard of me, but I'm afraid this is probably all my fault.

The sort of letter that is best left unwritten.

How did I know it was probably all my fault? Because, sometime in the blank numb weeks after his death, I'd remembered the odd little episode of the diary. At the time when it happened, I hadn't given it much thought; just vaguely dismissed it as inexplicable. It had been a couple of months earlier, in June, when I may have believed that I was unhappy, but I was excruciatingly happy too.

Martin had given me the diary as a Valentine present. He'd written in it: "May it record some happy days! To dearest G. from M."

A characteristic flowery Germanic sentiment.

Well, now, I had always kept the diary at my bedside in the toe of a pair of Turkish slippers that I didn't wear because they were slightly too small. (Sweden had brought them back from one of her trips.) Lodged in a slipper, the diary was handy for a late-night entry in bed; and to the casual eye, if seen at all, would look, I suppose, as if it had fallen there from the miniature bookshelf by the bed. But it hadn't, because I never kept it on the bookshelf.

That was why I was so puzzled, one evening in June, to find it on the shelf.

Nobody else had been in my flat. I had no char, window cleaner, TV repairman, or meter reader. I had given up seeing my friends. Martin didn't come there; I went to him.

I'd puzzled over the problem, vaguely, for a day or so,

and then gave it up as insoluble but of little consequence. Until after Martin's death; then it returned to haunt me. Had it been my diary that started the whole train of events? I couldn't be sure, but even the uncertainty was torturing.

Now, I was sure.

The scrap of my photocopied writing, from a book that had been in Sweden's possession, was incontrovertible proof. Sweden was the link between my diary and Martin's death.

Sweden had known that I kept a diary; way back in my early teens I can remember her teasing me about it. So Sweden might have said to somebody: "It would be worth having a look, if you want to know what he's doing. He's running round with my sweet silly cousin; she might have written something down."

And dear, sweet, silly cousin had.

Remembering farther back, I'd actually met Martin at a party given by an acquaintance of Sweden's, a sociologist called Maria Franklin; Sweden hadn't been there, she'd been abroad, but someone who knew her might have seen me and Martin together later, might have mentioned it. I'd never told Sweden anything about Martin, but she had a great gift for getting to know things.

And now it seemed likely that she was dead of it. No sense in hating her.

I laid the book down on a piece of blood-red handwoven material beside my mattress and worked it out logically: because of Sweden, Martin and his wife died and things won't be the same for me, ever again.

Is Sweden's death a corollary of this, or due to some other of her activities? At this point in the sequence my thoughts went back to Patrice Cruikshank, haunted by his load of guilt.

Was it the same guilt as mine?

Asking myself this question, struggling over the great gap in the question, the missing piece between his story and my own, I fell into one of those sudden spells of sleep that used to knock me out for ten-minute periods after Martin's death; exhausted but shallow, generally too near the surface for proper dreams.

This time, though, I did dream.

I had gone to his flat in Gower Street. Martin was lying on the bed. At first I believed he was dead, shot; then with immense relief I realised that he was merely sleeping. "Thank God," I thought, "I can wake him and ask him."

Ask him what? There was something I desperately needed to know.

So I said, "Martin! Darling, wake up. Please wake up, listen! Please tell me—"

He stirred, he muttered something, he was waking— then, suddenly, he let out the most appalling yell.

So, next moment, he was not awake but I was—exploded out of my dream with tears of frustration on my cheeks, and also dead scared. For it had been a real noise that had woken me from my knockout nap.

I stumbled out of bed, down the three wooden steps, and out into the court. Paper-white moonlight came stencilling through the vine leaves and gave a stronger emphasis to the black-and-white pattern of cobbles on the floor.

But the yard was empty, the camp bed untenanted, the door shut, the street silent; I'd have expected that, after a cry like that, half the population of Imandra would be outside, demanding to know what went on.

Then I saw the cats. A big skinny tabby pacing athletically along the top of the wall, its tail slashing from side to side like a sickle. And Gata, the resident cat, couchant, regardant, and militant, defending his home ground. His fur couldn't stand on end because he hadn't any more than a guinea pig, but his ears were flattened and his whiskers bristled. I moved closer and saw that he was defending property as well as his yard—under his paw writhed a caterpillar, the largest I'd ever seen, six inches from tail to tail, bright green.

"Cripes. All right, Gata, *I'm* not going to pinch your lunch, relax!"

Anticlimax.

It was plain now what had woken me: merely recriminations between Gata and the neighbour. It was also plain that I wasn't going to get back to sleep in a hurry. I had all the symptoms on me, now, of a sleepless night. Racing pulse, churning thoughts: my mind seemed revved up to operate at twice its normal pace. Plans, recollections, regrets for things done wrong, done too late, not done at all, unspoken retorts I hadn't invented in time for Capranis, and, above all, the aura of my dream, turned my consciousness into a kind of furnace every bit as torrid as Phyllora's pottery kiln.

Martin. Every single thing that had happened to me since I came to Dendros led me back to Martin. No wonder I had dreamed about him. But what was the significance of the dream? I was sure it had significance; every detail from it was stamped on my memory with a stormy clarity: the bed he had lain on, curled in his deep sleep, the pattern of the brocade counter-pane, his hands, relaxed on the cushion, the way he stirred and murmured after I had thought he was dead. My subconscious wanted me to notice one of these details particularly; which?

Why can't our subconsciouses *talk*?

Patiently I went over the whole short sequence again and again, reciting it in words, visualising it. No dice. All right, then. Put it on one side. Wait.

So I waited, sitting on the camp bed, watching Gata. The rival cat had retired in dudgeon (dudgeon might have been a word expressly coined to describe the manner in which he retired), so Gata was eating his caterpillar with a fearsome satisfaction. From the febrile buzzings in my brain a recollection floated up of the man who had given me a lift into Dendros from the airport—good heavens, hardly two days ago, it seemed a lifetime—"A valley full of butterflies. Caterpillars too, exceptionally large ones. There is an anchorage. You can sail your boat in."

Maybe this caterpillar had sailed round on somebody's boat from the anchorage. Or maybe the whole island was populated by exceptionally large caterpillars.

Never mind the damn caterpillars, a slightly more rational portion of mind protested impatiently. If we can't work out anything from the dream, let's get back to Sweden.

Sweden had a hand in Martin's death. Now, three years later, she has a hand in fetching me to this island. Is there a connection between one course of action and the other? It had seemed random enough; I was out of a job, I wrote Sweden; but perhaps she had been waiting until some such opportunity came up naturally. She wanted me to come to Dendros then—why?

'If anybody, I reflected with sour satisfaction, thought that I knew something useful about Martin's work, they were in for acute disappointment. Martin's death had been a ruinous, destructive waste of three lives—four, counting mine—but at least no one had, because of it, acquired any nasty information about how to turn a whole nation into schizos. Nor ever would; he had gone systematically through his lab, burning notes and charts, smashing test tubes, before returning to Gower Street.

Anyway, why wait till now?

Because something new had come up; two people, or two bits of information, had somehow been juxtaposed; some connection had been made; somebody had recognised a hitherto unrealised relevance; or a line of research had begun to lead in Martin's direction?

It was stiflingly hot in the little court; my burns and abrasions were beginning to nag at me in various accents of pain, despite Phyllora's tube of stuff, and I couldn't take a shower because some member of the Panas family seemed to be doing a month's washing in there. Suddenly it occurred to me that Imandra bay, that shallow, inviting crescent of sea, was probably less than five minutes' walk from here; there was nothing to prevent me from taking a moonlight swim. A dip in the sea might cool and marshal my scattered thoughts.

I grabbed a towel, put on my swimsuit, softly opened the courtyard door, and slipped out. Gata took the opportunity to slip out too; his enemy had disappeared and he sat himself down on the cobbles outside the door, vigilantly glancing up and down the alley for enemies. Nobody was in sight except a black-robed priest who was absorbed in contemplation of a poster for the Athene cinema in Dendros; he took no notice of me and I stifled the doubt, bred of my late experience, that all Orthodox priests were guerrillas in disguise.

Another alley left mine at right angles and dropped sharply in the right direction; I followed it down some rough steps, round a couple of corners and, by always choosing the downhill turn, emerged into a small, sloping olive orchard that ran directly to the beach.

Leaving my towel on the sand, which still felt warm even at this time of night, I waded thankfully into the mild, motionless water. I swam, and floated, and cooled off, and calmed down. There was nobody else moving on the beach, but a few lights and faint strains of bouzouki music from Imandra showed that its inhabitants were still awake and restrainedly cheerful. The sea sighed on the sand, the cicadas strummed away in the olive grove, and from one side of the bay a screech owl once in a while let out a single shrill, complaining monosyllable which was answered in due course, two notes higher, from the other side of the bay. Up above, the stars swam in the warm sky and Capranis's castle with its ragged line of battlements between me and the moon reminded me forcibly of his battered teeth; his wife *must* have left him a long time ago, I thought irrelevantly, or she would have persuaded him to have something done about them. Yet one could see Capranis would not be an easy subject for persuasion. I wondered *how* long ago she had left him, how old Paul had been at the time; no wonder he had a somewhat waiflike, pathetic air. It must be as difficult to be the child of a millionaire as to be brought up in an underprivileged and racially segregated family.

Aware that these random thoughts were merely a defense against memory, I came out and sat on the sand with my arms round my knees, staring at the moon's reflection and trying to think logically.

Sweden had wanted me to come to Dendros for some reason connected with Martin. Good or bad? She had been somehow instrumental in his death, therefore bad. But somebody had been equally anxious to circumvent Sweden—or to prevent her seeing me?—and had gone to the lengths of killing her. Good or bad? I couldn't judge. The same person—or someone else?—had then proceeded to have a try at killing me. Good or bad? Well, bad. I had—for reasons not fully clear to myself—refrained from following Martin's example. I wanted the end of my life, when it came, to do so in a reasonably dignified manner and not at the whim of some bravo.

The calcined remains of Miss Esther Summerson were discovered in a pottery kiln on the island of Dendros yesterday . . . No, definitely not.

Now: had the person who tried to kill me done so because they thought I could identify Sweden's murderer—

as Capranis seemed to think—or for some other reason?
If so, what? Had the same person committed both acts, or
were different parties and motives involved?

It was like one of those horrible puzzles: Mrs. Brown is
sitting next to the dentist; John is by the girl whose birth-
day is in January; Susan is by the host; the dentist's wife is
by Mr. Smith; does Mr. Brown wear dentures?

Such facts as I possessed seemed too random and
scanty to form the basis of any useful hypothesis; I wasn't
getting anywhere. And presently, cool now, more soberly
aware of my surroundings, I reflected that Capranis would
not be best pleased if he knew I was sitting alone in the
dark on the beach. He had been really annoyed at my
carelessness in letting myself be shut in his oven (and I
could see his point; it would be very undesirable publicity
for his school); he would think my present situation most
unjustifiably casual.

With guilty haste I twisted the towel round my waist
and started back across the beach. Suddenly I was nervous. Although nothing moved in the olive grove, it was full
of twisted shadows which might, for all I knew, have been
The Hunchback of Notre Dame lying in wait for me; I had
to make a definite and strong-minded effort before I could
bring myself to walk among them and into that knotted
tangle of dark. To make matters worse, as soon as I did
so, I tripped over something bony and living, which got up
and hobbled away with a loud bleat of alarm, equalled and
drowned by my own yelp of fright. All the assassins in
Imandra would now be alerted to my whereabouts, I
thought, disentangling myself from the sheep, which appeared to be chained to an olive tree, and glancing distract-
edly behind me down the silver slope of sand.

What I saw turned the blood in my veins to fish glue. A
black figure in a tall hat was moving in my direction across
the beach.

I took to my heels through the olive grove. Low whippy
branches with small sharp dusty leaves battered my face
and arms; I tripped over roots, and piles of rocks, and fell
into dried watercourses. *Oh Whistle and I'll Come to You,*
I thought, dragging myself over a crumbling dry-stone
wall; the creature behind me needs only to be white, su-
pernatural, and hopping, we'd have a complete half-hour

TV horror spooky. Why, why didn't I stay in that nice snug courtyard with Gata on guard and Mrs. Panas washing the blankets and all the Panas family in easy-shouting distance? Oh, how cross Capranis is going to be when my headless body is found dangling from a fig tree. Even though I'd be dead by that time, I winced at the thought of his predictable reactions:

"Like some heroine of romance this intrepid young lady must sally out in the dark, braving nameless dangers—"

Damn. I tripped over an old petrol can—it must be really old, or some thrifty Greek would be growing marigolds in it—and fell sprawling. Behind me I heard footsteps and the rustle of branches; I scrambled up, saw a gateway ahead, and bolted through it.

The gate led to a narrow path between walls; I fled along, it turned right up a flight of steps. In a moment I realised that I had gone wrong; this was not the way I had come down to the beach. The steps went up and up with no turning; there should have been one within ten yards or so. And when I looked back, there was the black figure down at the bottom, following.

A secondary alley presently led off to the left; I was now far too high up, but perhaps I could work my way round the village and down, back to the Panas residence; perhaps I would meet someone, for heaven's sake, the village wasn't deserted; I could hardly be murdered in the public alley in broad moonlight? Could I?

For a tiny village, Imandra was wonderfully mazelike; I doubled back and forth, sobbing and gulping, between high walls, up and down cobbled alleys, looking for number thirty-seven and not finding it. Furthermore the place really did seem to be deserted: not a step, nor a voice, not a sign of life except for that distant black figure which, without even seeming to run, appeared indefatigably round corners, at the tops of steps, flitting after me with menacing persistence.

Then, suddenly, doubling a corner, I came on an explanation for the deserted streets: the entire population of Imandra seemed to be jammed in the doorway of a little onion-roofed church, or straggling round the steps to get in. Immeasurably thankful, trying to stifle my panting breath, I slowed down and tried to mingle unobtrusively with the throng. Considering I had arrived at top speed and was wearing only a towel over a swimsuit, this was not notably successful; but kindly hands patted me on the back and I heard voices saying:

"It's the young English lady who's staying with Elektra Panas; naturally she wishes to go in; make way for her, let her through!"

I was shovelled through the crowd like a Rugger ball through a scrum, and, hurriedly shrouding myself togawise in the towel, arrived, through a smell of incense thick as porridge, inside the church. I had just time for one rapid, blazing impression of an interior completely tiled, enamelled, frescoed, painted, and gilded all over, like the inside of a Christmas pudding, before all the lamps went out and, onto a sheet which had been hung across the east wall, a rather unsteady projector threw a beam of light which presently turned into an early *Silly Symphony* about Donald Duck. He was trying to work in his garden and was being persecuted by huge champing beetles, voracious moths and birds, caterpillars which turned themselves into two feet and a U-bend and capered around on his seedlings while Donald pursued them, jabbering with rage, always too late, and the sympathetic Greeks shouted advice and fell about laughing.

The sight of Donald giving chase to a beetle reminded me of my own predicament. I turned to scan the crowd. One lamp still burned by the door and against its glimmer I was dismayed to see a high square black cap making its purposeful way in my direction. Sliding and wriggling I worked through the audience, across the church, towards a side door which stood open, presumably to let some air into the stifling interior.

"Oh, po, po, the poor young lady is too hot; help her out, let her through!"

Hands as kind as those which had passed me in now eased me out of the side door; but to my deep discouragement I found that I was now in a tiny square courtyard with no other exit. It did, however, have a handsome pomegranate tree, covered with fruit, growing against the left-hand wall. Nobody was looking; all heads were turned the other way, all eyes fixed on Donald; I clambered swiftly up the tree, which had low branches, and came face to face with Gata (or his twin) crouched on top of the wall. He certainly seemed to recognise me, and greeted me with a loud chirrup of welcome.

Amazed and relieved, I looked down into the Panas courtyard; there was just room to wriggle between the bunches of grapes and lines of washing and drop down onto the cobbles by the camp bed.

Mrs. Panas was sitting in the doorway mending a pair of trousers.

"Spondiko save us!" she exclaimed. "This young lady is mad about dropping from the sky! I thought you had gone down to the beach for a swim—Maria saw you start that way—and all the time you were flying through the air!"

"I—I called in at the cinema on the way home, kyría, and—and this seemed like a good short cut."

"I have used that pomegranate tree myself, in my young days," she said with a chuckle, "when the prayers went on rather too long and I was afraid the lamb stew would burn."

"You are up very late, kyría."

"I stayed up to warn you," she said, knotting her thread.

My heart scraped up and down like a seismograph. "Warn me?"

"Captain Cruikshank is here. He said he wished to speak to you. But he is very drunk. I was afraid it might be upsetting for you."

I looked again and realised that what I had taken for a pile of clothes waiting to be mended was in fact the captain, huddled in a patch of vine shadow leaning against the wall. I went and knelt beside him.

"Captain Cruikshank? You had something you wanted to tell me?"

He didn't answer, so I took his cold, cold bony hand. Then he slowly opened his eyes; I could just catch their faint shine, and the twitch of the mouth.

The hand clenched on mine, and I only just stopped myself from crying out.

"Captain Cruikshank? It's Georgia Marsh. Madame Panas said you wanted to see me? To say something?"

He stared at me for a long time in silence. The corners of his mouth twitched again, that was all. Suddenly I felt terribly tired; sleep seemed to be creeping up me from my toes; when it reached eye level I'd be done for. The sense of calm that accompanied this drowsy state made me wonder if I hadn't ridiculously exaggerated this notion that the priest was pursuing me; he was probably not after me at all, or, if he had been, merely wished to reprimand me on behalf of the Imandra Public Decency Committee, to tell me my swimsuit violated the local bylaws. Without doubt I had made a fuss over nothing. Anyway all I wanted now, and that passionately, was to go to bed.

"Captain Cruikshank? Patrice? What was it?"

"Oliver Twist," he said, rousing a little.

"I beg your pardon?"

This was no time, I strongly felt, for one of our literary discussions.

"Oliver Twist. All those orphans—but *he* lived on. They all died of smallpox—eight, nine, ten, those slum children had no resistance—but *he* lived on."

"Oliver Twist?" I was baffled. So far as I could recall, no one died of smallpox in that book; it was TB that had carried off little Dick.

"Are you sure you're not getting it mixed up with *Bleak House?* Those slum children had smallpox; Esther caught it from them."

"*No!*" He was so irritated by my stupidity that he almost ground the bones of my hand together. "Not in book at all! Not smallpox—diphtheria. Children on the ship." He paused for a while, as if his thoughts were wandering far back, and said sourly, "It would have been better if you hadn't come."

"I'm inclined to agree."

"Don't interrupt."

His articulation was very slurred; could you wonder, after heaven only knew how many brandies; no doubt he had several more after leaving me.

"I tried to stop it."

"Stop what?"

"Look," he said laboriously, "it was the only good thing I ever did. Don't—don't spoil it."

"Of *course* I won't, Captain Cruikshank." I put all the earnestness that I could into my voice because he sounded so despairing. He kept repeating, "Please, please don't spoil it. Don't let them take him now."

"Truly I won't! But you'll have to explain what you mean because I haven't the least notion what you're talking about."

"I never knew which one he was. I took care not to. Old wash-hands Pontius Cruikshank. I said he'd died though."

"Who had died?"

"The boy."

I began to tremble.

"Your son?"

"No, not my son," he said furiously, and muttered to himself, "I thought she seemed intelligent. If I'd known she was such a fool I probably needn't have bothered. But I thought she'd know him. That was why I thought I'd better stop her seeing him."

"Who?"

He suddenly gave me a smile of great and surprising charm that transformed his haunted face and, coughing, said,

"Well, well, I shall have to rely on you. After all, it is ironic that you should be alive and I should be dead." He coughed again and fell forward with his head in my lap. Disconcerted, I tried to raise him; he slipped heavily sideways. A small thread of saliva dribbled onto my towel, where his head now rested.

"Madame Panas! Kyría! I am afraid he is very ill!"

"It is not to be wondered at," she muttered, coming to look at him. "A man who takes that amount of drink every night—"

When she had examined him more closely she crossed herself three times.

"If he hasn't gone to God before sunrise, I shall be surprised. And really, it would be just as well, or one of these days he would certainly have run Kyrie Capranis's fine ship on a rock and then six men from the village would have been drowned too who have wives and children to support, whereas that poor fellow had no one. No, it's better as it is. But we had better get the priest to him; if ever a man seemed to have something on his conscience, he was the one. And I'll fetch my son, and a few neighbours to carry him to my daughter's; it is not very nice for a young English lady like you to have a dying man outside your bedroom door."

She hurried off. And I sat on in the little court, which had been hot but now seemed cold, watching over Captain Cruikshank, who lay speechless, looking up at the silvered grapes overhead; still with a small, ironic smile.

VII

The seven o'clock sun was already hot, and I was grateful for the shade of the big mulberry tree that stood on a grassy hummock in the middle of the flat space outside the village walls. Orange, and olive groves stretched away across the plain and the main road cut through them on a causeway bordered by cypresses. There was a two-way flow of traffic, for donkeys were coming into the village, laden with tomatoes and melons, and fishermen were carrying baskets of tunny and octopus from the little anchorage at the rocky end of the beach, while commuters, on their motorbikes, set off for daily-bread occupations in the city of Dendros. I sat on a rock watching them. The half-dozen tables set in the dust outside a morning-glory-covered café across the road did a brisk turnover in hasty coffee drinkers; slightly removed from them, under a grape arbour, a bearded, black-cassocked priest sat with his back to the road, absorbed in a newspaper.

A dusty little Fiat drew up beside me.

"You are the young lady who wishes to go to Dendros? Please to take a seat."

The unshaven, curly-headed driver gave me a gold-toothed grin and indicated ten inches of seat between the door and a box of mackerel.

"It's extremely kind of you but I've really come to say I've changed my mind and think I will stay here a little longer."

Far from being put-out, he was delighted. "Aha, you like our village!" he beamed. "It is the best village in the island, you are right to stay. Ask my cousin to take you fishing, his name is Aristides Markos, he lives at number forty-nine, he will be glad to do it for you, he has a fine boat!"

"Thank you, I'll certainly do that another day. This morning I have to go and see Mr. Capranis."

"Better still! You have decided to teach at his school?"

"I was thinking about it," I said cautiously. "I wonder, would it be a trouble for you to deliver this note for Captain Plastiras at the police station in Dendros?"

"Not the least trouble in the world! My sister's husband's cousin is a clerk there, I shall be glad of a chat with him. You write to Captain Plastiras about a residence permit, without doubt?"

"Without doubt," I agreed, and he stuck the note among the mackerel, gave me a last flash of his teeth, and roared dustily away. Next moment a Renault drew up beside me.

"Want a lift to the big city? I'm going in for a couple of hours' shopping. I hear you're leaving."

It was the blond Mixie Koolidge. I got no gilt-edged smile from her; she was curt to the edge of rudeness. Well, well, I thought, yesterday all the tea in China wouldn't have bought me a ride into town, today everyone is falling over themselves to be helpful. Quite a change.

"Thanks, but I've decided not to go. Heavens, you're up early."

"Oh," she said unconvincingly, "I like early morning. You just have to start early in this climate or you'd never get anything done. Sure you won't come? Well, okay."

Looking a little put-out she revved her engine unnecessarily loud and accelerated jerkily away. I could almost picture Capranis's smile as he looked after her.

I walked thoughtfully back along the warm, cobbled donkey-smelling alley that led to the Panas homestead, in search of a pair of sunglasses and some cooler garb; it was already hotter than it had been yesterday.

Last night had been fairly busy. It had been well into the small hours before I got to sleep. By the time that ten strong men plus the priest had come and ascertained that Captain Cruikshank was not dead, but unconscious, and had carried him off ceremonially up the hill to Aghios Georgios, and had then returned to drink ouzo and coffee and agree that considering his habits and the state of his health and conscience, the captain would almost certainly die within the next few months, I had been so exhausted that when I did at last retire I slept like a sloth and dreamed about nothing at all. But I woke with all the un-answered questions in my mind set hard as cement, and a fixed resolve not to leave Dendros until I had interrogated Capranis again and learned something more about the causes of all these apparently interconnected occurrences.

"You are going up to the abbey?" said Mrs. Panas, coming in with a lobster kicking under her arm as I put madras dungarees on over a thin muslin shirt. "Perhaps you would be so kind as to take this book, which the cap-tain must have dropped last night when he was taken ill."

"Of course, kyría."

It was a paperback copy of *Bleak House,* thumbed and dog-eared. I felt faintly touched—had the captain taken it out to read following our conversation on the harbour bench? I looked inside the cover and there was his name: Patrice Kroeksjank.

Not Cruikshank, Kroeksjank. Spelt like that it had a sudden optical familiarity. It was linked in my mind with a ship's name, the *Orfeo.* What did I know about Captain Kroeksjank of the *Orfeo,* and why was his story somehow associated with memories of my own worst period of un-happiness?

I slid the book into a capacious dungaree pocket, slung my handbag over my shoulder, and set off walking slowly up the hot hillside.

Kroeksjank of the *Orfeo.* Trying visual recall, I could see the name in Times Roman headlines. And the word diphtheria figured in the memory too. What had the cap-tain been saying about diphtheria last night:

They all died of diphtheria—eight, nine, ten slum children—but *he* lived on?

I sat on a rock under a cypress tree and stared down at the turquoise semicircle of Imandra bay.

DIPHTHERIA EPIDEMIC STRIKES
CHILDREN'S CRUISE SHIP

That was it. The *Orfeo* had crossed the Atlantic with
two hundred schoolchildren on a vacation cruise and had
reached the Mediterranean when diphtheria broke out and
some Italian port refused to let them dock; several children had died, and two or three of the adult counsellors as
well. There had been a lot of international ill will, criticism of the unfortunate captain—for not going on, for not
turning back, not defying the Italian port authorities.

Where had the ship sailed from? The *Orfeo's* misfor-
tune—that was it, of course—had coincided with the time
of my own worst grief; I had followed the headlines from
day to day with a kind of dreary apathy and in the end
had lost track of what became of the liner and her stricken
passengers. But—*wait a minute*—hadn't the ship sailed
from Boston? With two hundred mixed schoolchildren on
board—half from fee-paying homes and schools, others
from public schools in and around Boston, their fares paid
by some benevolent trade union with more cash than it
knew how to spend.

From Boston. Why hadn't that fact seemed of significance before?

So many discoveries are made because of a temporal
juxtaposition. You pass the hole A every day for three
years, and then on the one thousand and ninety-ninth day
you happen to be carrying the plug B in your hand, so you
try it in the hole.

And it fits.

*My Darling: By the time you read this letter I shall be
dead. It is a terrible pain not to be able to see you once
more, but I do not have the time. They have kidnapped
my Rudi. I have had a phone call saying that unless I return to East Germany and co-operate, I shall never see
him again. You can guess why—the Russians want the results of my Project A. Luise has telephoned from Boston.
She is desperate. Boston is the only place where she can
receive the right treatment. And I—I cannot go back. My
only hope is that if I am dead, they will not think it worth
while to keep Rudi, or that world opinion will force them*

to return him. *Otherwise this will kill Luise, and I have done her enough harm already.*

I am not a brave man, my darling. The thought that you will grieve for me makes me weep as I write this. If they caught me I do not think I could be resolute. So I have destroyed all my work and am taking the only action I can. I hope heaven will forgive me and make them send Rudi back. You and he are all I love—I shall be praying for you both at the last moment of my life.

Martin.

But they had not sent Rudi back.

It was possible that they had not been able to. The American police had a theory that a child's body, too badly charred to be identifiable, found in a crashed burnt-out Buick in a stretch of woodland in the Catskills, might be the missing Ettlinger boy; but there were several other missing boys he might have been. The case was never solved. And Luise Ettlinger's leukemia had taken a turn for the worse, and in due course she had died.

No one, apparently, had wondered about the cruise liner *Orfeo* with a cargo of mixed schoolchildren steaming towards Europe.

Too impatient to sit still any longer, I jumped to my feet and hurried on up the hill at a reckless pace.

I must see Captain Cruikshank again.

But supposing he was too ill to talk?

Well, he had said a certain amount last night. And what he had said now seemed highly meaningful. I had little doubt that he had been involved in the plot to kidnap Rudi and this had lain like a red-hot coal in his conscience ever since. No wonder he looked so haunted. He had reason to.

But he had also said: "It was the only good thing I ever did. Don't spoil it."

What had he meant by that?

Did he—could he mean that Rudi was still alive—was *not* somewhere behind the Iron Curtain but was safe, looked after, in good hands, and that I wasn't to interfere?

It certainly sounded that way. And if so, then the inference was obvious: he was here, in Capranis's school.

"That was why I thought I had better stop her seeing him," Cruikshank had said.

I sat down on another rock. If Captain Cruikshank's method of preventing me from seeing and recognising Rudi Ettlinger had been to push me into a pottery kiln, I felt it was only just that he should subsequently have suffered from a heart attack. So, from my point of view, the fact that he was now laid up and incapacitated, although it meant that I would probably have difficulty in obtaining access to and further information from him, at least meant that I was safe, for the moment, from any more lethal attempts of his to hamper my researches.

But what about the priest who had followed me about the village? He was certainly not the same priest who had been summoned to pronounce on Captain Cruikshank— the latter had been so remarkably fat that he had collapsed the Panas camp bed when politely invited to sit on it.

Well, the priest who had followed me could not have been Cruikshank in disguise, because Cruikshank had been waiting in the Panas courtyard in a collapsed condition for an hour before I returned. The more I thought about it, the more I was inclined to believe that my anxious imagination had exaggerated the whole affair; doubtless the priest who roamed after me had just suffered from harmless clerical curiosity.

Lightheartedly I dismissed him from my mind and went on through the massive wooden doors of Aghios Georgios.

The first person I saw was Capranis himself, engaged in serious conversation with the gardening Uncle Elias, who was pointing furiously at a pelican that sat with dignity on a nearby buttress of the castle wall. Capranis kept shaking his head, throwing it up with eyes half-closed; he looked like a supercilious goat. Then, seeing me, he gave me his beaming Mephistophelian grin and strolled over to intercept me.

"Ah, my dear Miss Georgia! I am so glad you have survived the excitements of the night."

Uncle Elias followed him expostulating.

"No, Elias! I will not have it. He wants me to shoot the pelican," Capranis explained. "He says it brings ill-luck. It has been sitting here for the last hour, casting the evil eye on his tomato plants."

Luckily at that moment the pelican solved the situation by launching itself languidly off the buttress. It rose, circled, planed down in an immense half-mile curve across Imandra bay, and flapped on northwards until it was merely a white speck vanishing in the direction of Turkey.

Elias shook an earthy fist after it and stumped back to his gardening.

"How is Captain Cruikshank?" I asked.

"Not at all well, poor dear fellow. But what can you expect if he will put away all that brandy? We are waiting for an air ambulance—ah, there it comes, in fact; Phyllora wants to get him to hospital in Nicosia for observation."

From the direction in which the pelican had disappeared, a vibrating dot approached our headland.

"I hope Patrice did not distress you too much last night? He can be very boring, I am afraid, when he falls into one of his depressions. I am sorry now that I suggested him for your escort."

Capranis did not look sorry. He darted one of his razor-sharp analytical glances at me.

"He didn't bore me a bit," I said. "On the contrary."

The helicopter's closer approach now drowned conversation, and Capranis bustled off to prepare for its reception. Newhouse, the handsome history master, was flagging it down onto the flat area at the top of the flight of steps which had once been the forecourt of Athene's temple; it seemed a suitable enough landing site for a vehicle of healing.

Down below, on the doorstep of the school building, a group of children sat watching absorbedly while Phyllora Tatula superintended the carrying-out of Captain Cruikshank on a stretcher and his careful insertion into the helicopter.

"I will say good-bye to you for the present, Miss Georgia," Capranis presently said, returning to me after conversation with the pilot. "I am going to Nicosia with the ambulance for a business conference. But I have told John to look after you; he will keep a most careful eye on you, I promise!"

"John?" Oh, the secretary, I remembered; he certainly gave the impression of an efficient, painstaking character.

Capranis was watching me as if he expected an outburst

of indignation from me at my being abandoned to the
perils of Aghios Georgios without his protection, but since
I had decided that Captain Cruikshank had pushed me
into the kiln, I was fairly calm on this head. I did feel a bit
put-out because I'd hoped to interrogate Capranis about
the *Orfeo,* but that would just have to wait for his return.

Phyllora came up to us biting her lip.

"I will have to go in with Patrice," she said. "The attend-
ant they have sent is utterly inexperienced. It is annoying, as Poppy has one of her migraines and I doubt if she
will be able to take classes today."

"If you are anxious about the children," Capranis said
gallantly, "I am sure you have no cause; just give Miss
Georgia a quick briefing and I have no doubt that she with
Newhouse and Sandstrom will be able to hold the fort till
you return. I shall probably fly back from Nicosia this evening if I can get my business affairs settled in time; I
promised Paul that I would be back for the picnic; so if
Patrice is all right you can return with me."

She still appeared far from happy but evidently there
was no alternative.

"Come and meet the children then," she said to me
worriedly. "I am sorry, it is not that I doubt your ability,
but to leave them with somebody they have not even met
is not at all what I would normally approve of doing.
However I am sure that, as Mr. Capranis says, you will
manage most excellently."

I felt none of her confidence.

"Supposing there is an accident—like the boy cutting
himself on the broken tile?"

"Oh, you need have no concern about that. Otto Firgaard has two very efficient Swedish nursing assistants in
the Athene wing; they are looking after Fernand, and if
there should be any accident of a physical nature, they can
cope. No, it is just that we take such pains to instill a feeling of confidence and security into the children by having
always at hand someone they know and trust; now, lately,
this has been so much impaired; first there was Miss Quindrell's accident; then your cousin, whose visits are always
popular, did not return when she was expected to do so;
now simultaneously Poppy has a migraine and I have to
be absent for the day; it is most unfortunate."

Feeling hideously inadequate, I followed her to the group of children who were sitting on the steps of the school building.

"Is Captain Cruikshank going to die?" demanded Suzanne Koolidge in her strident voice.

Phyllora gave this question her usual serious attention.

"No, I think not," she said. "He has had a bad heart attack it is true, but I think with good care he will get better. Now I have to go into Nicosia with him, to keep an eye on him in the plane, so here is Miss Georgia Marsh, who is going to take your classes today instead of me."

"Where's Poppy? Why isn't she going to teach us?" asked a burly dark-haired boy with a snub nose.

"She has one of her severe headaches, Mark; she is lying down. She may get better in the course of the day, but you are not to disturb her; she will get up if she can."

There were nods at this; evidently Poppy's migraines were an understood phenomenon.

"Miss Marsh is a cousin of Dr. Hannfelder," Phyllora went on, "so in a way she is not quite a stranger. And Robert and Jimmy will be here, of course, and Professor Firgaard."

"Blotto Otto," somebody murmured.

Phyllora ignored this.

"I must go now," she ended briskly. "The longer we keep Captain Cruikshank out of hospital, the less good his chances are. I shall probably be flying back this evening with Mr. Capranis—unless Captain Cruikshank should become very much worse during the next few hours—and will see you then. So have a happy day. I had meant to show Georgia all the things you do, but now you will have to do that and explain our ways to her. Good-bye."

She then embraced each child—there were about twenty, varying in age from five to ten—leaving out none, favouring none. In return they gave her heartfelt hugs. I was interested to observe that she did not ask them to behave well with a stranger; that she did not promise to bring them rewards or goodies from Nicosia; that she did not suggest they should prepare some lovely surprise for her return; that she expressed no anxiety for their welfare; that she did not smile at them. And that they seemed entirely satisfied with this treatment.

Capranis and Phyllora climbed into the helicopter, the doors closed, the staccato rumpus of the engine augmented to a blood-curdling crescendo and then swung up into the bright sky; they were gone.

I sat down on the steps with the twenty unknown children and took stock of them. They took stock of me. One thing, this day was not going to leave much time for worrying about Sweden's murder, or my attempted murder.

"Let's start with your names," I suggested. "I don't know anybody but Suzanne and Paul."

"Our names are Niko, Mark, Hans, Ninian, Salvador, Dino, Darius, Charlot, Andrew, Gregorious, Paul, Aristides, Elene, Sophia, Persephone, Artemis, Suzanne, Ariadne, Polly and Michelle."

"Right: now let's see if I remember."

I went through the group a couple of times naming and identifying, till I had them fairly fixed in my mind. And thought: one of these may be Martin's son; which? All the boys were dark, except for Hans, but he was about nine; too old, I thought, to be Rudi Ettlinger.

There had been photographs of Rudi at the time of the snatch, but he had been only two at the time; it wasn't even really possible to tell from them if he had been dark or fair. But Martin had been dark, and so, he had told me, was Luise.

A fig hit me on the back of the neck; I had let my attention wander from the group a moment too long and Mark, obviously a potential trouble-leader, was getting bored.

I picked up the fig; it was ripe, so I ate it.

"Now what would you generally do at this time of day?"

"Throw figs at each other," said Mark, giving me a mocking, measuring stare which had such a familiar quality that I instantly wondered if he could be an illegitimate son of Capranis; or had he picked up the expression by imitation?

"No we would *not* throw figs," said Artemis, a tidy, prissy little girl with her hair done in a knee-length plait. "Mark is just being silly. We'd have a PT lesson with Poppy."

"We have PT and dancing before it gets too hot, you see," instructed Ariadne.

"Bloody boring it is, too," muttered Hans. "Only fit for girls." He was speaking Greek, fluent but inaccurate; this, with a mixture of other languages when somebody was stuck for a word, seemed to be the common tongue.

"Oh. Well I don't know a lot about PT and dancing, but I do know quite a bit about bullfighting, so I suggest we have a bullfight."

"A *bullfight?* Have you lived in Spain then?" said Mark.

"No, in the South of France where they have bullfights too. Now, we'll want some people to be bulls—"

"I'll be a bull!" shouted Mark.

"And some bullfighters—they have to be very light and quick on their feet. The bullfighters should have cloaks, and I'll show you what to do with them."

Ariadne and Sophia ran off to get towels for use as cloaks, while the boys began charging each other enthusiastically.

"What should I be?" asked Paul, coming up to me. He had clung to his father by the helicopter until the last possible moment, and since then had been silent and subdued. I noticed for the first time that he had a slight stammer; it hadn't showed yesterday when he was talking to his father.

"Well, we need some picadors—they ride around on horses guiding the bull towards the matador—and some chulos, they distract the bull by waving cloaks at him."

"I'll be a horse!" announced Gregorious, a large, good-natured simple-looking boy. "You can ride on me, Paul, you can be a picador!"

"Okay." Gentle-natured Paul seemed relieved to be allocated a fairly neutral part in the game; I had a sudden qualm, wondering if undreamed-of bloodthirsty tendencies would be aroused in these problem children by my rash suggestion.

But, as so often with spur-of-the-moment improvisations, it proved a most successful activity. Having demonstrated the basic passes with cloaks, I sat back and let them organise the bullfight themselves, on the flat bit of ground under the big fig tree. In no time the sheer choreographic charm of what they were doing had me dumbstruck; it was hard to believe they hadn't been playing this game all their lives. The bulls charged with heads down and upheld arms to represent horns; the matadors, agile and light as gnats, vaulted over the outspread horns; the picadors and chulos gracefully darted in and out, waving their towels, bombarding the bulls with green figs. I wondered if possibly some of these children had Cretan ancestry; it seemed as if an inbred knowledge of bull-ring technique had suddenly sprouted and blossomed in them, imbuing all their actions with a perfection which one would have sworn must come from years of practice. They fell into their roles naturally; some of the girls preferred to sit round the outskirts of the ring, improvising mantillas from twigs and fig leaves, tossing geranium flowers and shouting *Ole;* but other girls were among the most skillful matadors. Gradually the game assumed more and more of a formal pattern; in the course of a couple of hours it was as if centuries of tradition had been assimilated, sifted, retained or rejected, and harmonised in something that might have been a sacred ritual.

John Smith, the secretary, wandered back and forth several times while the game was in progress; he had a preoccupied air, carried papers, and did not stop, but he cast a careful eye over the group each time; evidently he was carrying out Capranis's instruction to watch my interests.

When a bell sounded from the school building it seemed to shake us all down from some higher plane onto the mundane level of meals and lessons.

"Gee," said Suzanne, coming up to me, "that was really, really cool." She plumped herself down in the dust beside me, shaking the long tangled blond hair back from her scarlet face. Suzanne had been one of the most ingenious and intrepid matadors, inventing endless new permutations of feints and vaults. It had been interesting to see the transformation of a seemingly aggressive, sulky personality into something so dedicated and controlled.

"Liked it, did you?"

"Uhuh. When can we do it again?"

"I suppose when you have some more free time. Shouldn't you be going with the others now? What happens next?"

"Uh-uh." She shook her head, using the same grunt for me as for yes. "The others have an English class with

Bobby now but I don't; see, I speak English good already."

"Yes of course. So what would you do now?"

"Talk to my mommy I guess. But she's gone into Dendros. Shall I show you round?"

"Okay."

She grabbed my hand. "C'mon then; tell you what, we'll go and see how Fernand's getting on. I guess he may be a bit bored."

She led me through the school villa. In one of the airy classrooms, Robert Newhouse had his students all sitting in yoga position while he stood on his head and shouted questions at them; the doctrines of Ole Södso undoubtedly made for an unusual variety in teaching habits.

Suzanne took me on towards the building that Capranis had referred to as the Athene wing.

"Are we allowed in here?"

"Oh sure. This is where the sick bay is. And they keep the nuts here too, but they won't hurt you; see, most of 'em don't move around much."

Puzzled, I followed her up an outside flight of stairs. From what Capranis had said, I had gathered that the children in this wing were maladjusted, mixed-up, out of control, but Suzanne's words seemed to suggest that they were spastic or physically retarded. I felt a chill qualm of dread; suppose Martin's Rudi was one of these? And would it be so surprising—wasn't autism, for instance, thought by some to be the result of a drastic early experience? And what could be more drastic than to be kidnapped at the age of two?

But first we went into a big, air-conditioned sick bay, its walls painted in calm cheerful colours. A blond nurse was changing the dressing on Fernand's lip; she nodded to us. Fernand didn't pay much attention, either to us, or to the nurse and her activities; he was curled up in an armchair watching a film cartoon which was projected onto the ceiling.

"Hi, Fernand," Suzanne said rather bashfully. "Is your lip okay? I'm sorry I tripped you. Didn't think you'd hurt yourself so bad. It wasn't really my fault—Captain Cruikshank bumped up against me. Tell you what—when you're better I'll help you make another tile."

"You?" said Fernand coldly, taking his eyes from the ceiling for a moment. "You couldn't make a mud pie." But his rancour seemed to have died down during the night. "As a matter of fact," he went on loftily, "it doesn't matter because I've got plans for a much better tile; I'm going to tell Phyllora about it. When will she be back?"

"Tonight, I guess. *She*—" Suzanne nodded over her shoulder at me, "is looking after us. Poppy's got a migraine. Jeepers, Fernand, we had a bullfight. She showed us how. It was real great!"

"Bullfight, *hein?*" A gleam of interest showed in Fernand's eye. "Just you wait till I'm better and I'll show you a trick or two; there's not much about bullfighting *I* don't know."

"Time for your drink now, Fernand," said the nurse, and handed him a cup with a straw. Suzanne took me down some stairs and along a passage. Open windows along one side of it gave on to a shaded veranda with babies in cots; then she passed another big, cool nurserylike room with two glass walls.

"That's where they look after the kids who are too sick to do proper lessons," Suzanne said calmly. "Of course we do some things with them, but they don't talk so good and, like, some of them can't walk or sit up or anything. I guess they're real, real sick. And a few of them are pretty mean, too, but some of them are nice. There's Benny, he's my friend. He's *real* nice, only he never says anything. Hi, Ben!"

Leaving my side she darted through a sliding door and up to a boy in a wheelchair. "You getting on okay, Ben?" she said, and gave him a hug. "Look, I brought you a flower." She pulled it, rather squashed, out of her jeans pocket. "No, you don't put it in your *mouth,* Benny, you smell it—like this, see?"

A flash of recognition lit the boy's dark eyes as she held the syringa flower to his nose, and he smiled. I saw Professor Firgaard, who was moving about among the immobile occupants of this room, give Suzanne an approving nod; he made me a formal, Scandinavian bow, but did not come over and speak. Feeling an intruder, I moved on, but stopped, puzzled by the dreamlike, other-dimensional atmosphere of this place; why did it make me feel as if I were in a looking-glass world?

I looked at the dozen or so children who were here, in cots, in playpens, in baby chairs, in swings; playing with sand, with water, with plastic cubes, with wooden blocks. Like the bullfighting contingent, they were mainly between five and ten, but some were older still; they were too old for these occupations.

Then the real strangeness of the scene hit me: *each of these children had a replica in the other half of the school.*

Suzanne came back to me.

"Let's go play the organ," she said, grabbing my hand again. "Mr. Capranis told Paul you were going to play for him. And he doesn't like me to do it when he's around; he says I make a god-awful row. So this is a good time while he's away."

She pulled me along into the open, rock-studded ground between the two buildings. The normal, blazing outdoor midday Greek heat hit us; the real world asserted its existence again.

"Suzanne?"

"What's the trouble?" she said. "You sick, Miss Georgia? You look kind of green."

"Those children in there—"

"Did they scare you?" she said kindly. "We're so used to them we don't worry about them. But I guess they might be kind of scary to a stranger. They won't hurt you, you know."

"Are they brothers and sisters of the children in the other half of the school?"

This—it faintly occurred to me—might be the explanation; but could it account for such absolute, identical likenesses? Twins? Could those alert, silent, rayless children all be the twins of my bullfighters? My vital, inspired bullfighters?

But Suzanne was shaking her head.

"No, they're adopted."

"Adopted?"

"Mr. Capranis has adopted them."

"He *has?*"

Was he then, in reality, as benevolent as the village people asserted? Were my dark suspicions of him really groundless?

"Gee, Miss Georgia, it's kind of hard to explain." Suzanne sat on a rock under the fig tree; absently, I followed her example. "Well, see, that Benno you saw me talking to, he's Mrs. Radici's little boy. Well, he's real *nice*, I like him a lot, but he won't ever grow up very *bright*, you see?"

I did see. It was plain there was little, very little normal future for Benno.

"Well, he's *happy* here," pursued Suzanne. "Like, Professor Firgaard knows lots of ways to keep Ben interested, so he won't be just bored all the time. Mrs. Radici wouldn't *ever* have time to do all the things Professor Firgaard thinks up for Benny. She's kind of a cross lady; I don't like her much. She used to get real mad with Ben when he lived with her."

"How do you know that?" I asked curiously.

Suzanne turned and stared at me with her large pale-grey eyes.

"Why, Ben's my *friend*. It's like, when you've got a friend, you don't always have to talk in words, you know?"

"Yes, I see."

"Well," Suzanne went on, "Mrs. Radici still wanted to *have* a little boy, I guess. She was used to having one, see, and there'd been pictures of her in all the papers with Benny when he was born, 'cause she's kind of famous, isn't she, like my mommy. So she asked Mr. Capranis to find her another boy and he found her Dino."

Dino. One of the most inspired of the matadors; a lively, flashing boy with a wide grin and a mop of black hair; own twin, anybody would have said, to the speechless Ben.

"But—Dino's own parents—?"

"Dino's mommy and daddy, see, *they* were killed in an earthquake; Dino comes from a village called Pischia that all fell down."

I gaped at Suzanne, shocked silent by what I dimly began to grasp of the underlying function of Capranis's establishment. After a minute or two I found voice enough to croak,

"Well—well then, Suzanne, are you adopted too?"

"Oh, gosh no, Miss Georgia, *I'm* real! I mean, I really belong to my mommy. My dad ran off when I was a baby though," she added calmly. "That's why Mommy is going to marry Mr. Capranis."

"*Is* she?"

"Oh, sure. That's why she sends me to this school, you see? So she gets to see him a lot. I don't mind, I like it here. I don't like Mr. Capranis so much, though, and he doesn't like me."

More food for thought. I sat assimilating it.

There were a lot of questions I wanted to ask; but Suzanne, shrewd, dispassionate, and knowledgeable though against all probability she was, could not be the proper person to interrogate.

She went on with her revelations, however.

"Then, there's Salvador—*his* father's a prince, you see, and awful rich; it just wouldn't do for him to have a son who wasn't very bright. His real son's Juanito—he was the one sitting in the playpen playing with sand—"

"Good heavens, Suzanne," I said faintly. "Does Mr. Capranis *know* that you know all this?"

"Well," she said thoughtfully, "I dunno. It's not a secret, exactly. Only, nobody talks about it. Well, Benny and Juanito and the others *can't,* of course; and, see, it's nice for Salvador and Dino to be adopted by rich folks, isn't it, so they aren't grumbling?"

"No, I suppose not."

"Andy, his father and mother are pop singers, Major and Mynah, you know? They used to take their baby round with them—"

The Mynah birds and their little chick. I remembered. A pretty picture that would certainly be spoilt by the vacant-eyed stare of Andy's twin, sitting in a wheelchair, aimlessly rapping a wooden brick against his play tray.

Another bell rang.

"Oh, gosh, that's dinner," said Suzanne. "We'll have to go play the organ after."

"Are you sure we'll be able to get it open?" I asked, remembering the Grand Guignol mechanism that operated its doors.

"Oh, sure. Anyhow, I know another way in that I bet

even Mr. Capranis doesn't know. I know *lots* of things about this castle that other people don't know," Suzanne boasted.

We walked over to the main castle building.

Lunch, it seemed, was served here with some formality in a large dining room at the extreme other end from the wing that contained Capranis's study. It was a formally decorated room with dull blue walls and rococo gilt trimmings, opening on to a terrace with potted orange trees. There were white tablecloths, flowers, waiters (I recognised a couple of lads from the taverna, last night, and Maria, serving salad, gave me a grin). Children and visiting parents ate separately, at small tables. It occurred to me that of course this meal was organised so that adoptive parents and children should have a chance to get used to one another. I noticed Almina Radici and the lively Dino facing each other in glum silence over their souvlakia; from time to time she said something short and sharp, apparently in condemnation of his table manners, for he scowled and wiped his fingers on his napkin.

Parentless children ate together at a large table in the middle, presided over by John Smith, Sandstrom, and Newhouse. Evidently Poppy was still laid low with her migraine. Suzanne and I went and sat down.

"Hullo," said Newhouse. "I've been hearing about your bullfight. Seems to have caught everyone's fancy—they're all asking when they can do it again." He grinned. "Lord knows what old Otto will say when he hears about it, mind! Bullfighting's not quite in line with his pacifist views."

"Oh, good heavens—"

"Don't worry! We've got to channel their aggressive drive somehow. Listen, can you do a bit of language tutoring after lunch? Phyllora and Poppy and I generally take them in batches of four or so while Jimmy works with the ones who are backward at maths."

"Yes, of course."

"Hey, you were going to play the organ with me," complained Suzanne. "Paulie wants organ too, don't you Paul?"

Paul, eating his lunch on Suzanne's other side, at the end of the table, nodded, giving me a shy upward glance.

"Never mind, we'll fit it in somewhere I promise."

Mollified, Suzanne started chattering to Paul. It struck me that, away from his father's perhaps overprotective presence, he seemed to get on well enough with Suzanne.

But Paul and Suzanne floated only on the fringe of my thoughts, which were primarily occupied with the incredible—no, not incredible, all too credible—information about Capranis's school that Suzanne had artlessly poured into my ears.

A school to cater for celebrities who wanted to replace substandard children with samples more suitable for public display.

But what sort of people would those be, in God's name? People who would jettison their own flesh and blood, in exchange for a replica from heaven knew where?

People *do* jettison their own flesh and blood, though; babies are left in trash bins, in trains, on doorsteps. At least these children were left under skilled care, in beautiful, luxurious surroundings.

And people do adopt children; often, very often, they take pains to adopt children who have some resemblance to them or to their families.

And there are commercial adoption societies, arranging all the formalities and pocketing a percentage.

Taking all this into account, why did I find Capranis's scheme so cold-bloodedly shocking?

And how, in all this child traffic, had Sweden been involved? For involved I was certain she had been, her connection with it seemed to follow as the night the day. This last trip from Beirut, for instance—the child's scribbles, the toy, the pot—had she been fetching over a nice, normal matching one-year-old to replace somebody's unfortunate Mongol?

Feeling slightly sick I pushed away my plate of stuffed vine leaves. The big room was hot and noisy with the subdued chatter of children; I wished I could go off somewhere and think, put together all the things I had learned, try to squeeze them into a pattern.

Sweden had friends in clinics, in special schools, children's hospitals, faculties of child care in a dozen different countries; what better agent than she to seek out some handy replica for a juvenile misfit? Some orphan; or perhaps there were large families in underprivileged countries who would be glad enough to barter away a younger child to a secure future in return for a handsome consideration?

And where in this pattern did Rudi Ettlinger fit? Had he been dovetailed long ago into some moneyed or titled household, so as to preserve the entail or keep the family firm from passing into the hands of strangers?

"You okay, Miss Georgia?" said Suzanne. "Don't you want your dinner?"

"It's a bit hot in here, that's all."

"Never mind," said Paul kindly. "We'll take you swimming presently when we've had our language classes. I'm going to swim three lengths again today, maybe four."

VIII

Language tutoring hadn't sounded particularly alarming, but I was a little disconcerted to find that the parents were allowed to sit in on this part of the curriculum. My first four pupils, luckily, presented no parental problems. They were Paul, the saintly Artemis, little Persephone, and big, cheerful Gregorious. Paul's father was still off in Nicosia, and the other three had no parents, it appeared; conversing in faulty but willing French they explained that they were all three orphans of Greek *émigrés* to America whom Mr. Capranis had caused to be repatriated, was educating, and would send to the university in due course.

"He is a very good man," said Artemis. "God will reward him when he dies."

Gregorious looked obstinate.

"I liked it in America," he said. "And I don't want to go to the university. I would rather go to Detroit and get a job in the motorworks."

"What nonsense," said Artemis. "You can't remember what America was like."

"Yes, I can. I can remember fifty-seven different kinds of ice cream."

"Anyway you can always go back there after the university."

John Smith wandered by—we were sitting on the terrace, under a big ilex—stood listening to our conversation for a few minutes, and then said,

"By the way, don't go over beyond the artichoke hedge. The bees have arrived."

The children nodded, as if this were a regular occurrence, but I said, "Bees?"

"Travelling bees," Smith explained. "The beekeepers take them round, following the flower crops all over the island. Mr. Capranis has them for a month in his garden every now and then, and gets honey for the school in return. But they are Cyprian bees—very bad-tempered, and their sting is about the same as a hornet's. If you had an allergy or a weak heart you could even die of a sting. So it's best to keep clear of them."

"Oh, delightful. Just another of the amenities of Aghios Georgios."

"They make very good honey," he said seriously.

"Well we'll give them a wide berth." I looked towards the artichoke hedge and saw half a dozen mules standing at ease while straw skeps were unloaded from their flat wooden saddles. Uncle Elias was supervising; with a slight catch of the breath I also noticed a black-robed bearded priest sitting on an upturned wheelbarrow, watching the proceedings.

"Who's that?"

"Mr. Capranis has priests over on holiday from some mainland monastery; they come and go; I expect that one will conduct a service in the little St. George church on Sunday."

Although the bees were a fair distance away I could smell the musty scent of honey, over the musty scent of mule, in the strong summer heat.

"Suppose they take it into their heads to fly this way?"

He shook his head. "The hives won't be opened till dusk, and there aren't any flowers here; they only go where the flowers are. But Elias has bottles of special bee mixtures, a repellant, and one that he can lay in a trail to attract them in the right direction."

"I'm so glad to hear it."

Paul and his three fellow pupils finished their stint and left, but Paul lingered a moment before going.

"Do you know what time Papa will be back, Miss Georgia?"

"He said he'd try and get back this evening with Dr. Phyllora. But I'm not sure exactly when."

"When will you play the organ to me and Suzanne?"

"After swimming." He nodded, and ran off.

Suzanne, the pugnacious Mark, Dino, and Salvador arrived, plus parents. Mixie had returned from her shopping excursion, it seemed. She looked hot, cross and jaded after it. I felt decidedly reluctant to conduct French conversation under the mixed regard of Almina Radici, Mixie, and Prince Carlo of San-somewhere-or-other, a dried-up waspish little man who smoked cigars the size of a bass flute and kept clicking his false teeth in a disapproving way. Still, maybe the cigar smoke would discourage the Cyprian bees.

Trouble set in right away. Mark was in a restless mood; while I tried to discover how much French they knew he fidgeted, spun on his seat, fell off the edge of the terrace once or twice, and created as much disturbance as he could, eyeing me sidelong as if daring me to rebuke him.

"Right, now we'll tell funny stories," I said.

"Funny stories? In French?"

"Funny stories in French. Mark will begin."

"Me?"

"Don't you know any?"

"Oh, yes, I *know* some. Boy, that's a crazy kind of French lesson, though," said Mark. He was quite tickled at the notion, however, and told a very funny story indeed about how Uncle Elias, when drunk, had posted his live bait through the post office letter box and gone fishing in Imandra bay with a letter to his son in Providence, Rhode Island, and caught the largest fish ever seen in Dendros which he sold to a tourist for twenty drachmae. Mark had a tremendous narrative gift; by the time he had finished, the other three children were rolling about, helpless with laughter, and even the Prince of San whatsit wore a wintry smile. But Mixie Koolidge and Almina Radici remained unimpressed; dismal pair of hags, I thought resentfully, and wished they were at the bottom of the sea.

"Now it's Salvador's turn."

Salvador, a sad, stupid-looking little boy, was totally tongue-tied. No amount of prompting or helping could wring more than a couple of phrases out of him. He blushed painfully and writhed under the ironic gaze of his adoptive father, and I began to regret my latest impulse.

Mark tipped a deck chair off the edge of the terrace with a disruptive clatter and then cried in a loud resentful voice.

"I'm bored!"

Dino instantly echoed him, black eyes sparkling with original sin.

"I'm bored, I'm bored. You bored, Suzanne? Come on, say you're bored, then there'll be three of us, we can have a penalty lesson."

My heart sank. But Suzanne replied.

"Ah, nuts, who wants your old penalty lesson? I want to tell my funny story."

"Who wants to listen to *your* story? Come on, Salvador, say you're bored; you're boring, anyway."

"Bored," Salvador muttered, staring at his bare feet.

"Hard lines," said Mixie Koolidge, sending me a great big false smile. When she grinned her black eyes tipped up at the corners, giving her a faintly Chinese look. She gave a conspiratorial wink at the boys; suddenly I wondered if she had put them up to this.

"So, okay, what is this penalty lesson?" I said shortly.

"We have to decide. In private." The children retired to the other end of the terrace and conferred. Mixie, Almina, and the prince meanwhile chatted in a desultory way. He had a rumpled copy of the airmail *Times* folded back at the centre page.

"I see the Russians are making another try for Celia's brother," he remarked, in a weary Winchester voice that came so startlingly from his middle-European face.

"Celia's brother?" Almina sounded as if this person were her least interest in life. "Why do the Russians want him? Is he a chess champion?"

"Come, come, my dear Almina. He's Sir John Pitshill."

"Oh, that man." She yawned. "He got sent to the Tower of London or something? I never met him."

"She's not proud of the connection." Prince Carlo's malicious little black eyes twinkled. "His family all disowned him, I believe; wife got a divorce."

"So why do the Russians want him?"

The prince shrugged. "Who knows? Perhaps he still has secrets to confide. They are hinting that they have an important exchange in mind."

Almina seemed massively uninterested. Mixie Koolidge yawned, patted her blond beehive of hair, and called irritably.

"Hey, kids, hustle it up a bit, can't you?"

The children came back, looking as solemn as a Trade Union delegation, and announced with due formality,

"She's to scrub the kitchen floor."

I jumped to my feet.

"Oh, no, I darn well am not! I know about that floor and its cosy little booby trap. That's one of your games I'm not getting involved in."

"Ah, heck, dearie," said Mixie, "you don't have to be scared of Cappy's trap door." She gave me a pitying smile. "It's all gussied up with a safety net underneath nowadays; nobody could fall to their doom through it any more. You don't have to worry the least little bit."

"All right, so there is a safety net; very funny I'll look falling into it like a—like an octopus. Just think of something else, will you?" I said to the children. They shook their heads.

"Honest, honey, you don't have to be so scared," said Mixie. "Why, good heavens, the trap doesn't even open unless someone's in Cappy's study pulling the lever."

Her pitying, patronising tone exasperated me, specially in conjunction with the scorn of the children.

"Chicken," I heard Mark mutter in an experimental way. I could see I was losing ground fast.

"Oh, good *lord*. Where's Mr. Smith?" Capranis wouldn't approve of this development, I thought. Or would he? Had he maybe organised the whole affair, to take place when he was out of the way?

"God knows. What's it got to do with him?"

"Come on, come on," shouted Dino, jumping up and down. "It'll be time for swimming soon."

"Oh, all right. But you're all to come and stand where I can see you. I'm not having someone nipping off to pull the lever when I'm not looking."

All sunny good cheer and giggles now they had gained their point, they dragged me away to the kitchen, and the grown-ups followed with the bored, dutiful, reluctant smiles that grown-ups wear while they watch the play that the children have made up themselves and act after tea on a wet Saturday.

The kitchen, with its Sahara-size expanse of black-and-white marble paving, was just as I had seen it before. Aged Ariadne was now listening to the Rolling Stones (rather off-station) as she slowly sliced up a mighty heap of tomatoes. She peered with disfavour at all these intruders in her territory and, when asked to provide a mop and bucket, hobbled off, shaking her head, muttering:

"Not satisfied with their own quarters they have to come and get under *my* feet. Give them an egg, they expect an elephant."

Returning with a kind of witch's broom which had rags lashed round its head in a combined knob-cum-tassel, and a Snowcem pail half-full of cold water, she snarled at Mark,

"Anyway, *you* ought to know better, descendant of a donkey! Wait till your uncle hears about this, he'll give you a proper ticking-off bothering me."

"Ah, come off it, Great-aunt Ariadne, he won't mind. Your kitchen floor can do with a scrub anyway," Mark retorted.

It could. The elegant black-and-white marble was covered with a layer of sandy dust, tomato skins, shrivelled grapes, artichoke leaves, and other kitchen detritus.

Before I could stop them, the children bustled about, piling all the little chopping tables one on top of another at the far end of the room, so that I had lost my only guide to where the trap door might be concealed. Under all that dust it was not going to be at all easy to spot.

"Is Mr. Capranis your uncle, then?" I asked Mark, as he politely carried the pail of water for me to the back left-hand corner of the kitchen.

"He's my aunt's cousin's son," Mark said after thinking it out.

"French, please."

"French!"

"This is supposed to be a French lesson." That eliminated Mark from my list of possibles, then, and accounted for the likeness to Capranis.

"Oh, all right!" He grinned good-temperedly. *"Très bien!"*

The parents were leaning against the wall in attitudes of tolerant ennui, watching as I crossly swished about with the besom. It gave me some satisfaction that there was nowhere for them to sit down.

"My stars, you sure are making a difference to that floor. I'll get you some more water," Suzanne said, and grabbed the bucket.

"Thought you weren't supposed to help teachers with their penalty lessons!" Mixie called when her daughter returned with the pail.

"Ah, go climb the Eiffel Tower," Suzanne muttered, darting a glance of dislike at her mother.

I sloshed water over another dusty stretch of marble. My activities could not really be said to clean it, as the dislodged dust merely floated along and settled on the wet area.

"What this place really needs is a giant Hoover. I suppose with all those electronic foot scrapers and sliding walls, they wouldn't have thought of a simple thing like that."

"There's one in the school building," Mark said. "And they have electric stoves in the kitchen where they cook the lunches. But Great-aunt Ariadne doesn't like modern gadgets in her kitchen; she cooks over a charcoal grill and she says the vacuum cleaner is a devil's invention and would have to be buried under a running stream before she'd touch it."

"Under a running stream? What does that do, for Pete's sake?"

"Takes off the devil's power. They do it with donkeys sometimes, when they're bewitched, or if it doesn't rain for a long time."

"How perfectly fascinating."

"I'm bored," complained Salvador dismally.

"So am I!" shouted Suzanne. "Let's go back to the terrace. I want to tell my funny story."

"Oh, I'm sure Professor Firgaard would say she ought to finish her stint; otherwise it would be a bad example for you all." Mixie gave her daughter an annoying retaliatory smile; her black eyes remained inscrutable as lumps of lava.

At this moment John Smith arrived.

"Oh, there you all are," he said hurriedly. "New York on the phone for you, Miss Koolidge." Abandoning all interest in me, Mixie darted off.

"Is this a penalty lesson?" John Smith said to me, frowning. "I don't know that Mr. Capranis would approve—"

"Oh, but it was perfectly in order, my dear John," Almina Radici assured him. "The children voted about it most correctly—didn't you, Dino?"

"Si, signora."

"Call me Mama!" she snapped at him.

"*Scusi,* Mama."

"So I really think they should be left to organize it themselves, don't you?" Almina went on sweetly. "I'm sure Professor Firgaard would disapprove if they were to break off in the middle. And Miss Georgia is taking it in the most sporting spirit and is not complaining at all—are you, dear Miss Georgia?"

I shrugged; John Smith worriedly began, "Just the same I don't think—"

"Ah, c'mon, let's quit!" said Suzanne, and grabbed the witch's broom from me. Either her sudden weight, or mine, or something else, dislodged the slab that I had just stepped onto. It and the one next it tilted together like cellar flaps. The result of this was that Suzanne, the broom, the bucket, and I all fell into the hole, tangled together uncomfortably, in a shower of dirty water.

"Oh, gee!" Suzanne gasped, as we hurtled into the dark well. I heard a shriek from above; Almina doubtless; myself I just had time for one heartfelt curse as we plunged into the chasm.

Anyway, Mixie Koolidge had been right. There was a safety net. But it was a good long way down. We must have dropped twenty to thirty feet before a web of springy, tough nylon received us, bounced us, and entangled us worse.

Overhead the trap doors, worked by a spring or counterbalance, tilted quietly up into place again, leaving us in total dark.

I'd have expected howls and carryings-on from Suzanne. But I'd have been wrong. She began to giggle.

"Oh, gosh, that was really, really cool! *Gosh,* won't the boys be mad that it happened to me and not to them. You okay, Miss Georgia?"

"When I get this broomstick out from under my elbow," I growled.

"Wasn't it wild, though! Wait till I tell Paul."

"Are you all right? Not hurt at all?"

"I guess not. The bucket banged my ear, that's all. Paul will be real sore that he missed this."

"How do we get out of here?"

"There's a doorway somewhere just by here, and a passage. And a flight of steps that goes round and round, right down to the bottom. I guess in the old days they used to go down to collect the money and secret papers and stuff off the dead bodies," Suzanne said with robust matter-of-factness.

"Delightful." I felt around, crawling on hands and knees over the unstable netting. "You start on the wall nearest you, Suzanne, and work round clockwise, and I will too; one of us is bound to find the doorway."

"Found it!" Suzanne announced with satisfaction almost at once. I crawled over to where her voice came from and found an arched opening in the stone wall and just by it, under the net, the top of a flight of spiral stairs leading down the well. Suzanne was perched just inside the doorway; I joined her.

"It's kind of spooky, isn't it?" she said cheerfully. "You don't smoke, do you, Miss Georgia?"

"Why? To keep off the bats?"

"If you smoked, you'd have a lighter, is all; we could see a bit. Still I guess they'll come down after us quite soon."

Suppose they don't, though, I thought to myself.

"Did you know this was going to happen, Suzanne?"

"No, I didn't, honestly, Miss Georgia. But I kind of guessed; see, the boys were acting all mysterious before the lesson, like they'd got a secret and wouldn't tell; they kept giggling and carrying on, so I reckoned they were planning something."

"But who could have pulled the lever? The boys were right there all the time."

"Maybe Paul or somebody else did. Or maybe my mommy pulled it; maybe she fixed to have them do it."

"Is your mom very fond of practical jokes, then?" I inquired dryly.

"Well, see, Miss Georgia, she sure doesn't like you!"

"For heaven's sake, why not? What did I ever do to her?"

"I dunno, Miss Georgia." Suzanne sounded really puzzled. "The way I figure it, maybe she thinks you're keen to marry Mr. Capranis too. I heard her saying to him last night, 'Why don't you send her away, Cappy? If she's anything like Sweden, she'll be a real pain in the neck!' and he was saying, 'No, no, I assure you, my dear Mixie, she is a very nice young lady.' I could tell Mom wasn't a bit pleased. Maybe she did this to kind of warn you off."

I was speechless with astonishment for a minute. Presently I found voice enough to say, "She can set her mind at rest on that head. I wouldn't want him if they were giving him away free with twenty years of extra life."

"Oh well, I'll tell her," Suzanne said kindly.

"I'd be so grateful if you would."

"They're awful slow coming to find us, aren't they?" she remarked presently. "Shall we start off to meet them?"

"All right. Have you been down here before, Suzanne? Do you know the way?"

"Yup; I guess so. Dino and me found a way in from a hole in those old ruins up by Athene's temple; see, it doesn't show, 'cause it's under the roots of a big old fig tree so no one knows about it but us, I reckon. We didn't tell anyone in case Mr. Capranis would say it was dangerous and we weren't to come here. But we always had flashlights when we came in; it isn't so easy to find your way when it's real dark like this. There's lots of passages; one goes down to the jetty at the bottom of the cliff where Mr. Capranis keeps his boats, and I think one comes out in the village somewhere."

"Oh well then, if we keep on going we're bound to hit on some way out."

"I guess so," Suzanne said, sounding hopeful rather than certain.

"Here, let's hold hands; then we shan't get separated."

"Okay."

We moved along with care. If the passage had been dug out by fourteenth-century Turks, they must have been of small stature and had very amateur notions of passage making; the floor was remarkably corrugated and every few yards one banged one's head on a knob, protrusion or stalactite from the ceiling.

"I'd like to know what Esther Summerson would do in here," I muttered.

"Who's she?"

"She comes in a book."

"Did it have a secret passage? I think books with secret passages are cool."

"Damn." I hit my head on another knob.

"I'll go in front, shall I, as I'm smaller? Then I can warn you about the low bits."

"Okay. Thanks, Suzanne."

She led me along quite nimbly. It was still completely dark; like walking with one's eyes full of soot.

"I'll tell you my funny story, shall I?" she remarked presently. "It's about this old man, see, and one rainy day he's out walking with his umbrella and he comes to this river where there's a crocodile swimming about and he—"

She screamed.

It was a scream of real terror; she flung herself back against me, shaking all over, and gripped me with frantic hands.

"Oh, *oh!* It's a body! There's a p-p-person, a *dead* person—"

"Easy. Easy honey." I tried to soothe her, though by no means in a state of unruffled serenity myself. "Here, why don't you sit down while I have a look-see—feel, I mean—"

"Don't let go of me, *don't!*" Her small fingers digging into my wrists had the strength of steel bolts.

"No, all right, but I've got to do *something*—"

With considerable difficulty, holding both her small trembling clutching hands in one of mine, I felt ahead with the other, and discovered that it was just as she had said: there was a body blocking the passage, doubled up and crouched over. A man. His feet were pointing in our direction: shoes, trousers, jacket.

Dead or unconscious?

Well, one or the other. He wasn't moving around at all.

"Look, Suzanne, this poor chap isn't going to hurt us. Just let go of me a minute, there's a love, while I try to feel and see if he's breathing. Maybe he's just knocked out— banged his head on the roof, the way I've been doing."

"All r-r-right," she said, teeth chattering.

"That's the girl."

It wasn't hilarious fun crawling past the recumbent man so as to be able to reach his chest. He was curled over, lying on his front. I had to slide past his back, and in doing so, put my hand first on the back of a grizzled neck, then, accidentally, on a bald head with a considerable gash in it; my fingers came away sticky. Whatever had given him that bang surely had not been just the roof!

With a lot of reluctance I worked a hand under his chin, inside his shirt. Warm. And after a minute or two I felt a faint heave of breath, which was pretty much of a relief.

"It's all right, Suzanne, he's not dead, he's breathing."

"Oh, gee, that's good. Gee, Miss Georgia, I'm sorry I made such a fool of myself."

"You did fine—after all, one doesn't reckon to find dead bodies lying around all over the place." Except at Aghios Georgios, I thought. My exploring fingers had found something else; an elaborate triple crucifix on a chain.

Now, where—

Captain Plastiras.

Captain Plastiras had certainly worn such a crucifix.

With even more shaky hands (and feeling also that I was taking an unwarranted liberty) I felt all over his face. Little moustache, cleft chin, high, balding forehead. It certainly could be Captain Plastiras.

Only, what the devil was he doing in an underground passage at Aghios Georgios?

"What are we gonna *do* about him?" asked Suzanne,

whose equilibrium and practical sense was beginning to reassert itself.

"We certainly ought to get help for him."

"Can't we shift him out of here?"

"He's probably too heavy for us. And it might be bad for him, if he's hurt."

But, I thought, it might be even worse to leave him. Whoever had given him that bash might feel inclined to come back and finish him off.

And anyway he was going to have to be shifted from where he was sometime; the sooner the better.

"I wonder if we *could* move him?" It was clear that taking action to help the stunned man would be the best way to soothe Suzanne's fears; weighing two possible goods against one possible evil, I decided to try.

"If we can only get him through this narrow place, the passage seems to widen out a little farther along."

"I could take his feet and you could take his head," Suzanne proposed, her confidence returning by leaps and bounds.

Getting him through the narrow place was no joke, though; not much easier than extracting a cork without benefit of corkscrew. If I put my hands under his armpits and yanked, his head scraped along the ground; I was extremely tempted to try pulling him by his ears which I remembered (if it *was* Captain Plastiras) to be particularly large, useful-looking ones.

He seemed to be half wrapped in some kind of voluminous cotton cape—a shroud?—which got frightfully in the way until we had him dragged clear into the wider section of passage. Then, muttering, struggling, and cursing, rather impeded than helped by Suzanne's well-meant efforts, I managed to work it straight and spread it beneath him.

"Now we can use it as a kind of carrying hammock."

"That's neat," Suzanne said approvingly, scrabbling to get the material pulled down under his feet. "What d'you reckon it is, a sort of cloak?"

"I can't imagine. Yes I can—it's a cassock—or whatever they call those priests' black robes; good heavens, I suppose *he* was the priest who's been mooching around for the last couple of days. Well, my goodness—of all the silly, unhelpful bits of play acting—"

The poor fellow let out a grunting moan, and I supposed that I ought to feel sorrier for him. But if his plan had been to keep an eye on me and simultaneously watch for more murder attempts, it had been singularly ineffective, not to say tiresome.

"Good, the floor turns to sand here, it won't be such a bumpy ride for him."

It was either sand or dust; half lifting, half dragging, we were able to haul him slowly along, through a choking cloud of the dust we raised. Unfortunately, it was also an uphill slope; hot work, even in this rocky underground place. Still, I was glad of the slope really; it must mean that we were on our way towards ground level.

We had to stop every couple of minutes; I am fairly wiry, and Captain Plastiras (or whoever) was a smallish man, and Suzanne was tough and strong for her age, but even so it was like trying to get a large roll of carpet up a particularly awkward flight of stairs. I perfected a technique of squatting and then pushing myself back with my heels; my hamstrings began to feel as if they had been used for tethering barrage balloons; I have never been in the least interested in pot holing and never shall; people who get themselves stuck in underground passages deserve to be left there, in my opinion.

Still, at last, painfully rounding a rocky corner, we were cheered by a tiny gleam of light, ahead and up above.

"Oh, goody," Suzanne said. "It *is* the way I thought it was. Shall we leave him here now? The entrance isn't far from the school building and we could get the boys or Mr. Newhouse to come and fetch him from here."

"That's a good notion. Tell you what, you go up to the entrance and shout for help; I'll stay here with him just in case he starts to come round and gets scared."

Once we could see daylight, Suzanne was bold as a lion; she agreed to this plan and went ahead.

The unconscious man, now that he was left still, began to mutter and groan. I tried to make his head comfortable on a wad of cassock. His heart was beating more strongly now; he must have a tough constitution; or perhaps all the jolting had been good for his metabolism.

"They'd undone the safety net, you see," he suddenly enunciated quite clearly.

"Had they, by God?" I was exceedingly startled. "Who had?"

But his mutterings became incomprehensible again. I sat there feeling more kindly disposed towards him; if it was he who had fastened up the net again, Suzanne and I certainly owed him a good turn. It was much better to be crouching here in the sand, albeit with aching calves and dust-filled lungs, than lying in a heap at the bottom of that deep, deep well.

Why hadn't whoever coshed him also thrown him down the well and undone the net again?

Perhaps there hadn't been time; he was jammed in the narrow passage, they'd have had to unjam him and get him back along an even narrower section; it would have been a slow job.

Suzanne was waving from the entrance. A moment more, and it was blacked out; footsteps and voices filled the tunnel. At closer range they resolved themselves into Robert Newhouse, cautiously leading the way, holding up a large cigarette lighter, and behind him was the redheaded Poppy, recovered, apparently, from her migraine.

"Hallo!" I called. "I'm here."

"What the devil is all this?" Newhouse said. "We thought at first it was one of Suzanne's tall tales—that child has a wild imagination—"

"Hush," Poppy murmured. "She's right behind me here."

"Something about a hurt man—"

"Yes, he's here. Can you give me a hand to carry him?"

"Good lord," muttered Newhouse, stopping short, holding his lighter closer—and it *was* Captain Plastiras. "How very extraordinary. You found him here?"

"A bit farther down. Look, it's a long story—can we get him out before we chew it all over?"

"Yes, of course. If I take his shoulders and you two each take a leg—"

This proved feasible and we made steady if not very fast progress up the final slope. Suzanne was at the entrance, talking eagerly to someone just outside.

"How's your head?" I asked Poppy, by way of distracting my attention from my wrenched arms and aching legs.

"Eh? Oh, it's fine now, thanks," she said absently. "I

hear that you were an absolute wow with your bullfight; the kids are all begging to have another. How did you and Suzanne get down here, for goodness' sake, and who is this guy?"

We were now in the muted daylight of the entrance, which was a narrow gully overhung by a giant fig. Beyond, sun blazed on scattered rocks; I recognised the area. We were down near the main entrance to the castle, inside the wall.

Suzanne, jumping up and down with excitement and importance, awaited us in the gully with Professor Firgaard and—to my huge relief—Phyllora Tatula.

"It's a priest!" exclaimed Newhouse in surprise.

"One of Cappy's pals from the monastery; he's been here a day or two, I've seen him around," said Poppy. "Silly sod must have gone wandering down inside and given his head a biff. Here, Phylla, you'd better have a look at him. Jolly lucky you're back."

Up above, on Athene's forecourt, I could see the helicopter outlined against the brilliant sky.

"Suzanne," said Phyllora, compressing her lips as she looked at the long, dirty, congealed gash on Plastira's bald dome, "have you got the strength to run very fast up to that helicopter and ask the pilot—that man standing on the rock—to wait and take another stretcher case back to Nicosia? Ask him if they'll bring a stretcher down here."

"Sure!" Suzanne said proudly, and galloped off across the open rocky space to the wide stately flight of steps that led up to the ruined temple.

"It was exceedingly fortunate for this man that you found him." Phyllora glanced round at me as she knelt by Plastiras, checking his pulse and breathing. "He could easily have lain down there for days without being discovered, and if he had done so—" She shrugged.

"Guess he owes you his life," Poppy said laconically.

"Will he be all right?"

"Oh yes. He may be a bit confused, but I do not think there is any severe damage."

I ought to have felt good at that, but there was a kind of chill coming from behind my right ear; I looked round to find the weight of Professor Firgaard's disapproval hanging over me like a glacier.

"Miss Marsh," he began formally, "I appreciate that you have not been here very long and are not a permanent member of our staff. But I am afraid that you do not seem fully to have assimilated the doctrines of our august founder, Ole Södso—"

"Oh, blimey," muttered Newhouse, into the boughs of the fig tree.

Poppy's handsome brown face took on a kind of alert blankness, like a sprinter waiting for the starting pistol. Phyllora glanced calmly up the hill to the stretcher bearers now approaching.

"For instance, this bullfight which I understand you organised this morning," pursued the professor, looking at me over the tops of his glasses as if I were a specimen of Bacillus typhosus, "now that was a most undesirable element to introduce into our peaceful community, Miss Marsh, most undesirable indeed. You have caused to be born into these children's consciousnesses the concepts of violence, fear, competition, trickery, and by implication, death—"

"Professor Firgaard! If you had seen the bullfight, I don't think—"

"Can you wonder," he continued, without acknowledging that I had spoken, "that in retaliation for opening their innocent minds to these dark influences, some of them should have—I understand—played a trick on you with the oubliette—"

"Professor, I'm pretty sure it wasn't the children's idea—"

"If you care to come with me to my study, I shall talk to you more on this theme, and also lend you a copy of our founder's most important treatise, *Anti-Björnsen*—"

At this moment, thank goodness, the stretcher bearers arrived and, helped by Newhouse, with Phyllora organising, loaded Captain Plastiras, cassock and all, neatly on to their stretcher and bore him off to the helicopter.

"I suppose I ought to go back with him to the hospital," muttered Phyllora worriedly.

"Is Mr. Capranis back?" I called after her.

"No, he had to stay behind in Nicosia; someone he wished to see had not yet turned up; he said he would be back tomorrow—" she called over her shoulder.

I felt rather dashed.

"Heavens, it's the children's swimming time, come on Bob, or they'll all be jumping in the deep end," Poppy exclaimed, looking at her watch. "Want to come and cool off, quickest way to clean off the dust after your underground excursion?" she said to me and I realised that, as usual at Aghios Georgios, I must look a sight, filthy, dishevelled and scraped. But Professor Firgaard took my arm in a firm clasp, and saying austerely, "Miss Marsh is coming with *me,*" led me most unwillingly away.

He took me to a cheerless Scandinavian study in the Athene building; it was furnished with graphs, laminated wood in characterless curves, and some huge heavy pieces of grey glass. One wall was all soundproof window, looking into the Athene nursery, where the usual activities were in progress.

"Sit down, Miss Marsh." Although different, his chairs were no more comfortable than Capranis's pink leather and gilt studs; sliding about on that unwelcoming wood I felt like the boy who went to school on a dolphin. But at least there'd be no need to worry about dust on the upholstery.

"Would you care for a glass of milk, Miss Marsh? You look heated."

I was surprised by the kind thought, and gratefully accepted. But the milk, when it came, proved a bit of a shock.

"It is a mixture of hydrolised, homogenised nuts and goat's milk," said the professor. "More nutritious by far than ordinary cow's milk."

"I'm sure it is. It was just the flavour that startled me."

"You soon get used to it. Now, Miss Marsh, here is this book"—he handed me a forbidding black tome about the size and shape of Cruden's Concordance to the Bible—"please study it carefully and I will have a conversation with you about it each morning at 7:30 A.M. There are fourteen chapters; if you read two chapters each day, we shall be through it in a week."

"So we shall." I tried to introduce an air of pleased surprise into my reply.

"Miss Marsh." The professor stood mournfully regarding me; he looked like a great northern diver stirring up

clouds of pollution in some lake whose waters were probably befouled beyond recall. "Miss Marsh, I am not angry
with you, for anger, I am happy to say, is an emotion that
I eliminated from my emotional spectrum some thirty-five
years ago."

He paused, apparently for me to congratulate him, so I
said, "That's nice."

"But you have brought trouble to our peaceful little
colony; you have brought aggression, jealousy, malice; the
Muddle Principle is rampant and it is all due to your intrusion."

"Oh, look here, Professor Firgaard," I said indignantly,
"how unfair can you get? All these things must have been
here before I came—"

"Can you deny that since your arrival your cousin has
died by violence, Captain Cruikshank has suffered from a
severe heart attack and now lies upstairs gravely ill, that
man whom you discovered underground has been hurt—
to say nothing of the irremediable harm done to the children's psyches by all this unloosed anarchy—"

Bypassing the injustice of his reproaches I started to
say, "How did you know about my cousin?" when the second of his remarks hit me.

"Captain Cruikshank is here? He's upstairs?"

"Apparently his condition was not so serious as to war-
rant hospitalization, and he was very anxious to return.
My medical orderlies are looking after him."

"Is that so? In that case, Professor Firgaard, if you'll
excuse me I—I have a book of his that I promised to return to him. Thank you so much for the milk." Making
Stakhanovite effort I gulped down the nauseating stuff and
stood up. "I'll think carefully over what you said and—
and I'll look forward to our conversation at half-past
seven tomorrow."

He looked even more disapproving.

"Miss Marsh I cannot agree that you visit the captain.
This might cause a severe setback in his physical or psy-
chic sphere—"

"I shan't stay long."

Before he could interrupt me—which he showed every
sign of doing—I nipped to the door and through it. Luck-

ly at that moment the professor's phone began to ring; while he was answering it I escaped up the openwork-style stairs to the upper storey.

IX

At the top of the stairs I had the impulse to try the door that said *Dr. Hannfelder;* I'd have liked to look in that portfolio on her bookshelf and see if it was the one that had been on *L'Aiglon.* But the door was locked. And there was no time to lose, really, if I was to talk to Cruik-shank—supposing he was fit for conversation—before Professor Firgaard finished his telephone conversation and took preventive action. I hurried on, along a wide, rubber-floored corridor, turned a corner, and found myself in the sick-bay zone. Through an open door I saw little Fernand and waved to him; he waved back. Since there were no nursing staff to be seen around I went in and asked,

"Do you know where they put Captain Cruikshank?"

"He's next door, I think. I saw them carry him by. They didn't go far."

Fernand, bandaged but cheerful, was making a wonder-ful mess in his bed with occupational therapy: sticky paper and plastic putty; glue, sticky tape, and glitter powder. "Look, I made a machine gun," he said proudly, and held up a squat toadlike symbolic object. Oh dear, I thought, something else Professor Firgaard will surely lay at my door.

"It's lovely," I said. "Now make something useful. Make a—a cultivator."

Fernand gave me a look of scorn. "Machine guns *are* useful. You use them to kill people. Now I'm going to make a rocket-propelled missile."

I tiptoed out, leaving him admiring his work. The trouble is that rocket-propelled missiles are so much easier to make than cultivators.

The door of the next room was shut but I quietly opened it. Sure enough, there lay Patrice Cruikshank in bed, propped on a lot of pillows. The room was in shade, voluminous blue curtains pulled across the balconied window, but he was not asleep; I saw the gleam of his dark melancholy eyes turn slowly, recognise, and consider me.

Closing the door behind me I stepped softly up to his bedside.

One might as well translate one's pretexts into truths; I pulled *Bleak House,* somewhat the worse for dust, out of my dungaree pocket and laid it on the bedside table.

A faint, very faint smile came into the haunted eyes.

"An—unusually—interesting—narrative method," whispered Captain Cruikshank.

"You said that once before."

"What—are you reading now?"

I silently exhibited Ole Södso's treatise on the Muddle Principle and his lips twitched again.

"So you—decided—after all—to accept a position here?"

"I had reasons. Look, Captain Cruikshank—Patrice—you were in command of the *Orfeo?*"

His eyes left mine; his face stiffened. But after a minute he said,

"So you were as intelligent as I thought at first. Yes—I was."

He looked so ill, so terribly drawn and white, that I felt considerable guilt at what Professor Firgaard would undoubtedly regard as another rampant example of applied Muddle.

"And Rudi Ettlinger was on board?"

A long silence followed. I longed to plead, urge, cajole, threaten; I longed to shake him. I sat still, clenching my hands together. At last he whispered coldly,

"I have—reason to believe so."

"You were paid for taking him as a passenger, anyway?"

A faint angry flush momentarily stained his cheekbones. He did not reply.

"And now you have reason to believe he is here?"

"Mr. Capranis—adopted—all the Greek orphans."

"Rudi wasn't Greek—"

"Some—died of diphtheria—there was—confusion.
Three of the adult—counsellors—died too—"

"The one who brought Rudi on board?"

He didn't answer. I said, half to myself,

"Easy to muddle the identities of a living two-year-old
and a dead two-year-old."

He gave the faintest possible nod.

"By then—you see—I'd heard of—my wife's—death.
It—was like—a judgment. So I thought—better for
him—be adopted by Capranis—than fall—into *their*
hands. I told them—he died."

As usual, I thought glumly, repentance too late to be of
practical use, just causing a lot of trouble. Martin died,
Luise to die of grief a couple of years later—but still, no
doubt Rudi *was* better off adopted by Capranis than falling into *their* hands.

"Captain Cruikshank—Patrice—which of them is he?"

His eyes flickered about the room. One of his thin, bony
hands came out from under the covers and took mine in
the well-remembered grip. This time it was not cold; it
was hot, dry, feverish.

"I do not know." And I'm bloody well not *ever* going to
know, if I can help it, the dark eyes said. He did have a
large streak of Pontius Pilate, it was quite true. "Nobody
knows. That was why—your cousin decided to bring you
here."

It was a warm room, but suddenly I felt cold. It wasn't
any possible knowledge of Martin's work they thought I
might have, then; something much simpler.

Thank heaven I had never met Rudi, never even seen a
picture of him till the newspaper reports.

I must have said something aloud. The sad eyes came
back to mine.

"They know that."

"Well then—what can they hope for?"

"You knew Ettlinger—well. Otherwise—no one did.
He was—solitary. Some likeness—inherited—gesture—
perhaps would not even—remember—till you saw it
again—"

Oh God, I thought. So that's why I dreamed about Mar-

tin. Something one of the children did reminded me of
him—

"Captain Cruikshank—Patrice?"

He looked at me in silence.

"How do *you* know so much about my history?"

His lips gave the slightest ironic twitch.

"Your cousin and I—had a little fling."

"Oh I see." Faintly disgusted—heaven knows why—I
tried to slide my hand away. But he clenched on to it even
more tightly.

"Mutual—self-interest." He grinned his sour grin. "She
—wished—to learn what I knew: I wished to—learn what
she knew. So: bed."

And I hope you gave each other a miserable time, I
thought angrily. My feeliing must have communicated
themselves to him; he brought out another hand from
under the bedclothes and touched my cheek. To my horror I saw that his eyes were full of tears. After a minute he
said quietly,

"Here we are—both in hell."

"Too right."

"Georgia—will you marry me?"

"For heaven's sake!" I exploded. I tried to jump up, but
he still gripped my hand like Death. "That's the worst reason for a proposal I *ever* heard. Talk about the Muddle
Principle—"

"We might—redeem one another."

I doubt it, my friend. More likely push one another over
the final precipice.

I shook my head.

"I'll never marry now."

"Don't—say a final no. Think—about it."

I thought, but didn't say, the plain thing that whoever
married him had an odds-on chance of being a widow before the first-wedding anniversary.

"Patrice—do you truly not know which is Rudi? Surely
you must have some idea? And who killed Sweden? Was it
you? Was it you who pushed me into the kiln?"

"Sorry—now," he whispered. "Not—sensible."

Good grief, what a character. Pushes you into an oven
one day, proposes the next.

He was looking terribly weak from strain; sweating.

felt like an executioner, persisting in my catechism, but I might never get the chance again; any minute now Firgaard's myrmidons would come bursting in to give him a blanket bath or something, and throw me out.

"Who did kill Sweden? Who are *they?*"

"Two different lots."

"Both after Rudi, you mean?" My heart sank.

He gave the faint nod again. His eyes slipped past me to the window.

All of a sudden it struck me that the gently pervasive smell I had subconsciously been absorbing for the last few minutes was not disinfectant but the patchouli-flavoured sweetness of Pink Jade. I followed Cruikshank's gaze to the blue curtain and thought I saw it move slightly.

Oh, Polonius. What have we given away?

Well, at least we haven't given away the main thing.

Exhilaration at that thought struggled with annoyance about everything else. Really I was having a lot to put up with. Pushed into ovens, dropped into oubliettes, accused of embodying the Muddle Principle, made to scrub floors, eavesdropped on, and what do I stand to gain from it all? Not a thing, except a proposal of marriage from this melancholic Flying Fleming.

In a spirit of four-parts scientific curiosity to six-parts cussedness, I picked *Anti-Björnsen* off the floor and hove it hard at the swaying curtain. One thing about having six elder brothers is that you learn how to throw overarm.

The book hit the curtain with a solid sort of impact and then thudded to the floor. It was followed by a massive, reeling body which dragged the curtain half off its rail: British floral cotton, Pink Jade, and a blue rinse.

I stared at her aghast like the angler who, fishing for tiddlers, accidentally hauls out the Lady of the Lake.

"Po po po," whispered Captain Cruikshank, quite aptly.

"Lady Lurgashall! Are you all right?"

I hoisted her up as best I could and put her in an armchair. She had a large blue bruise on her brow. A spray of gladioli lay scattered on the balcony.

"What happened?" she murmured. "Just coming up outside way—ask after dear Captain Cruikshank—"

That was the moment when Professor Firgaard chose to

arrive. Oh dear, I thought, just in time for another first-class example of undistributed Muddle.

Luckily the professor did not instantly observe Lady Lurgashall's collapsed condition. His attention was all for me.

"Miss Marsh, you should not be here. I must request that you leave Captain Cruikshank in peace. In any case Mr. Capranis is on the telephone wishing to speak with you. In my study."

Given a first-class excuse to leave the scene, why hesitate?

"Thanks, Professor," I said, darted out, and took the stairs in three jumps.

"Mr. Capranis?"

"Is that Georgia Marsh?" He sounded very brisk indeed. "Where are you speaking from?"

"Professor Firgaard's study."

"Is the door shut?"

"Yes, I shut it as I came in."

"It is the first sensible act I have known you to perform. Miss Marsh, what *have* you been *doing?* Firgaard is in a rage because you teach the children how to fight bulls—you let yourself be pushed down the oubliette—really, have you no sense at *all?*—and, worst of all, what do I hear about Captain Plastiras whom I had left to watch over you? You knock him out and drag him along an underground passage so that poor Phyllora has to take him back to hospital; now there is nobody left to keep an eye on you."

"*I* didn't knock him out. I found him like that. And he was lucky I did find him."

"If you hadn't let yourself be manoeuvred into the oubliette there would have been no need for him to be down there," Capranis said unfairly. "Professor Firgaard is in a terrible state of mind: demanding that I get rid of you at once if I have to send for a Concorde to fetch you away. And I can tell you, even if I managed to soothe Firgaard, you will have to keep a sharp lookout now that Plastiras is no longer around to protect you."

"A lot of use he was," I said sourly. "Who's he supposed to protect me from?"

"How shall we be able to discover, now you have been so careless?"

I didn't persist in my question; I heard a click on the line; for all I knew, the entire population of Aghios Georgios might be listening in on other extensions.

"Anyway," I said spitefully, "so far as I can make out my being manoeuvred into the oubliette was nothing to do with—what we thought—but a little joke arranged by Miss Koolidge, to warn me off any matrimonial intentions with regard to you."

"I *beg* your pardon? Who gave you that idea?"

"Someone who should know. And I thought Mr. Smith was supposed to be keeping an eye on me?"

"Listen, Miss Marsh—Georgia. Will you please be sensible. Keep away from heights. Don't go swimming. Avoid electrical gadgets. Be careful what you eat. Stay with a group of people, not just one—trust nobody till I get back."

"Where are you now?"

"Nicosia. Is Firgaard there?"

"No, he's upstairs. I just knocked out Lady Lurgashall with his treatise on the Muddle Principle and I expect he's giving her first aid."

"What?"

I looked over the phone; the door was opening quietly.

"Here are Miss Koolidge and Signora Radici coming in—do you wish to speak to either of them?"

"Heaven forbid," said Capranis impatiently. "What was that about Celia?"

"Who?"

"Celia Lurgashall. What did you say you did?"

"I'll tell you when you come back," I said slowly. "When will that be?"

"God knows," he snapped. "In time for the children's picnic tomorrow—that is all I can say. I promised Paul I would be. Mind what I said now. Good-bye."

He rang off.

Mixie Koolidge and Almina Radici tiptoed into Firgaard's study, all giggles and rolling eyes and exaggerated caution. Just a pair of frolicsome schoolgirls.

"Where is he?" breathed Mixie, peering from side to side out of her slitted eyes.

"Who?"

"The professor, of course. We've come to *rescue* you!"

"We heard he was giving you a rocket for falling down the oubliette."

"So we came to 'fess up that we did it and tell him not to scold you."

"You got the children to say they were bored, and ask for that particular penalty?"

"Yes," cooed Almina. "I'm afraid it was very, very naughty of us. Just our joke. Will you ever forgive us? We knew that the net was there, of course, so that you couldn't fall far."

"Forgive? All friends?" pleaded Mixie, head on one side, Daddy's Little Girl owning up.

"Of course," I said politely. "It must have been a bit of a shock to you when you heard that your own daughter had fallen in too."

"Oh, honey, it was." Mixie's tone didn't carry conviction; she looked as if she could have spared Suzanne without overmuch grief. "But she's a regular little Tarzan anyhow; I bet she had a whale of a time down there."

"You haven't talked to her since we came out?"

"No, she's gone swimming with the other kids. Why?"

"You didn't know she'd found a man's body down the tunnel?"

Mixie's mouth fell open.

Almina said, "A *body*? Whose?"

Deciding to forget my recognition of Plastiras, I shrugged and said, "Oh, just one of the regular bodies that one finds lying about Aghios Georgios I expect. Phyllora's taken him to hospital."

"Hospital? You mean he was alive?" Almina's dark eyes were alight with interest but Mixie looked ready to faint. Muttering, *"Poor* little Suzanne—why didn't anybody *tell* me? I must go to her right away," she blundered from the room and could be seen through the window running awkwardly in her high-heeled sandals across the rock-studded ground to the main castle building.

"She forgot that Suzanne's in the swimming pool," said Almina dryly.

Remembering Capranis's injunction to avoid tête-àtêtes, I surveyed her with careful attention, wondering if she was about to whisk a poison-gas pistol out of her white wild-silk bikini and let fly at me.

While Mixie was talking, though, a pleasing notion had come into my head. After all, I had been fetched here by devious means to identify Rudi Ettlinger, if Patrice Cruikshank was to be believed. And I thought he was; on this head, anyway. Therefore, until the identification had been effected, it was in the interests of all parties, whoever they were, whatever they represented, to keep me alive. So all *I* had to do was maintain a carefully blank façade no matter what happened, and I'd be as safe as a numbered account.

There was only one flaw to this theory: the undeniable fact that someone had already tried to do me in. But if—but if Patrice had pushed me into the oven, to prevent my seeing and identifying Rudi, and if Mixie had organised the oubliette lark in order to eliminate possible rivals for Capranis's hand (why *me*, in the name of St. Spondi-ko, I wondered in passing, and also, remembering his ironic eye on her, she's got a hope if she really thinks she can land him), and if the priest who dogged me round the streets of Imandra was merely old Plastiras keeping a fatherly eye on me (why hadn't he *said* he was going to, the silly knothead?), that seemed to eliminate most of my would-be murderers, unless Mixie was good for another try.

All I had to do was refrain from recognising Rudi Ettlinger.

"When's the picnic?" I asked irrelevantly.

Almina Radici was staring through the glass wall into the room beyond.

"Picnic?" she said vaguely. "Oh yes, I believe the children are to be taken to this Valley of Butterflies tomorrow. Dino spoke of it. Professor Firgaard takes them . . . why?"

"Mr. Capranis said he'd be back for it."

She did not seem to be paying attention. I saw, with shock and some compunction, that silent tears were running down her cheeks. She was staring at Benno who, inert in his wheelchair, was ignoring pictures being shown him by a girl nurse.

"They really are happy there. Don't you think they are happy?" she said with the overemphasis of disbelief.

"I'm sure they couldn't have better care."

"No they couldn't," she agreed tonelessly. "We—parents are not supposed to go in there, once they have settled, for fear of unsettling them again. That is why this window—so we may at least look a little."

Her hands knotted and unknotted. Well, you chose to do it, I thought, rather unkindly.

But one shouldn't sit in judgment on others.

Unfortunately just at that moment Ben, not interested in the pictures, turned his head and saw Almina. His lustreless eyes lit up.

"Mama!"

"Benito! Benno mio!"

Regardless of Firgaard's prohibition she shoved open the glass door, ran through, and crouched down by her son's wheelchair to hug him and cry over him and hold his poor little unresponsive hands.

Not surprisingly this started up a tidal wave of unrest among the other children. There were piteous cries of "Mamma! Mutti! Mommy! Maman! Mum—where's *my* mum?"

Two more nurses scurried in and simultaneously Professor Firgaard, who had the capacity of a real old Demon King for appearing at the worst possible moment, came loping down the stairs, took in the situation with one hawk-eyed glance, and decided without loss of time where to lay the blame.

"Miss Marsh!" he hissed. "Yet again I find you at the bottom of a scene of evil disruption and chaos. Without doubt you encouraged Signora Radici to visit her son. This is too bad, too bad! I must ask you to withdraw immediately."

"I did no such thing!" I said, outraged. "Why blame me?" But wondered, in the same breath, if maybe it *had* something to do with me—if perhaps I'd allowed a shade of disapproval to slide into my expression?

"Do not argue with me, Miss Marsh; we will discuss all this at a later date. Meanwhile, I wish you to have nothing more to do with the children. *Nothing.* You understand? You are like a plague carrier—please remain apart."

He thrust *Anti-Björnsen* into my hands, said, "Go and read this somewhere quietly. You could not be better employed," and dived into the wailing scene, calming a child here, soothing another there, organising the nurses, bringing instant order and hush. He did, I was obliged to admit, know his job.

Well, I was only too glad to retire. I went up the stairs, two at a time, and found my way to Phyllora's room; I was sure she would not begrudge me a second use of her shower, and I could certainly do with one after the mixed mental and physical exactions of the last couple of hours.

First taking care to lock myself in, I stripped, washed my shirt and trousers (luckily in that climate a sodden yak would be tinder-dry in half an hour), took a long, leisurely shower, and then lay flat and relaxed on Phyllora's rush matting, doing my best to apply myself to the teachings of Ole Södso.

"To lay down precepts for an orderly code of conduct, we must first define terms. Since language is not logically perfect, we must make it so, or we shall convey, not truth, but falsehood."

The first sentence brought me up standing. After all, how can you make language logically perfect? Any fool can see that is an impossibility.

I looked gloomily through the chapter headings: Definition of Terms. First Principles. Application of Logic to Emotion. Application of Logic to Memory. Application of Logic to the Future. Fallacies in Björnsen's Philosophy, Part I, Part II, Part III. Logical Structure of Society. Logic and Religion. Logic and Poetry. Logic and Art. Education of Children.

Logic and Poetry looked like a very short chapter, so I thumbed along to it.

"Since a statement in a logically perfect language conveys pure information in the most concise terms possible, poetry must inevitably fall outside the terms of reference of such a language, for poetry seldom conveys information, and, if it does, never in the most concise terms possible. Since neither poetry nor its function can be defined in exact terms, we find it inessential for a logical existence, and therefore outside the scope of this treatise."

So much for poetry. So much for Milton, Ogden Nash,

and Mrs. Harold Wilson. Inessential to the logical existence. Why should we have a logical existence anyway, I
thought rebelliously? Just because the stars carry on in a
mathematical way doesn't mean all the rest of us have to.
If I choose to eat breakfast before I go to bed, live my life
backwards, jump over a cliff when my ship comes in, and
laugh with Little Audrey when I'm all knotted up in a
tragic situation, who the hell's got the right to forbid me?
Not Ole Södso, for one.

However I was supposed to be making myself acquainted with this humourless stuff, so I went doggedly back to
the beginning and started learning his definitions. They
were pretty soporific; presently I drowsed off into a short
catnap. But I hadn't slept for more than about fifteen minutes when I was roused by the school bell, and almost at
once heard two familiar voices outside the window.

"Man, it was crazy! We fell and we fell and it was all
dark and we fell into this net, it was even better than a
trampolin, and then Miss Georgia said look for the door
so I started looking and I found it, and we went along the
passage and we bumped into this hurt guy—it was all dark
and I thought he was dead so I yelled—gee, Paul, it was
real cool, I wish you'd been there."

"Where's Miss Georgia now?" Paul sounded decidedly
less enthusiastic about the pleasures of underground adventure. With a pang for him I remembered that Capranis
had said he would probably not be back till tomorrow.

"Dunno," Suzanne said. "I haven't seen her since we
got out."

"Hey!" Wrapping myself in a terry robe of Phyllora's I
leaned over her balcony. "Hey, you two!"

"Oh, hi, Miss Marsh." Suzanne beamed up at me. "We
were just looking for you. Can you come and play the
organ for us now? We're all through swimming."

"Okay." Then I remembered Firgaard's prohibition.
But, damn it, who was boss round here? Capranis had
specifically asked me if I'd entertain Paul, and he owned
the place after all. Besides being the boy's father.

"I have to get dressed, I'll meet you in the organ room,"
I called. "Be down in five minutes."

X

Running down the stairs I met—inevitably—Professor
Firgaard escorting a weeping Almina Radici sternly away
from his study. Evidently he had been giving her a long
lecture.

"Never do such a thing again. How can you expect your
Benito to settle down if you return and disturb him with
your presence?" he was saying severely. "You chose to
bring him here, so far, good. That was a wise decision.
Here he will be treated with more care, more wisdom,
more true goodwill than you could have given him."

"Oh it's not true, it's not true," wept Almina. "I love
him! None of those nurses will ever be able to give him the
love that I do."

Firgaard looked about him impatiently, as if hoping to
see the Holy Ghost descend like a dove with a sprig of
logic in its beak. A fresh burst of wailing came from the
nursery; simultaneously his eye lit on me coming down the
stairs.

"Miss Marsh. Where are you going?"

"I'm going to play the organ," I snapped. "Any objec-
tions? Mr. Capranis gave me permission. In fact he asked
me to."

"So. You would be better occupied reading the book I
gave you."

"I have read a couple of chapters. I need time to digest
them."

"In that case," he gave me a cold glance, "I should be
grateful if you could escort Signora Radici to her room.
She is still affected, as you can see, by that most foolish
and unauthorised visit to her son."

"Of course I'll take her. Where is the room?"

"In the main castle building; on the first floor. I am

161

obliged to you." He gave me another piercing look, relinquished the sobbing prima donna, and walked off along the hallway.

I put an arm round Almina and steered her across the hot rocky space to the main building.

"Look, honey, try not to take on so. I know Firgaard seems rather a chilly old skeleton, but he's very likely right, you know; after all, they can give Benno twenty-four-hour care, they do know their job, they have dozens of ways to keep him amused and interested; and you've got your career to think of."

"Damn my career," she wept. "What do I care that my *Aida* is the best in the world has ever heard? I would rather live with Benno in a cottage on the shores of Lake Garda —what do I care about money or fame?" Her words, to my ears, had the slightly hollow ring of cliché, then she added, more convincingly, "Anyway, singing is very hard work; I would be quite happy to give it up."

"Think how boring life would be without all those gala performances and meeting crowned heads all the time."

We had passed through a stone-arched entrance into a square vestibule hung with what looked like and probably were Canalettos; a flight of stone stairs led upward, trodden into shallow curves by the feet of countless Knights Templar stomping up to bed in full armour. We followed them and reached a huge bedroom, decorated in some more of Capranis's terrible taste, with green-satin swathings and drapings, and a green glass floor, and a green glass four-poster topped by a mirror, and a fountain playing in a mottled marble trough which looked like the sort erected for underprivileged cab horses by philozoic Victorian industrialists.

"There you are; why don't you have a nice lie down? Is there anything you'd like? A drink? Smelling salts? Eau de cologne? Shall I ask Ariadne to rustle you up a cup of her tea? It's got the kick of a mule."

"Scusi?" she said absently; her eye had been caught by the blue square of an air letter on the glass dressing table. Freeing herself from my supporting arm she swiftly crossed the room and opened it.

"Dio mio! La Scala, the day after tomorrow! Why did that fool Claudio not tell when he phoned? La Scala.

Lucia di Lammer-moore! Ligeti has broken her leg. I must pack, I must pack directly, Cappy will have to phone for a plane, oh, why did I not know of this when the helicopter was still here?"

She began feverishly opening drawers and cupboards, tossing tropically coloured heaps of beach clothes out onto the green glass. I felt I ought to offer to help, but the children would be waiting for me—besides, she seemed fully recovered now, boiling with energy indeed.

"Shall I send Dino along to help you? Will he be going too?"

"Grazie tanto! Not likely! What use would he be? In any case his table manners are still quite hopeless—he is not fit to take about."

Somewhat out of charity with her I retired, shutting the door briskly behind me, and ran down the shallow stairs again. The organ room, with its Medusa's-head mosaic, lay somewhere through a sequence of rooms to the left. Passing under arches, crossing great checked plains of marble, I presently found it, guided by a rhythmic sound which, when I reached it, proved to be Paul, seriously jumping with a skipping rope along the border of sea monsters that surrounded Medusa.

"Hallo, Paul. That's a handsome rope."

"It's Suzanne's. Her mother came and fetched her away. Suzanne didn't want to go, but Aunt Mixie said she'd had a fright and must lie down on her bed for an hour."

"Oh, too bad. Maybe she'll come along later. So now, can you open this organ?"

"It's easy," he said seriously. "Papa has often shown me how."

Crossing to Medusa he jumped two or three times with his whole weight on her battered stomach, and at the last jump the organ doors creaked open.

Paul switched on a grove of lights inside the organ compartment and displayed the massive pipes towering up to terminate in elaborate baroque capitals topped by gilt figures who might or might not have been Bacchus, Apollo, and the Nine Muses, up to some complicated acrobatics. Paul glanced up at them tolerantly.

"Papa says the pipes are made of tin, isn't that funny?

Papa can hardly play the organ at all, but he wants me to learn, he says every son should be able to do things his father can't."

"A very good principle." I surveyed the bank of keyboards. "Now, how do we pump this monster, or is it electric?"

"No, you pump it like this," he said, and showed me. "I always do it for Papa. Signora Radici was surprised we didn't have it electrified, but Papa said he didn't want to die just yet. Papa takes a lot of care."

"He shows sense."

"So many people would like to murder him, you see," Paul explained. "Papa says that is always so when somebody is very rich. So he is always on the lookout."

"I see." That accounted for his sparse eating habits, I thought. Presumably millionaires did acquire a lot of enemies: business rivals and people who stood to inherit. That would account too for Paul's constant air of watchful anxiety.

He turned now and shoved down a gilded lever inside the sliding doors; they slid back into place, folding us into a cosy inner closet with the organ.

"Papa likes to do that so no one can stab him in the back while he is playing."

"I'm all in favour of it too. Now, 'Baa Baa Black Sheep' and 'Chopsticks' are about my limit, but I'll be pleased to play them for you if you'll pump."

I sat down on the quilted gold-velvet seat.

But Paul had hardly started pumping when I heard a giggle behind me, and spun round in astonishment. Suzanne's head was protruding through a narrow crack in some painted Venetian panelling at the side of the closet. She burst out laughing at my surprise.

"Bet that gave you a fright, didn't it, Miss Marsh? I told you I knew a secret way into the organ."

"*I* told you about it," said Paul, pumping away. "And mind you don't tell anyone else."

"Course I won't," Suzanne said impatiently. She pushed the panel open a bit wider and squeezed through entirely, gave Paul a friendly thump, then came and leaned heavily against me. "Come on, Miss Georgia—play a tune. Play something from *The Sound of Music*."

"Paul's choice first," I said firmly. "What would you like, Paul?"

"I don't know what it's called." He hummed a familiar nursery tune and I played it, trying to think of its name.

" 'Did You Ever See a Lassie Go This Way, Go That Way,' " said Suzanne, fidgeting around behind me. "Now me, now me, Miss Georgia! Play 'All You Want Is Love.' "

I didn't, but I showed her how to participate in "Chopsticks"; she caught on with lightning enthusiasm and we were working up to a real jam session when steam began spouting out all over the organ. At least it was smoke really: a thick, suffocating white cloud, spurting out in tendrils, activated, it seemed, by Paul's operations on the bellows.

"Help! You'd better stop a moment, Paul, you're choking us."

The organ closet was filling up with fumes like cotton wool; our eyes streamed and we were all beginning to cough and gasp.

"Quick! Out through the little door, it's easier than working the lever."

I shoved the children ahead of me; Suzanne was nearest the panel, so she went ahead. "I've got a flashlight this time," she said proudly. "I took Mom's when I sneaked off to come here. Gee, Miss Georgia, don't we have adventures? I never had half such fun before you came."

She pulled the torch from her jeans pocket and switched it on, while Paul carefully shut the panel door behind us. We were in a narrow flagged passage, walled with reddish stone. The air was fresh enough in here; we took big gulps of it and I pulled out a handkerchief and wiped the children's eyes; gradually our fits of coughing abated.

"What was it, Miss Georgia?" said Paul worriedly. "Do you think the organ was on fire?"

"I don't think so. It didn't smell quite like ordinary smoke."

"*I'll* say it didn't," Suzanne said. "One time when we were living in California we had termites in the house and a man came and put gas bombs under the floor to kill them. It smelt just like that."

"Pyrethrum! I believe you're right, Suzanne. It did smell something like that."

"Maybe there are termites in the organ," Paul pondered, "and Papa arranged to have them smoked out."

"I daresay there's some perfectly simple explanation."

"Still, don't let's go back yet awhile," Suzanne said.

"Oh no; we'll leave the termites to enjoy it." Privately I wondered if the explanation wasn't even simpler; another of Mixie's lighthearted pranks. "Where do we go from here?"

We had come to a kind of T-junction of passages; only it was more complicated than that; ours led into a wider one, off which two others branched. Just at this moment Suzanne's torch, none too healthy at the start, flickered, gulped a couple of times, and went out. Paul, who had not taken the extrusions of smoke from the organ with Suzanne's carefree zest for adventure, let out a slight whimper.

"Darn it," Suzanne said. "Still, it doesn't make any difference. We know the way. Don't you worry, Paulie, I'll hold your hand," she added kindly. "There, I've got you. And Miss Georgia's right behind, aren't you, Miss Georgia? Just follow after us and we'll be out in no time."

"Okay. I'm right behind you," I said, hoping Suzanne's confidence was well-founded.

Whether it was or not instantly became of no more than academic importance to me. I was caught short by a final cataclysmic burst of coughing; I gasped and rasped, my eyes streamed in the darkness, I missed my footing and lurched against the side wall. By the time I'd managed to gulp sufficient air into my lungs to cool them down, and had recovered my centre of gravity, the children were a long way ahead. I could no longer hear their voices or footsteps.

"Hey, kids!" I shouted. "Suzanne! Paul! Where are you?"

No answer.

"Paul! Suzanne!"

Silence.

Well, they probably were all right, I hoped. After all, Suzanne had been both calm and resourceful during our previous subterranean foray; and it seemed plain that both she and Paul were fairly well acquainted with the underground byways of St. George's castle. All I had to do was get myself out and then, if necessary, I could start a search for them from aboveground. Someone, probably John Smith, must have a complete plan of the estate.

All I had to do was get myself out.

Easier said than done.

Down under the old city of Exeter there are some sinister little narrow passages, old water conduits, like magnified ant runs, which wander in a mazelike way through solid rock. I find them claustrophobic and felt the same about the back access to Capranis's organ. More light and space would have been definitely acceptable, and besides, for Pete's sake, it was the second time I'd been driven underground since lunch. Too bad little old one-track Mixie couldn't think up some other joke. But of course it was quite possible she hadn't known about the back exit; merely expected me to share the termites' fate.

Well I hoped to deprive her of that satisfaction.

Having no idea which way the children had gone, I decided to follow the slightly wider passage along to my left; theoretically I was now aimed in the general direction of the big castle kitchen, but the passage bent about in a discouraging manner. I moved cautiously along with a hand on either wall, feeling for entrances.

Anyway it must be going *somewhere*.

Mustn't it?

Presently it forked. By now I was uncertain enough of my sense of direction to have no very clear views as to which fork I ought to take; furthermore I was getting pretty tired and fed up. I stood still in the dark and brooded.

After all, can I trust anyone?

How do I know Capranis didn't lay the groundwork for the whole affair, inviting me to play the organ, inciting Paul and Suzanne to urge me, arranging for Mixie to plant a gas bomb?

No, but Capranis would never have run the risk of Paul's being in there too.

But Firgaard had forbidden me to associate with the children; perhaps an order from Capranis lay behind that.

Oh, come on, Georgia, what's the use of standing here in the black dark building card houses with ideas that won't stand up on their own? Let's make a start in some direction, eh? What would Esther Summerson have done?

Esther would have bustled up and down the passages doing a great many household errands and embroidering half a dozen yards of ornamental work and jingling her bunch of keys. But I hadn't any bloody keys and it was definitely too dark for embroidery in this rat run. All I could do was try and come to a decision about which turning to take. I put in a bit of listening, in the faint hope that Paul and Suzanne might have started back when they discovered that I wasn't behind them after all, and might be calling for me.

I didn't hear their voices, but after aurally combing the darkness and silence for a while, I began to think that I heard some kind of a faint sound, far away along the right-hand passage. It could have been the wind wailing, or somebody groaning; not Plastiras *again,* for heaven's sake? They hadn't removed him from the air ambulance and stuck him back underground so as to give me the exercise of hauling him up to the surface twice over?

Whether Plastiras or not, life of some kind ahead there definitely was, and I started off along the right-hand fork. Of course—I suddenly halted—it could be that this passage led back in the direction of the oubliette and the sound was intended to lure me to my doom. I slowed down after this notion struck me, and went more carefully, checking the ground ahead with a foot and the wall with a hand before taking each step. The faint gusty sound ahead rose and fell in a regular way, like a psalm chanted in church; its rhythmic pattern began to have a certain familiarity. After a while I became sure that it was a human voice; songs the sirens sang, maybe? Or some marine monster that Capranis kept immured in the middle of his castle rock; Caliban, or the Minotaur. Perhaps that was why Firgaard was so obsessively set against bullfighting; he knew that the real thing, Old Horny himself, was somewhere not far away, shut in underground, ready to rush out roaring, seeking whom he might devour, as soon as somebody penetrated his labyrinth; first he would eat them, then he would track backwards along their trail until he came to the outside world. Only in this case he'd come to the organ full of termite fumes, which might also be Minotauricidal, but that wouldn't do me any good; I'd have been eaten already.

Georgia, old pal, your thoughts aren't making a lot of sense, and Esther Summerson would tell you the same.

Being in a cave underground never does have a clarifying effect on my thoughts; they get very archetypal.

So let's not think, about minotaurs or anything else.

Instead I whistled "Baa Baa Black Sheep," and "Chopsticks," and Paul's little tune which was not, of course, "Did You Ever See a Lassie Go This Way, Go That Way," as Suzanne had suggested, but "Ach, du lieber Augustin," as anyone ought to know; I knew it perfectly myself, just hadn't thought of it at the time. One of Martin's favourite tunes, it used to be.

The chanting was much nearer now, and it was definitely chanting; St. George himself, perhaps, or a hermit sailed across from the African desert in a stone trough, and now inhabiting a cell in the heart of the rock.

Suddenly my passage came to a blank stop; there I was, up against flat solid darkness. The chanting, now quite loud, almost divisible into words, seemed to be just beyond the barrier, interspersed with swishing, sploshing, watery sounds; a water Minotaur, a hippopotamus? Cautiously investigating the dark ahead with both hands I realised that it was wood, not rock like the side walls; a door therefore. A door implied a handle or fastening of some kind; Minotaur or no, I explored the smooth surface up and down, all over, like a surgeon palpating a stomach; I hoped for some lever such as the one inside the organ compartment but found nothing of the kind. Then, stepping closer to reach higher, I must have trodden on a foot button, for a section of the blackness ahead of me pivoted on a central axis, creating two narrow exits like a turnstile. The chanting stopped abruptly. I walked through the turnstile into such a dazzle of green, blue, and gold light that my first instinctive reaction was to shut my eyes and face round towards the dark passage from which I had just emerged. Already the pivot door had swung back into place, displaying, on its reverse side, an elaborate representation of Diana surprised bathing by Actaeon and his hounds. Some nymphs were darting away between laurel

groves with maidenly gestures; Diana herself was looking
not so much surprised as very angry indeed.

"May I ask what the *devil* you think you're doing
here?" said a familiar voice.

I turned again, blinking against light and a powerful ef-
fusion of pine bath essence, and got an eyeful of Capranis,
rosy as a huge strawberry (much the same shape too),
discovered reclining in a capacious square sunk bath
which contained about twenty inches of brilliant green
water topped with pea-coloured foam. The effect was very
sybaritic—like a Neapolitan ice. Capranis had been leaning against an air pillow at the opposite end, reading the
Financial Times; now the *Financial Times* was floating on
the green foam, and Capranis was sitting bolt upright,
looking even angrier than Diana.

We were in a bathroom. A narrow green marble cat-
walk encircled the bath and was protected by narrow gold
railings; two gold-railed sets of steps led down into the
water. The walls were lapis-lazuli; rather pretty. There
were some mullioned windows with stained-glass versions
of Io, Leda, Danae & Co; rather hideous. All in all the
room was striking; it reminded me of those tough red,
blue, green and yellow beach balls there used to be before
blow-up ones were invented.

"I didn't know you were back," I said, startled by this
very sudden change in my situation.

"I hired a plane," Capranis said coldly. "I didn't want
you raising civil war and mayhem in my castle before I got
back. It seems I was wise to do so—"

"You didn't want *me* starting civil war! I like that!"

"It is usual to explain and apologise when you walk into
someone's private bathroom."

"Listen, have Paul and Suzanne been through here?" I
said ignoring this red herring.

His expression changed.

"No, why?"

"They were in front of me, back in there—" I gestured
towards the painted panel on which poor abashed Actaeon
was sprouting horns. "We got separated. I'm worried in
case they—"

He had already picked out a green malachite telephone
from a niche in the wall.

"Niko—get me Ariadne will you please?" He waited, listening. "Ariadne? Have you seen Paul? He and Suzanne Koolidge are there with you eating grapes? I see. That is all right then. No—no, Miss Marsh merely wished to know where they were. No thank you, no tea just now."

I let out a breath of relief as he replaced the phone in its niche.

"I suppose one of these narrow passages comes out in the kitchen."

"That is so," Capranis agreed. "Now, Miss Marsh, perhaps you would be good enough to give me some brief indication as to why you and those two children were wandering about underground in this extremely foolish and reckless way when I had given you explicit instructions to take every possible precaution?"

"Explicit instructions? You said I could play the organ, didn't you? You as good as ordered me to."

"Organ?" The bald dome of forehead crinkled itself upward. "What has that to do with the case?"

"I'll tell you—" I was beginning, when it struck me that a kind of insistent hum overhead which had steadily been growing louder was not the bathwater running away—as I had vaguely apprehended—but some exceedingly large bees which were cannoning about up above me in the manic way of their kind. Furthermore, additional bees kept arriving. Following their course back to the window, I noticed that in the Leda scene a section of the swan's midriff seemed to be missing; bees were pouring through this hole like a stream of dark brown cough syrup from a bottle opening.

"Look, there's a hole in your window," I started to say, when a sharp burning jab on my left arm caused me to let out a yell.

Simultaneously Capranis shouted,

"Get under the water! *Quick!*"

I was quick. It is wonderful how fast one catches on in some circumstances. Shaking off two more bees who were just about to settle I hurled myself into the bath, clothes, sandals and all.

Capranis reached out an ungentle hand and shoved me right under; I came up gasping and he did it again.

"Hey!" I gulped, finally getting nose and mouth just above water, "you don't have to drown me."

"I assure you, it is a preferable death to being stung all over by Cyprian bees," Capranis said grimly. Nothing was visible of him but two bushy brows, the bent nose, and a few of those amazing teeth.

Bees were now invading the bathroom in a solid black cloud; the noise they made sounded like motorcycle scrambles, only more high-pitched and continuous. One had to speak fairly loud to make oneself heard.

"What can we do? Can you phone for someone to come and smoke them out?"

More gas bombs, I thought.

"I might if the phone were not occupied at present by about three hundred bees."

I saw what he meant. Three feet away from the water, blanketed by bees, the phone might as well have been in Tasmania for all the use it was to us.

"We will just have to relax." Capranis came out of the water just enough to give me a malicious smile, then quickly submerged again. "And it is not often, after all, that one has such an interesting opportunity to share one's bath with a beautiful young lady."

"No? What about your pal Mixie?" I snapped. "Don't you ever share a friendly bath with her?"

The eyebrows shot up.

"Certainly not," he replied frostily. "There is a proverb that says, 'Share a bath, a mango, and a prayer mat only with the love of your heart.' "

"Well, I apologise for *my* intrusion."

However, embarrassing though in some respect it was, to be sharing a bath in this compulsory seclusion with Capranis did constitute a first-class opportunity to try and get a little information out of him. And the hum of the bees would substantially diminish the chances for eavesdroppers, if any.

Abandoning any pretences of modesty therefore—in any case, *I* was fully dressed—I wriggled closer to Capranis and got an old-fashioned look.

"Mr. Capranis, while you were away I had a conversation with Captain Cruikshank and learned, as I'd thought that he had been in command of the *Orfeo*."

"Indeed?"

"Yes." If he could be noncommittal, so could I. "And that, among the Greek orphans from Boston that you were charitably repatriating, adopting and educating, it is almost certain that you included another child who was not Greek, a boy who had been taken—"

Capranis sighed. He leaned over, gently enough this time, and laid a finger on my lips.

"No names, please."

"Mr. Capranis. Do you know which this boy is?"

"How could I have discovered?" he said, looking at me slit-eyed. "How could I know, when even Cruikshank did not?"

"No, but did you?"

"Even if I did I would have no intention of telling you. Indeed, what right have you to know?"

A simple answer seemed best.

"I loved his father. I'm anxious about him."

"What could you do for him that is not already being done?"

He had a point there. But I said miserably,

"It was partly my fault that he was taken. Unintentionally I let through some information about his father. I feel responsible."

"Your self-accusations help nobody," Capranis said, briskly but not unkindly. "They are no more than self-importance. Unjustified! If not through you, the people who took the child would have acquired the information some other way. Guilt is not only useless but harmful. Look at Cruikshank: on account of his morbid tendency to self-reproach and brooding over the past, your cousin was confirmed in her suspicion that the boy had not died after all. She had been hanging around Cruikshank for a couple of years, like a cat over a mousehole. By good luck he really did not know which of the children was—was the boy in question. She could get nothing from him beyond the fact that the boy still lived. But that has caused trouble enough! So she waited for a chance to send for you."

"Why did you let her?" I was really puzzled.

He shrugged. "By the time I had learned of her plan you were on your way."

"Why allow *her* to come here?"

"I did not know until this year of her part in the original snatch." Capranis seemed rather put-out at having to admit this.

"But when you did find out, why let her come, if she was such a danger?"

"Everything is a danger," Capranis pronounced. "She had been helping me for years, visiting the school, bringing children. So if I suddenly got rid of her, that would arouse suspicion in itself. Better to keep her, keep an eye on her activities. But then she got herself murdered, and *you* turn up—"

"You're sure you didn't murder her?"

"Miss Georgia," he said patiently, "what would be the point? You were already on your way. She had certainly kept her colleagues in touch with developments; you too for all I knew—"

"So you got your friends the police to bundle me on a plane that was going to be hijacked as the simplest way out of that little dilemma?"

Capranis tipped up his head to grin at me. A bee settled on its bald crown and he submerged with an oath.

I had adopted a sort of Récamier posture, reclining on my elbows, looking at the ceiling where the bees hung like a cumulus cloud. Their first shrill buzzing had by now simmered down to a slumbrous rumble, and they seemed, on the whole, less restless and frantic; but still, I wouldn't lay a thousand drachs on our chances of getting as far as the door. Absently studying their endless permutations and circlings, I reflected that this was a very peculiar interview; I doubted if Esther Summerson would approve of it.

Capranis surfaced again, and put up a cautious hand to rub his head.

"Mr. Capranis."

"Oh, why not address me by my first name?"

"What is it?"

"Dionysios-Enneacrounos."

"Well, I don't know. I think I'll go on calling you Mr. Capranis."

"What were you about to say?"

"Do you think someone encouraged those bees to come into your bathroom with that bee-trail stuff?"

"Oh, without doubt," he said indifferently. "Such things

are happening to me all the time. A man in my position has so many enemies."

"Yes, so Paul was saying."

"You were talking to Paul?"

"Playing the organ. That was how we came to go underground. A little trouble with the organ. Goodness." An idea suddenly struck me. "Perhaps I've been misjudging Mixie. Perhaps all that poison gas in the organ was really intended for *you*."

"Explain, please."

So I explained, first about the oubliette, and Mixie's confession, then my interview with Cruikshank, and finally about the abortive organ recital. Capranis heard me in silence. I'd have liked to try and gauge his thoughts from his expression, but the expression was all under water.

"Very interesting," was all he said when I had brought us along the underground passage.

"Mr. Capranis?"

"Yes?"

"Patrice said there are two different sets of people after —after the child. Do you know who? Do you know why?"

"Partly I do," he said, and maddeningly said no more.

"Well, aren't you worried about the situation?" I burst out. "Don't you think you ought to—to hide him?"

Capranis sighed.

"Where can I hide him better than here—a child among the other children? What do you suggest I do—lock him up in Fort Knox? Worried?" he said impatiently. "Of course I am worried. That is why I set a trap"—using me as bait, I thought—"to try to find who of the people here may be involved. Of Sweden I knew—but who worked with her, who against, that I do not yet know for sure."

"And Captain Plastiras—what did he know?"

"That we shall not be able to find out till he recovers. He is mildly confused—it will not be long."

"I wish you'd told me that Plastiras was going to be masquerading around dressed up as a priest," I said crossly. "It would have saved an awful lot of trouble."

Capranis preserved a neutral underwater silence.

Suddenly I felt I'd had enough of sitting in a gold-rimmed bath with a millionaire.

"I'm going to try a bit of persuasion on your bees."

"*Oriste?*"

"My mother was a bee woman."

"I understood she was a biologist."

"Both. Bees were her recreation. When she died, all her bees died too. She used to sing to them, when they were upset about something, or in thundery weather. Like this."

I hummed Mother's funny, archaic tune; whistled it; hummed it. Over and over. Countless times I'd heard her doing it, wandering up and down between the lavender bushes in her old jeans and Madras shirt. Mother never bothered putting on hats and gloves and bee veils, like most apiarists; she said she wouldn't do anything so wounding to the bees' feelings. But she wouldn't ever let me go very close to the hives; children's characters, she said, were too unformed, on the whole, for them to associate safely with bees; children might do something rash and sudden that would cause a misunderstanding.

I hoped my character had formed sufficiently since those days.

The acoustics of Capranis's bathroom were splendid; I could quite understand why he took such pleasure in chanting Orthodox psalms, or whatever he had been doing as I came along the passages. The sound rolled up from the water in vibrant, melodious surges; soothing and hypnotic, I hoped, for homesick Cyprian bees.

"My goodness," said Capranis.

It did seem as if the bees were calming down. At least they were flying in a much more orderly way, in flocks, in waves, instead of single. And then, no doubt of it, they did begin to settle, dangling themselves in heavy black clots on the gilded sconces that held wall lights, alighting in dense black mats on bottles of cologne, soaps and sponges and the garishly coloured towels that were flung down by the steps.

"Your mother's tune appears to be quite efficacious," Capranis murmured with what might even have been respect in his tone.

Very slowly, moving an inch at a time, I lifted myself out of the water and sat dripping on the rim of the bath, avoiding a small nexus of bees who were rising, falling, hovering, making up their minds to settle on a discarded sandal. They ignored me, so I ignored them.

"Pray be careful, my dear Georgia."

"I think it's okay."

I went on humming. Very few bees were in the air now, nearly all of them had found somewhere to sit and have a kip.

"Get yourself as near to the steps by the door as you can."

There was a proper door opposite the concealed entrance by which I had come. It was bolted. Capranis moved carefully through the water, looking like a piece of intercontinental drift. When he reached the steps I surveyed the bee scene. They were all sitting now; a reflective silence fell as soon as I stopped humming. I slid back into the water and followed Capranis.

"Now: when I nod, go up those steps and out of the door. Don't move suddenly, don't think about the bees, just go out calmly and steadily and shut the door behind you."

I began humming again. Capranis gave me a thoughtful look, checked some remark he had been on the point of uttering, and set himself in motion again. Glossy, pink, and dripping, he emerged from the water, mounted the steps with a kind of massive dignity, unhurriedly undid the door, passed through, and closed the door again behind him. Not a bee stirred. A trickle of sweat went coldly down between my shoulder blades. I gave with a few more bars of the bee tune, just to be on the safe side, then rose from the water myself and followed Capranis at a careful, deliberate speed, not too fast. The back of my neck prickled as I stepped past black motionless hunks of bees, absorbed in silent contemplation on a rumpled bath mat, piled like a portion of caviare in marble soap dish and ashtray. I opened the door, stepped through, shut it . . .

Beyond the door was a dressing room furnished with yakskin and silver fittings; Capranis, rough-dried and wearing one of his more lurid pairs of shorts, had a silver telephone receiver jammed under his ear and a glass in one hand; with the other hand he was pouring from a bottle into a second glass.

"As soon as you can, please, Niko," he said to the phone. "No, no, tell the beekeeper that of course I'm not in the least angry, but I have left my favourite gold watch in the bathroom and I want it; besides, I do not think the damp atmosphere will be good for the bees. Also ask Ariadne to come to my dressing room, if you please."

He laid the receiver back, filled the second glass, and approached me. But instead of handing me the glass he put it down on a silver commode and gave me a hug instead.

Just like old Mrs. Panas.

"Brandy. I should think you need it. Are you all right?"

"Fine, thanks. Only rather wet."

"Here." He removed his arm and flung several large towels round me. "Drink the brandy, it will stop you from getting cold. Really you are a capable young girl, Miss Georgia, one must admit; even the bees have a respect for you, it appears." His grin, for once, seemed more affectionate than derisive. "Now, you will be needing some other clothes; it is curious, is it not, how almost every time I see you, some disaster seems to have overtaken your wardrobe?"

Ariadne came in.

"Po po po," she said. The situation in a nutshell.

"Ariadne, Kyría Marsh needs some clothes."

"Only a robe," I said. "My things will dry in ten minutes."

"Take them away, then, Ariadne, and dry them."

"If the kyría will come through here."

She escorted me into Capranis's bedroom which, unexpectedly, proved to be a thoroughly utilitarian kind of room with peasant-weave rugs and bedcoverings.

"I should think Kyría Koolidge's robe would fit you," Ariadne said, and fished a white velvet negligee from a closet.

"I'm allergic to velvet; it makes me come out in a rash," I said hastily. "Any old towelling thing will do. Or a shirt of Kyrie Capranis?"

"That would not be suitable. To go to bed with a person is one thing, to wear his shirt is something else."

I reflected that she seemed to share her nephew's unusual and rigid notions of the proprieties.

"I didn't go to bed with him, kyría; we had trouble with some bees."

"Better a wineskinful of bees than a headful of evil fancies," she said enigmatically, went muttering from the room, and presently returned with a tremendous embroidered shawl, evidently her own. I thanked her humbly and slung it on over underwear, which was nearly dry already.

"I have hung your other things round my charcoal range," she said. "They will be dry in a few minutes. Your arm looks rather swollen; would you like me to do something for it?"

"Thank you, kyría, that would be very kind; it is rather sore."

It had swelled up to the size of a leg of mutton, and was throbbing so loudly that I felt anyone else must be able to hear it too.

Ariadne had a look at it, sucked the point of sting, po-po'd a bit more, hobbled away, and came back with a small earthenware pot of blackish paste which she spread liberally over the epicentre of the swelling and all down the arm. At once I felt a wonderful easement; the throbbing died down from *ff* to barely audible.

"Goodness, that's marvellous, kyría. What is that stuff?"

"Wild doves' manure mixed with honey. And a pinch of powdered sea horse," she said.

Homeopathic medicine. I wondered what Phyllora would think of it.

Ariadne then produced my jeans and shirt, ironed and dry.

"Kyría, you are too good."

"It is nothing. My great-nephew tells me you saved his life." She unbent enough to give me another voluminous Greek hug, and added, "When you are ready he asks if you will go through to his study."

When I had tidied my hair I did so to find Capranis, somewhat more formally dressed in that he had put on trousers and shirt, writing a note, not by any of his elaborate electronic gadgets, but on a simple piece of paper with a pen. When it was done he handed it to his nephew Mark who stood waiting, gave Mark a nod, but no verbal instructions, and gestured him towards the open french window. Mark flashed me a grin and ran off.

"It's very odd that Mark's so much more like you than"—I began, and then stopped, staring at the tasselled, brocade-covered settee on which Paul had lain sleeping the previous evening. It was the cushion, the brocade of my dream. And the sleeping figure—that tense, fidgety sleep, the muttered words, the sudden startled awakening—how familiar they were: a behaviour pattern I had seen repeated countless times.

I said without thinking, the words jolted out of me: "What a fool I've been. It's Paul, isn't it?"

Capranis slapped me. Not as hard as he had Suzanne; it's possible he merely intended to lay his hand over my mouth. I just gaped at him, utterly dumbstruck; more with my discovery than his action.

Paul. Everything fell into place. The age was right, the physique, Paul's insecurity, his desperate dependence on his adopted father. And—how could I have been so unobservant?—now I thought about it consciously, I could see that everything Paul did, every action, every movement, recalled Martin; the way he stood slightly leaning back, with his head poised at an angle on his neck; the way he frowned over a difficulty; the very intonations of his voice, only, as he had been speaking Greek, not English or German, I had failed to catch the resemblance in the sound pattern. Good lord, there was the tune even—"Du lieber Augustin"; Paul must have unconsciously memorised it when a baby, Martin was always whistling it. Intelligent? Cruikshank was wrong. Far from being intelligent, I must be the thickest, most insensitive dolt in the whole of the eastern Mediterranean.

I was still staring at Capranis; he had pulled out his telephone from behind the works of Lord Lytton and was speaking to Ariadne, asking her to bring a bottle of champagne. I was vaguely puzzled, since brandy and ouzo already stood at hand. When I opened my mouth to speak, Capranis gave me such a silencing scowl that, instead of the intended apology, I said,

"If Kyría Ariadne is your great-aunt I'm surprised you let her cook and run errands for you."

"We are in Greece, not England, Miss Georgia. Besides she is the only person in this place that I trust."

Ariadne came in with an ice bucket and bottle on a tray.

"Can you send Paul to me, Ariadne?" Capranis said in a low voice.

The old lady shook her head.

"Not possible."

"How do you mean, not possible?" he snapped.

"He and Suzanne, Kyría Koolidge's daughter, have gone off with the teacher."

"Which teacher? What for?"

"To make things ready for the picnic tomorrow, they said. They went with Kyrie Smith in the Volkswagen. To the Valley of Butterflies."

Capranis let out a barely audible but vehement and comprehensive oath.

"I must go after," he muttered. "Tell Niko I want the Alfa right away."

Ariadne nodded and hobbled out.

"He'll be all right with Smith, surely?"

Capranis turned an expressionless face to me: mouth set thin, brown eyes opaque as caramels.

"Now the cat is out of the bag I trust nobody."

"But, good heavens, it's not five minutes since I—"

"You think they wait till there is a *Times* editorial about it?"

"What can I do?" I could have wept; I was utterly wretched and at a loss.

When in doubt, Raymond Chandler says, have a man with a gun come through the door.

"You can stay just where you are, Miss Marsh, for the time being," Lady Lurgashall said. She walked through the french windows with that unstressed air of being so superior to her surroundings that the fact is hardly worth remarking, peculiar to the English landed gentry; she might have been the president of the Women's Institute, moving unassumingly to take her presidential seat on the platform and tell the local ladies how to vote in the next by-election.

But, unlike the run of W.I. presidents, Lady Lurgashall held a gun, a thickset workmanlike looking pistol which carried instant conviction. She had it pointed at my navel, and said to Capranis,

"Keep quite still or I shall shoot the gel in the stomach. Put your wrists together behind your back."

If looks speak volumes, his spoke the whole *Malleus Maleficarum,* but he stuck his hands behind him as instructed, and Lady Lurgashall, pointing the gun at me all the time, laid down her large tapestry bag and extracted from it with her left hand a family-sized roll of adhesive elastic bandage. An end of the bandage was already loosened with a corner doubled over to prevent its sticking to itself; still one-handed she expertly whipped this round Capranis's wrists, pulled it tight, and proceeded to wind on the whole reel of bandage so that his hands were solidly clamped together. It must have been uncomfortable.

"Now you," she said to me.

"I can't get my arm behind my back." It was too swollen.

She tried to push it but it wouldn't go.

"In front then," she said, compressing her lips.

Most of Aunt Ariadne's dove-manure poultice fell off as she fixed my wrists together in the same way, with more bandage.

"May I ask what you plan to achieve by all this?" Capranis inquired.

"Now we know that your adopted son is the Ettlinger boy, we are taking him," Lady Lurgashall briskly replied.

"And what makes you so sure?"

"Oh, my dear man! We have two microphones in this room; we've been tapping your conversations for months. The moment the gel identified him, I sent Smith to pick him up. We want the gel too."

"Why?" he said coldly. I was amazed at his apparent calm; myself, I didn't feel so serene. Firstly, I would have liked to kill myself for my thoughtless stupidity; secondly, my arm had started to throb again; and also I had taken quite a powerful dislike to Lady Lurgashall, who reminded me of the headmistress at my prep school. Lady L. had the same bleak stone-grey eyes and Roman nose, thickly powdered skin and lips that were several tones paler than her florid complexion. Her stout, no-nonsense foundation garment creaked when she moved, expelling an unwelcome waft of Pink Jade.

Looking more closely at Capranis, I saw that he wasn't really so calm; his pulse was rapid and his breathing tumultuous, as they say in nineteenth-century fiction.

"My opposite numbers won't take just my word that the boy is Ettlinger's son; the gel will be needed to establish his identity."

My heart leaped up; perhaps I could fool them. But then it sank again as sense and realism prevailed; no doubt they had all the interrogation resources of modern technology at their command.

"Why not take me?" Capranis said.

"You didn't know Ettlinger."

"So what are you going to do with me?"

It struck me that Capranis was being uncharacteristically chatty; did he care so much? Was he trying to acquire information? Or stalling for time?

"Shoot," Lady Lurgashall laconically replied. "We shan't leave your body here, though; we don't want a hue and cry till we're away. Everyone here thinks you're still in Nicosia."

"Ariadne knows he's back. So does Niko," I put in. So, presumably, did the character who led the bees into the bathroom.

Capranis shot me a baleful look, but Lady Lurgashall was unruffled.

"Ariadne is locked up in the wine cellar. Niko is asleep; Smith gave him a shot of morphine when he took the Land-Rover."

Quite coolly she raised the gun and took aim.

"Hey, wait a minute," I said hastily. "You're really laying up trouble for yourself if you shoot Mr. Capranis, Lady Lurgashall."

"Why?" Her tone of cold disinterest suggested that I was the tweeny-maid, offering an unwanted opinion about local politics.

"Paul absolutely adores his father. I don't know what you want Paul *for,* but once he hears you've shot his— shot Mr. Capranis—"

"Who's going to tell him?" she snapped.

"Even if he weren't told," I said slowly, "without his father he feels so insecure that I honestly wouldn't bet on his chances of survival. He'll just die of grief."

It needed no effort to put conviction into my voice; I was convinced. The vision of Paul dragged off by strangers for the second time, once more bereft of the prop and focus of his existence, was one I could hardly bear to contemplate.

I met Capranis's eye and quickly looked away again.

Lady Lurgashall frowned.

"Rubbish, absolute nonsense," she said. "He'll adapt, just as any boy does when he goes to boarding school." But I thought she seemed slightly irresolute.

"You are wrong, you know, Celia," Capranis said quietly. "And Miss Marsh is right. Paul, after all, is not an ordinary boy. He is the son of a genius—"

Lady Lurgashall's lips curled; I fancied it formed the word "milksop."

"And furthermore, he has had already a deeply disturbed childhood. Your East German friends, Celia, will not be particularly grateful to you if the child you produce for them is on the verge of a mental breakdown."

"Why *do* you want him, in heaven's name?" I burst out. "What good is he to you now you've destroyed his wretched father? Why can't you leave him in peace?"

"They want him for his exchange value," Capranis told me in a colourless tone. "Have you ever collected stamps, Miss Marsh? If so, you will know that sometimes you buy one simply for its use as a swap, because you know that somebody else is after it, who has something that *you* want."

"What do they want, then?"

"Celia's brother, who is doing forty years in a top-security prison for handing over state secrets."

Sir John somebody. I remembered a snatch of conversation from earlier in the day.

"And they intend to offer Paul as a swap?" I said, horrified. "It sounds crazy. Why not swap someone they've got already."

"Just now they have no agent of comparable value. Whereas, you see, there was a lot of international outrage at the time of Paul's disappearance, and of course most people believe to this day that he is in East Germany somewhere; it must have been quite annoying for them that in fact they did not have him and were ignorant of his whereabouts."

"So it would be a double coup to get him back and exchange him for their own man. Treating him like a match-box."

"The boy would be perfectly well treated," snapped Lady Lurgashall. "I can't think why you are kicking up such a fuss. Come on, we're wasting time."

Apparently, however, she had decided to abandon her intention of shooting Capranis immediately; she gestured him towards the french window with the gun.

He glanced at me and I saw his lips move; it might have been the word "Delay."

This was not difficult for me. The elastic strap round my wrists was playing Old Harry with my bee sting; for the last few minutes there had been a mysterious singing in my ears, not unlike the buzz of the bees themselves, and a beelike swarm of black dots had been dancing up and down in front of my eyes. The fierce pain in my arm had started off a king-size headache; in fact my head felt like the beacon of a pedestrian crossing: a sunset-coloured in-candescent glow up in behind my frontal lobes kept switching on and off at irregular intervals.

"You'll have to excuse me," I said, in between urgent efforts to get a bit of air into my lungs. "I'm afraid I'm going to pass out."

And I did so.

XI

If this is a hospital, I thought, jouncing along with my head hanging over the edge, stretchers have certainly changed since fifty-seven when they took my tonsils out; maybe they have vibro-stretchers now, to stimulate pa-tients' circulation, and this head-down business is doubt-less to encourage the flow of blood to the brain; but what have they been doing to my arm? It can't be typhoid shots, I had them in the spring.

The next jounce shook my eyes open and I was surprised to find that I was in the dark.

Stars shone overhead. I began to notice a strong musky smell, quite unlike the antiseptic whiff of a hospital corridor. So where was I, if not in hospital having my arm amputated? What the devil was going on?

A noise like a ship's siren blasted off in my ear and really roused me; it also brought home to me the unpalatable truth of the fact that this leisurely jerk-and-sway motion below me was that of a mule; I was lying strapped to a wooden pannier platform on its back. Another mule walked behind, whinnying; I could see the glow of its eyes, luminous as a fox's in the dark, and the twitch of its big furry ears against the moonlit sky. Somebody was astride the rear mule; I screwed my head round to try and make out who.

A low voice said, "Georgia? Can you hear me?"

Capranis.

"Where are we?" I muttered. But my throat was dry and sore; speaking made me cough. A mule in front, which I had not noticed, slowed down till mine drew alongside; somebody caught its bridle and shone a flashlight into my eyes. I let out a protesting squawk.

More mule-braying from farther ahead, and another one jolted up beside us.

"All okay?" said a man's voice. "No trouble?"

"None." That was Lady Lurgashall.

"Very efficient, my dear Celia. But why is Capranis alive?"

"The girl said"—her voice was a mutter and they had drawn aside, but I could just hear—"the Ettlinger boy is so devoted to him, he'll collapse if Capranis dies."

"We weren't instructed to bring him." I thought I recognised Smith's voice.

"Instructions! You're a real civil servant," she said scornfully. "Well, you'd better get in touch and tell them this; see what they feel."

"All right; let's get on."

The mules broke into their shuffling stride once more. We were now going steeply uphill so that my whole body was tipped at a forty-five-degree angle. It was uncomfortable, but in a way the discomfort helped take my mind off my arm. And other things. And that was an advantage.

I tried to employ my mind usefully. Lady Lurgashall was taking us to her opposite numbers, her East German friends, Capranis had called them. Where were they to be found? Doubtless time would show.

Now we were crossing the top of a scrubby, rocky hill, and a moonlit stretch of sea showed over to our right; we were, I supposed, therefore going north along the coast of Dendros. I looked back—no trouble about doing this, I was tied that way round—and saw the unmistakable pinnacle of Aghios Georgios behind us and a glimmer of light near the top that must be from the castle. Old Firgaard having his nightly read of Ole Södso.

I heard Lady Lurgashall, who was riding a half-length ahead of me, say,

"What have you done with the children?"

"Locked on the boat. I left the girl for the time. She keeps him from panicking."

"Well, we don't want a lot of fuss; these two can go in the shed for the night. I'll take them. You'd better go straight back and send the message about Capranis."

Her tone was so much that of duchess addressing butler that I half expected him to reply, "Very well, madam. Will that be all?"

Instead, rather sourly, he said, "All right. Here's the key of the shed. Can you manage?"

"Yes," she said, shortly but with great conviction.

He kicked his mule to the right, and disappeared down what looked like a cliff face.

Lady Lurgashall, riding straight ahead, led the way down a path that was slightly less steep. Literally led; she had my mule and Capranis's on long headropes and was towing us all along; Capranis, although at least in an upright position, was tied to his mount just as tightly as I was.

The straps round my wrists had been loosened a bit, presumably when I fainted, but my arm wasn't giving me any joy. To liven up the party a bit I said,

"Where are we going, Lady Lurgashall?"

"There's a ship coming in to pick you up," she said briefly. "The *Moskva Rika*."

"A Russian freighter," Capranis said thoughtfully. "She was in the Black Sea last week. Going back there?"

"She'll take you to a Black Sea port; you'll go on by air."

"Quite a little jaunt," I said.

"Lady Lurgashall," Capranis suggested, "has it ever occurred to you that they might be playing you for a sucker?"

"What nonsense!" she said, and then, "I can't imagine what you're talking about."

"Suppose they don't really want your brother? Why should they, after all? Suppose they want Paul for some other reason?"

"You're talking rubbish," she said shortly. "What other possible use could a child his age have for them?"

But just the same his suggestion had made her slightly uneasy, I could tell from her tone; she gave her mule a sharp slap with a stick and trotted on ahead, accelerating the pace of all three.

"Do you think that's really so?" I whispered to Capranis. He gave a shrug—I saw his shoulders move against the pale sky—and murmured,

"Who knows? How is your arm?"

"Sore. Where are we going, do you think?"

"To the Valley of Butterflies. There's a little harbour. I suppose the *Moskva Rika* will send in a boat for us."

Up to now, I had hardly taken our plight seriously. I felt too feverish, and the moonlit mule ride was too dreamlike, for the experience to be measured in terms of reality; but Capranis's glumly matter-of-fact tone brought me up short. To a man in his income bracket, presumably, kidnappings, piracy, and moonlight flittings were an everyday probability; for all I knew he had been kidnapped and ransomed several times over. But this was different from an ordinary commercial snatch; when the people who wanted Rudi Ettlinger had him, and were confident of his identity, what would happen then?

Was Capranis right in his guess that the boy was wanted for some other reason than his exchange value? And—a minor question, but one that nevertheless held some personal interest—what would happen to Capranis and me? Would we be politely returned, C.O.D., when our purpose was achieved, or would we be sewn in sacks and dumped in the Bosphorus as the *Moskva Rika* passed up that way?

We were in a little wood now, not unlike an English bluebell wood. The path descended, meandering among rocks; smallish trees, olive or oak or wild plum, climbed up the sides of the narrow glen and obscured our view of the sky. Nearby a stream ran chuckling over rocks; farther off I could hear the roar of a considerable waterfall. I could also hear Capranis behind me, swearing as every now and then a branch slapped him in the face; lying prone on my mule I was spared that at least. But I was beginning to be very tired of the head-down position; furthermore it had struck me that the reason for my curious state of stickiness was not blood from some unnoticed wound, as I had thought at first, but honey. These were evidently the mules that had been used to bring the hives to Aghios Georgios and I was now just about as tacky as a bit of baclava; I hoped that when we were unloaded Lady Lurgashall did not think fit to deposit us within smelling distance of a colony of the rapacious Dendros ants.

After about ten minutes' descent through the wood we reached a flat open place. The mules jolted to a stop. Ahead of us the trees came to an end; the stream ran over a crag and vanished in a cloud of spray. Beyond the trees one could glimpse the sea again; below the waterfall, I presumed, lay the anchorage.

A stone hut stood between us and the cliff edge. Lady Lurgashall dismounted and tethered all the mules to a spike in its wall. Then she unlocked the door and went inside. A torch-beam shone briefly about, she emerged again, came over to me, and started cutting through the straps that tied me to my mule with a triangular blade like a Stanley knife; it seemed to be very sharp. The mule backed a bit and I rolled off and fell heavily to the ground, Lady L. making no effort to break my fall. The pain in my arm was dazzling; I felt as if I were on the point of atomic fission.

"Well, get up!" she said sharply. "Don't just lie there."

"Lady Lurgashall," Capranis said, snapping off his words like icicles, "Miss Marsh is suffering from an inflamed bee sting. Also in the course of the last twelve hours she has fallen down an oubliette, crawled through several underground passages—"

"I'm all right, don't give it a thought," I said, rather embarrassed, lurching to my feet. "Can't move very fast, that's all."

"Into the shed," Lady Lurgashall said, gesturing with the knife.

"Is there a loo in there? Because I could do with one."

"Good heavens no, gel. If you wish to relieve yourself, go under the trees. And don't try to run, because I have you covered with this gun and it's a .357 which will stop a car engine and would certainly blow your leg off. I'm a first-class shot," she added.

Born and bred on a grouse moor, I thought.

The next few minutes were painful as well as undignified—it's remarkable how few things you can do properly with your hands tied and a sore arm—but Lady L. needn't have bothered to keep her lethal weapon trained on me, I hadn't the least intention of trying to make a dash for it. Presently I hobbled into the hut, which was full of rusty wire-mesh lobster pots, and in a minute Capranis followed me.

Lady Lurgashall paused a moment in the doorway, giving the place another once-over with her flashlight to make sure that it contained no razors, ladders, machine-guns, files, or pick-axes—which it did not—then she said,

"You'd better not shout because the only people who'd hear you are Smith and myself and it would only mean that we'd have to gag you."

She went out and locked the door.

There was a window, quite high up, about two foot square. When we had heard the mules clink and plod off, and Lady L. with them, presumably, I moved with care in the direction of the window, having plotted out a course between the lobster pots while the torch was on.

Poking the fingers of my joined hands between their crisscrosses, I piled three pots one on top of another, and scrambled up onto them. They all slid from under me, and I rolled onto the dirt floor, banging my arm, which could have done without this new cause of grievance.

"Damn!"

"Valiant Miss Georgia," said Capranis—I could tell

from his voice that he was smiling, but he came over and helped me up, as well as he could with hands tied behind him, "I fear the window looks out over a cliff."

"It does, doesn't it? But still, I think one might get out that way."

I'd had a rapid glimpse, before I fell, of the little cove down below, with a single boat moored in it. Over to my right the waterfall bounced splashily down the cliff, its spray rising in a white moonlit cloud.

"Alas," Capranis said, "my circumference is too great for the aperture, even if my hands were not tied."

"Yes, that's a pity. We might be able to do something about our hands, but maths is maths."

In fact I didn't feel too sanguine, myself, about the chances of escaping through the window. And he certainly had a point about his circumference. It would be like trying to get a melon into a match box.

I sat down, rather dispiritedly, on one of the lobster pots.

"What do we do, then, just wait for the Russian freighter to come and tow us away?"

"If they take Paul, I prefer they take me too."

"Yes."

"But I shall try to delay as long as possible."

"You think your friend Plastiras will come galloping along with a posse?" I said rather unkindly.

"Not Plastiras, no; heading a posse is outside his scene just now. But I have other friends."

Mixie? I wondered. Would she come rushing to the rescue like Pocahontas? Somehow I didn't see her in the role. But of course if she thought that saving him from peril would fix Capranis's hand and heart, she might feel inclined to. Changing the subject, I said,

"When *did* you get back from Nicosia, anyway? You must have come back awfully fast after our telephone conversation. I thought you were fixed there for the night."

"I heard about the *Moskva Rika*'s movements and it made me anxious. And I had an excellent opportunity to hire a plane, so I took it. Besides, I was worried about you, Miss Georgia. You are such an impulsive young lady."

"I'm most terribly sorry—about being such a fool. About goofing like that in the study," I said haltingly.

"Po, po. Forget about it. It must have happened some time, sooner or later."

"I can't think why you ever let me stay in the first place. It was bound to lead to trouble."

"I did, if you recall, do my best to prevent your arrival at Aghios Georgios! But then, when you arrived, I thought, ah well, let her stay."

"Why?"

"You reminded me of the nurse I had when I was a little boy."

"Charming!"

"You mistake. She was aged twelve, beautiful as a goddess; she could stop a bolting donkey with one flash of her eyes."

"No, but seriously, why did you let me stay?"

"Seriously, I thought you might help to clarify the situation. As you have."

"You must be worried to *death* about Paul," I said, uncomforted by this view of the matter.

"Yes," he said simply.

We were both silent for a while. I had discovered that the mixture of honey and pigeon dung in Great-aunt Ariadne's embrocation had prevented proper adhesion of the strapping to my arm; I was thoughtfully rubbing the edge of the plaster against a lobster pot, trying to pry it loose.

"I'm glad anyway they've left the children together," I muttered presently, when I felt the need of a breather from this occupation.

"Paul and Suzanne?" He sounded sceptical of the benefit to be derived from her company.

"Paul's fond of her. She'll keep him from being too scared. She's really a nice child, you know." Specially when she's away from her mother, I added inwardly. "And *very* brave."

"Children are your profession. You should know." But he sounded unconvinced.

"Mr. Capranis."

"So formal still!"

"Why in heaven's name do you run that school?"

It was certainly not the most tactful moment to ask him, but he could probably do with some distraction. Besides I wanted to know.

"You disapprove?" He seemed surprised. "But it fills a most useful role."

"For spoilt sweet-lifers who can't stand having a below-normal child?"

"Ah. So it is not really the school you object to? It is the replacement service."

"Yes. Yes I suppose so."

"The school, after all, does much good." He sounded quite detached about it.

"Yes, the orphans and the refugees; it's just—"

"The replacement service—which, incidentally, was conceived and put into practice by your cousin—accounts for less than 3 per cent of its pupils."

"Sweden invented the replacement idea?" Characteristic of her, I thought. I ought to have guessed; it had her stamp all over it. She'd enjoy making capital out of people's weaknesses. And having a hold over them ever after.

"I am afraid she began to use her knowledge in order to blackmail people," he said, echoing my thought. "I was in fact considering how best to put an end to the connection —which would have been a very delicate, complicated business—when she added to the complication by getting out of Patrice the fact that Rudi was not dead. But then she solved the problem by getting herself murdered."

"If you knew all about this—"

"I have not known for very long. When Patrice had a heart attack a couple of months ago and was reduced very low, he had a fit of repentance and told me all he had discovered about your cousin. He had not known, until their affair, of her connection with the Ettlinger kidnapping."

"It seems so extraordinary that, if she knew Martin, she could not have identified Rudi herself."

"She had never met Martin Ettlinger."

"But—she had a sketch of him."

"The one in your handbag?" Capranis chuckled at my gasp of outrage. "Well, you left the bag in my kitchen when you fell down the oubliette; really you are decidedly careless! Ariadne brought it to my study so naturally I looked at the contents. I like the colour of your eye shad-

ow very much. That sketch was done from the *Times* pho-
tograph—did you not recognise it? She probably did it to
familiarise herself with Ettlinger's features in hopes of recognising his son. No use: Paul does not take after either
his father or his mother."

"That's another thing that puzzles me," I burst out.
"How could you be so callous as to leave that wretched
Luise to die under the belief that her baby had been stolen
as a political pawn—"

"You think *that* of me?" He sounded really upset. "My
dear Miss Georgia! I had hoped our relationship was getting on to such a comfortable footing. Of course I went to
see Mrs. Ettlinger."

I gaped at him. The moon was setting, but our square
of window faced east; a green dawn light was growing in
the patch of visible sky and I could just see the outline of
Capranis's face; it widened in a smile of indulgence for my
amazement.

"I went to see her in the hospital in Boston. The visit
was kept very quiet, naturally. I even wore a false beard—
most undignified. We both knew she was to die soon. She
agreed that in the circumstances, it would be better for
Rudi to be left with me altogether, with the Greek orphans, not to be removed again, not to be exposed to risk.
Harder for her, better for the child."

"Good grief." I sat silent, assimilating this: assimilating
the fact that I would have to revise my estimate both of
Luise and Capranis.

"Patrice, filled with remorse, had told me of his crime.
Rudi was already with me. So I promised Luise that I
would adopt him and look after him as a son."

I didn't say anything.

He looked at me thoughtfully for a minute and added,
"She was a brave woman."

"I never doubted it."

"I saw you at her funeral."

"*You* were there?"

"In the beard again," he said apologetically, and added
without apparent relevance, "Another reason why I was
not entirely averse to your arrival at Aghios Georgios."

"So you really knew the whole story? Luise told you everything?"

"I knew about your love for this man. If that is what you mean." He waited a moment and then said, "Ettlinger was a weak character, you know. You would have felt that, in time."

"What do you know about it?" I snapped. "Anyway, he was a genius."

"I don't deny it. But—to desert his child! He knew his wife was dying. And yet he chose to kill himself and leave his son without any defender."

"What could he do? He was in a terrible position."

"Well," Capranis sounded positive, "all I know is that in his position *I* should not have acted so."

I wondered what he would have done. All of a sudden I felt profoundly dissatisfied with myself, with my own self-pitying grief.

"It is true," Capranis went on reflectively, "that Ettlinger had unusual qualities."

"He had one quality," I began slowly. "I've been thinking about it. If they believed that Paul takes after him in that respect—if they think Paul has it too—"

He turned his head sharply.

"Hush!"

A foot scrunched on rock outside. Footsteps approached. Somebody fumbled with the lock, then the door was opened. Some grey, predawn light filtered through.

John Smith came in looking as trim and alert as if he were arriving in Whitehall with his briefcase at 9:29 A.M. Only instead of the briefcase he carried Lady Lurgashall's .357 or its twin.

"You're to come now," he said to Capranis.

"Good morning, my dear John!" Capranis said genially. "What a refreshing reversal of roles you must find this. I sometimes felt that, as a secretary, you were slightly too perfect."

He stood up, leisurely.

"Be quick," Smith said. His voice held no expression.

"Where are you taking us?"

"The girl's not wanted yet. Only you."

I didn't like the sound of this. Capranis gave me a quick look, and shook his head. I noticed that, as Smith urged him through the door, he limped a little. He also looked the worse for our sleepless night: face all pouches and hollows, grey hair rumpled, what there was of it.

"What happens to Miss Marsh? She is in considerable pain from her swollen arm."

"I'll come back for her presently. Hurry up."

"I'm afraid I can't go very fast," I heard Capranis say, and then the door was slammed and locked again.

Without wasting a minute I scraped the final twist of dung-and-honey-smeared bandage from my joined wrists. They were pretty sore from all the work I had been putting in on them while we talked, but the bee sting was no worse. Which wasn't saying a lot. Some pain, but less throb.

Restacking the lobster pots I clambered up and stuck my head out of the window. Smith and Capranis were a far way off now; I could hear them scrunching down the rock path and a short remark from Smith, words inaudible.

Seen in growing daylight the drop under the hut window looked no more attractive than before, but in fact it wasn't sheer; there was a rock shelf at ground level, before the cliff proper began. And a wild fig extended a tangle of thin but wiry branches round the corner; if I could reach sideways and grab hold of them . . .

And there was no time like the present. No time to lose.

Without devoting any more thought to the drop underneath, I levered myself up onto the window sill, doubled into a foetus shape, and got my left leg through. Then there was an awkward moment when it looked as if my right leg wasn't going to follow. Then there was an even worse moment when my whole centre of gravity tipped outwards and it seemed likely that I'd take a short cut and go bouncing down the cliff to the anchored boat. There was need for hurry. A little more daylight and I'd be highly conspicuous from below.

Luckily my vertiginous lurch brought me within reach of the wild fig. I grabbed and got an armful of slender whippy branches, enough to bear my weight. Toe in crack between two stones in the shed wall—a few negligible scrapes on arms and knees, torn trouser leg—and I was on the rock shelf, squeezing past the main growth of the fig and out onto the dusty level ground in front of the hut, where a fresh morning breeze cooled my scrapes and bruises.

I couldn't help feeling fairly triumphant. True, I was a bit feverish and abraded, and I could have done with a cup of coffee, or even several, but at least I was an independent protagonist again. I bet Esther Summerson would not have been equal to that window; for one thing, all those bunches of keys would have got in the way.

My bet is, she wouldn't even have tried.

To add to my self-satisfaction, I saw something gleam in the dust, Lady Lurgashall's Stanley knife, which must have been dropped in the dark when she was cutting us loose from our mules. I pounced on it, and set off, running, but quietly, down the cliff path, which was sunk between banks. There were big spiny bushes of the purple-and-white flowered shrubs growing along the sides, so not much chance of being seen from below. And the lower I went, the louder the sound of the waterfall became, satisfactorily drowning any noise I might make.

At the bottom there was quite a thick little grove of olive and fig and wild plum. Ahead of me the path came to an end on a little gritty beach, so I scrambled sideways and worked my way in among the trees. Just as well, for Smith and Capranis and Lady Lurgashall were there, standing on a kind of natural rock quay. Smith was still pointing the gun at Capranis.

To my left a boat was anchored: *L'Aiglon,* I observed without surprise. And to my right, beyond the rock pier, was a rowing boat with small outboard; towards this—which did strike me as odd—Smith was urging Capranis with the gun. Surely he didn't intend to take Capranis out to the *Moskva Rika* in such a cockleshell? If the Russian ship was hove-to somewhere outside the territorial limit, it would take them a hell of a time to reach her; I'd have thought there must be half a dozen more efficient craft round the headland in Capranis's anchorage.

A much nastier possibility came into my mind and I knew why I'd had such an instinctive urge to hurry after them, not to waste any time.

"You go straight to the boat and send the message," Lady Lurgashall had said last night; presumably she and Smith had a transmitter on *L'Aiglon* and were in radio contact with the *Moskva Rika*. Suppose they had been told to stop playing about, to dispose of Capranis and sink his body in the sea? Now Paul was identified as Rudi, they'd have grounds for believing they had a double prize; not only Martin Ettlinger's son, but Capranis's adopted heir.

They moved a bit my way and I heard Lady Lurgashall say,

"I still think we ought to use him to interrogate the boy before you shoot him. We'd get results quickly that way."

"May I be spared from ever working with a woman again!" Smith said. "Our instructions are quite explicit. They don't want the boy to arrive in a completely frantic state."

"I always did say," remarked Capranis dispassionately, "that for sheer cold-blooded ruthlessness you have to go far to beat the British landed gentry. Torturing a father in order to extract heaven knows what reactions from his five-year-old son—"

"He's not your son!" barked Lady Lurgashall.

A piteous cry came from *L'Aiglon*.

"Papa!" Paul, shut in somewhere on board, had heard his father's voice.

"Now you've done it," muttered Smith.

"Oh, for goodness' sake, take him off out of sight and finish the business then," she said.

I judged it was time for me to act so, with a prayer to Athene, who was a handy markswoman in her day, I took aim and let fly with the rock I had been nursing. Thanks to my six devoted brothers it hit Smith just nicely on the side of the temple and toppled him off the end of the pier. The gun flew out of his hand into the water. It was all highly satisfactory. Lady Lurgashall ripped out a very unaristocratic word and made for *L'Aiglon,* presumably in search of another gun.

Capranis ran in pursuit, I nipped out of the bushes to intercept her. But she was a massive, powerful woman— breeding tells, all those generations of beef eaters, port drinkers, and hard riders—she laid me out on the beach with one clump of her powerful right. While I was picking myself up she swung on board. Capranis arrived, much slowed down by the fact that his hands were still strapped behind him.

"Here—half a second—you can't do much like that," I gulped, and pulled the Stanley knife out of my overall pocket.

"No cutlass, my dear Georgia?"

The blade was so sharp that I was terrified of slicing through an artery, I sawed through the last half-inch, he gave me a nod of thanks, and ran for the boat. But meanwhile Lady Lurgashall, maybe acting on orders from the *Moskva Rika,* had apparently decided to cut her losses and, without waiting to check on Smith, had cast off and started *L'Aiglon*'s engine. The boat drifted into mid-channel, Lady Lurgashall appeared in the cockpit with another gun and took careful aim at Capranis. The boat slewed round; she missed him, but not by much. A chip of rock flew up from the ground between us.

For the second time in ten minutes I was knocked flying; Capranis dealt me a clip on the ear that sent me to the ground.

"*Stay down!*" he bawled at me, and ran to the water's edge.

"Don't!" I jerked out, as one might to an approaching express train.

How could a middle-aged millionaire hope to stop a boat by swimming after it when there was a hostile member of the British upper classes shooting at him from it with very fair aim and definite intent to kill? But this seemed his wild intention.

Luckily at this juncture our affairs suddenly took a startling turn for the better. The stutter of *L'Aiglon*'s engine had prevented our hearing another outboard; a small bright-pink launch now came bustling round the headland and swept up to *L'Aiglon.* Two boys were visible on board, Mark steering, Dino perched in the bows, holding some kind of weapon. Lady Lurgashall, taking aim for the second time at Capranis, had her back turned and was unaware of their approach until the launch rammed *L'Aiglon,* throwing her shot wide. Dino leapt on board; next moment I saw Lady Lurgashall topple sideways into the cockpit and vanish from view.

"Gosh!" I muttered, scrambling to my feet, "He hasn't killed her, has he?"

"No, no," said Capranis impatiently. "Mark! Bring *L'Aiglon* in again—quick!"

Mark nodded, grabbed *L'Aiglon*'s trailing painter, and towed her back to the landing, where he efficiently made fast. Capranis leapt on board and, ignoring Lady Lurgashall slumped on the cockpit floor, unlocked the cabin door and went inside.

"What *is* that thing?" I asked, looking at the tubular weapon which Dino was handling with such assurance.

"Oh, it's a dope gun that Uncle Dion takes when he goes on safari," Mark said cheerfully. "It doesn't kill the lions and tigers, just stuns them so he can take pictures. People use them to catch animals for zoos. Patrice always keeps one on *Phaedra* in case of mutiny or pirates."

"I see." It seemed highly appropriate that Lady Lurgashall should have been knocked out by the equivalent of an elephant gun. "Well, you were a big help, Mark and Dino! Thanks."

"Parakaló," said Mark politely. Dino grinned like Little Dog Fo.

Capranis came out of the cabin, tightly holding a tearsodden Paul in one arm, leading Suzanne with the other. She, though white and big-eyed, had kept something of her usual buoyance.

"Gee, Miss Georgia, did you *see* what *happened?* Wasn't it *cool?*"

"No time to chatter," said Capranis briskly. "On shore, all, and up the cliff."

"But, Uncle Dion, wouldn't it be better to go back to Aghios Georgios by sea?"

"No it would not. Move!"

"Why not?" persisted Mark as we all hurried up the cliff path, Capranis still carrying Paul. I took one of Suzanne's hands, Mark took the other and pulled her along; Dino still carried his dope gun.

"Because there's a Russian ship somewhere out there," his uncle explained. "Presently they may wonder why *L'Aiglon* has stopped transmitting and come in to see. We don't want to meet them."

The boys accepted this, though Dino looked regretful.

"What gave you the idea of coming round here?" I asked the boys.

"We'd gone to the wine cellar—"

"What for?" said Capranis suspiciously.

"There's lots of old leather stored there. I wanted to make a sling."

"Well, well! A likely tale."

"And we found Great-aunt Ariadne tied up and Niko fast asleep, we couldn't wake him."

"Did you take my message to Mr. Suleiman?"

"Of course. He and some of his friends came to Aghios Georgios and Aunt Ariadne told them you'd said you were coming here looking for Paul and Suzanne who'd gone with Mr. Smith in the Land-Rover, but we were a bit puzzled because you hadn't taken the Alfa."

Mark was telling the story all back to front as children do; I couldn't make head or tail of it, but it seemed intelligible to Capranis.

"Where's Mr. Suleiman now?"

"I don't know, Uncle Dion. We wanted to go with him, but he said we were too young," Mark said injuredly. "And last Easter you promised you'd take Paul and Dino and me round here in the launch, and we were fed up that you'd forgotten your promise, so we asked Aunt Mixie to take us, and she wouldn't so we went to Captain Cruikshank to get the key of the boathouse."

"But he was ill in bed," I said.

"Yes. But he got up. He said he couldn't let us go by ourselves, so we helped him down. He asked us a lot of questions and then he started the boat for us."

"God above. Where is he now?"

"On the boat. When he heard about Ariadne being tied up and Mr. Smith coming round here with Paul, and you going after, he got worried and said Mr. Smith could be trying to kidnap Paul. *Was* he?" Mark asked.

"Yes," Capranis said shortly.

"But what about Captain Cruikshank?" I said. "We ought to go back for him!"

"Actually he's asleep," Mark told me. "He went like he does when he's drunk and then he went to sleep."

"We'll pick him up later," Capranis said.

We were still toiling up the valley, as fast as the varying

strengths of the party would allow. Which was not all that fast.

The sun had not yet risen, but, way up above us, at the head of the valley, the tops of the trees were beginning to turn pink. It was an extraordinary place—like some romantic Scottish glen, with crags of cliff thrusting through the vegetation here and there, and the stream in the middle dropping from one cascade to another. From time to time the path crossed it by means of log bridges. Some of the trees here were quite large and gave the place, along with the overhanging cliffs and splashing water, an oppressive, claustrophobic quality. Still, up above, the sun was rising. It would be better when we got up there, out of the deep shadow.

"Why's it called the Valley of Butterflies?" I panted, picking up Suzanne, who was beginning to flag.

"Why? Because of the butterflies, of course."

"Well, so? Where are they?"

"Can't you *see* them, Miss Georgia?" Mark gave me a teasing grin. "Look!"

"Look on the rocks. Look in the stream. Look in the trees," chanted Dino.

I looked. And realised that the things like dead leaves floating downstream, caught in backwaters, were in fact dead butterflies. They were a dark mole-brown colour, with cream-coloured diagonal markings. Once I had recognised them for butterflies I looked again, as Dino had suggested, at the rocks, at the branches, at the trunks of trees.

"*Heavens*. There must be hundreds of them. *Thousands* of them."

Wherever I looked, now that my eye was in, I saw butterflies perched thick as barnacles, thick as coral mites, covering every available surface. Thousands? There must be millions, billions of them.

"What a fantastic place. It's a bit spooky, isn't it?" I said, and shivered a little. My arm was throbbing again from carrying Suzanne, but in spite of it I felt chilled to the bone in this dark shadowy canyon.

"Don't they ever fly about?"

"Oh yes, at noon, when the sun shines down here. Or if you shout or whistle or bang a gong."

"Well don't let's. I'm not mad about butterflies. Though I suppose they are better than caterpillars. What it must be like here when they're at that stage!"

"Ah!" said Capranis, cocking his head. "Didn't I hear voices? That must be the others. Come along. Can you manage?"

He might well ask. We were going up a most awkward place. I certainly didn't remember coming down this way on muleback and could only conclude that the canny mules must have taken a longer way round. The path here met a sheer, twenty-foot cliff, down which the stream cast itself in smooth, shining sheets of water. Evidently some winter landslide had carried away part of the track, and to remedy this lack a kind of Jacob's ladder made from dead branches had been constructed diagonally across the fall by some ingenious local with a good head for heights; it looked decidedly rickety and insubstantial, but the boys ran up it like squirrels. There was one nasty little moment when a branch cracked under Dino's foot and, recovering himself, he grabbed at a root and dropped his dope gun, which fell into the waterfall; but such mishaps can occur at any time.

"Come on, Suzanne," I said, setting her down. "This is where we grip the rail and shut our eyes. I'll hold one of your hands, you hold one of mine."

She paled till her freckles stood out like giraffe spots and gripped my hand hard, but said gamely,

"Gosh, Miss Georgia, this is *great,*" and followed me from one log step to the next without faltering.

Capranis came behind us, still carrying Paul, who had fallen into the total sleep of emotional exhaustion.

"Are you okay?" I whispered, and he nodded.

"Are you?"

"We're just having a ball, aren't we, Suzanne?"

She grinned, and Capranis did too.

"Nearly there."

But when we reached the top of the ladder and came round a corner of rock onto a flat mossy arena beside a large clear pool and below yet another wall of cliff, his expression changed laughably.

Whoever he had expected to meet there, it plainly was not Professor Firgaard, solemnly dispensing rolls, grapes, tomatoes, and goat's cheese to twenty or so well-behaved children sitting round a white tablecloth.

"Now in Nature," the professor was saying, "we see no muddle, no muddle whatsoever. Everywhere is order, seemliness, pattern, law. You see this butterfly"—he held up a dead one, which had stuck to the fig he was eating— "you know that last year it was a caterpillar, then a cocoon, now presently it will lay eggs, then the beautiful cycle will start again."

"Papa's going to give me a beautiful cycle," Paul muttered, rousing a little from his sleep. "When I can swim— when I can swim six lengths. Papa! Are you there, Papa!"

"Yes, yes, chicken, don't worry."

"We know just what each butterfly will do next—" Professor Firgaard was going on, when suddenly the effect of Capranis's voice impinged on his consciousness and he swung round to gaze at us in disapproving amazement. His bleached-blond eyebrows shot up into his straw-coloured mop of hair: he looked like an outraged cassowary.

"What's all this?" Capranis said.

Paul struggled out of his arms. "It's the butterfly picnic, Papa. Don't you remember? We were supposed to walk here, really—"

"Each child carrying his own provisions and conducting a conversation about Lepidoptera along the way," Professor Firgaard said severely. "It is not at all fair if some come the easy way by boat. Nor do I think there will be food sufficient for six extra."

"Never mind about food, I suppose you wouldn't have any coffee?" I said hopefully. I'd have given the Hope diamond for a cup of instant, just then.

"Coffee, Miss Marsh, is undiluted poison. Accelerates the heart-beat, warps the judgment, pollutes the whole system, and a pot a day shortens your expectation of life by fifteen years."

"Oh, never mind. I'll suck a grape. I'd certainly hate to lose fifteen years."

"If you are thirsty I can give you a vitamin C tablet; that may be more quenching."

He pulled a tube from his pocket and offered it to me. At the same time a bit of paper fluttered to the ground. Suzanne picked it up. *"Mode d'Emploi.* Instructions for

Use," she read. *"Bombe insecticide.* Insecticide bomb. Gee, Professor Firgaard, was it you that filled the organ with gas? You nearly choked us! At first we thought the whole castle was on fire."

A somewhat glazed expression came over Firgaard's austere countenance; he looked embarrassed. But before he could speak a voice from above said, "Don't anybody move."

"Don't anybody move."

I looked up and saw Mixie Koolidge, elegantly clad in dark-brown, gold, and white hot pants, descending the winding path that led down from the top of the valley. She was carrying something that must surely, I thought, though I had never seen one at such close quarters before, be a submachine gun.

XII

"Let's keep this short and simple," Mixie said. "All we want is Paul and we're in a hurry, so just pass him over, will you?"

I looked at Capranis. He did not move, his face remained impassive, eyes half closed; he might have been listening to a routine boardroom report.

"Papa!" Paul shrank up against his father, who laid a protecting arm round him.

"Don't worry, my treasure. I am afraid however impatient your Albanian or Chinese friends are, they will just have to manage without him," Capranis said politely to Mixie. "I find I can't do without Paul."

She came farther down the path and addressed him angrily in a lower tone.

"Don't be so stupidly obstinate, Cappy! He's not your own child, why should you care what happens to him?"

"What does she mean, Papa? I am your son, aren't I, *aren't I?*"

Capranis stooped and picked Paul up again.

"Of course you are, treasure."

"Heck, when we're married I'll give you three or four just as good. Better!"

"I really do not think we are going to be married, my dear Mixie."

"But you as good as—"

"I doubt if I did. And I practically never marry women who point machine guns at me. This is not diplomatic of you, Mixie. What happened? Did your employers begin to think you were not attending strictly to business? Got worried about the *Moskva Rika* cruising down the coast, did they?"

"I must object very strongly to all this!" declared Professor Firgaard. "Here we come on a peaceful picnic to observe Nature—"

"And you are indeed observing Nature, my dear Professor," Capranis said genially. "And may it be a lesson to one and all. Miss Koolidge, sent here by the Chinese government to search for a particular child, became tempted from her duty by the hope of matrimony—"

"Shut up!" she said furiously. "Just hand over the child."

"No, Mixie."

She jerked the gun, but Paul clung tighter to Capranis and she could not get one without the other. Her face went ugly with rage, lips thinned, eyes narrowed, its oriental cast suddenly much more pronounced; if she couldn't have Capranis, I realised, she'd take great pleasure in blowing him to bits.

"Gionaj, go and get that boy."

A man came down the path from behind and passed her.

"Now listen," she said. "If you don't hand over the boy I shall start shooting the other kids. And your friend Miss Marsh too."

She turned the gun towards the group of children, who had all drawn together. I noticed Suzanne among them, pale as a tissue, her huge horrified eyes fixed incredulously on her mother.

"Miss Koolidge—I must register my view that this is a gross example of Muddle."

"Be quiet, you silly old goat. Hurry up, Gionaj!"

Paul then did an astonishing thing. As the man approached, as Mixie pointed her gun at the children, Paul scrambled down from his father's arms and ran to join the group.

"You're not to shoot them, you're not to shoot them!" he screamed. "They're my friends!"

Gionaj, a tall, burly dark man with the hawklike, aristocratic profile of some nomad warrior chief, hesitated and glanced at Mixie.

"Hurry up, you can get him now," she repeated.

But Gionaj didn't find it so easy. As he followed, Paul retreated, ducking and dodging among the other children, who moved to screen him. Gionaj made a grab for Paul, but Mark jumped in the way, while Paul skipped back. Gionaj grabbed again and got nothing but a handful of Suzanne's hair.

Fantastically, the pattern of the bullfight was repeating itself. Nimbly as a *corps de ballet* the children darted in and out, protecting Paul, impeding Gionaj, getting in his path and making him stumble.

"Ole!" shouted Mark irrepressibly.

They were beginning to enjoy themselves.

But I was looking at Mixie who, white, furious, her eyes slitted in concentration, had turned the gun towards Capranis again. He took a step towards her.

"Don't!" I whispered, as on the beach. My mouth was dry, acid with terror.

Capranis jumped sideways behind a rock as her gun began clattering; the white tablecloth was ripped to shreds and a rain of grapes and tomatoes spattered in my direction; Mixie, I saw with some relief, was not such an expert hand with a firearm as Lady Lurgashall. But anyone can find a target with a machine gun sooner or later.

Professor Firgaard suddenly fell into a towering rage. The discipline of thirty-five years flew asunder from his emotional spectrum.

"Harpy! Hyena-woman!" he shouted at Mixie. "How dare you violate our peace in this manner?"

He started towards Mixie but stopped with a groan clutching his arm, which had begun to spurt blood.

A strange thing happened then.

The whole green, brown, and mossy glen suddenly turned scarlet. A blinding, blood-coloured cloud surged up, out of nowhere it seemed; for a moment I thought I was hallucinated from bee-sting fever, but I could also *feel* the cloud, fluttering, tingling, titillating, buffeting against my face and arms and legs.

It was the butterflies. Disturbed from their motionless early-morning repose by the gunfire, they had unfolded vermilion-lined wings and taken flight. It was like being in a sandstorm—we were blinded, almost suffocated. One was afraid to move, one could see nothing, feel nothing but the dry turbulence of their wings.

I could hear cries of fright from some of the children. The gun's clatter had stopped abruptly. Then Mixie screamed. It was the high, mad scream of someone completely unstrung by terror: shriek after shriek in a rising series; the sound moved my way, jerkily, as if she were staggering to and fro; through the flickering cloud I caught a glimpse of her, insanely trying to beat off the tempest of wings; then she vanished from view. A moment later the screaming stopped as abruptly as the gunfire had.

I began groping my way towards the group of children and encountered Suzanne, who clung to me.

"Miss Georgia! What *happened?* What happened to Mommy?"

"Don't be scared, honey. It's only the butterflies. They'll settle in a minute if we keep quiet."

Through the red whirl I thought I saw Capranis, over by the waterfall, looking down; I couldn't see Mixie anywhere.

"Look, we must do something about Professor Firgaard, he's hurt."

Now I could dimly make out the shape of the professor sitting clutching his arm amid the ruins of his picnic.

"Find a stick, Suzanne—quick; oh, that's great, thanks."

Using the stick and some bits of tablecloth I twisted a hasty tourniquet round his arm.

"I am obliged to you, Miss Marsh," he grunted. He was pretty subdued.

The butterflies were gradually settling down, apart from an occasional scarlet fluttering swirl. I looked between them for the man Gionaj but could not see him.

"Where did that man go?" Suzanne asked anxiously, echoing my thought.

"When he saw that Mr. Capranis had got the machine gun he bolted back up the cliff," Mark said.

"What did Mr. Capranis do with the machine gun?"

There was no sign of it now.

"Dropped it in the pool." Mark's eyes sparkled. "Boy, I've never seen the butterflies go up so fast! Mostly, Professor Firgaard won't let us make too much noise for fear of scaring them."

"Scaring them? They scared *me*," Suzanne said. "And Mommy just can't *stand* butterflies or moths or anything with wings. Where is she, Miss Georgia? Where did she go?"

"I'm not certain. Maybe she ran up the path too."

But my guess was different. I made my way over to the waterfall and looked down. A gap had been smashed in the ladder of branches. At the foot of the fall, Mixie lay with her head doubled under her.

Capranis was scrambling down the side of the gully, through the bushes. I saw him reach Mixie's body and carefully move her. Then he looked up, saw me, and shook his head. Presently he came climbing back.

"Broke her neck," he reported briefly when he reached the top. He looked towards the band of children who huddled, subdued by shock, round their injured professor.

"We had better get that lot home."

"It's going to take some doing. I'm not sure that we can manage without help."

But at that moment help arrived. A group of fantastically dressed men came bounding down the path from the head of the valley. They wore turbans, they had sweeping black moustaches, they had big gold earrings, they wore picturesque rags in the most amazing colours, orange, viridian green, shocking pink, acid yellow.

"Gipsies, it's the gipsies!" Paul exclaimed, his face

lighting up. "Papa promised that gipsies would come and dance for us at the picnic."

"*There* you are, Mr. Suleiman!" said Mark. "Uncle Dion was wondering where you'd got to."

"Well you're a useless lot!" Capranis remarked with exasperation as the leading gipsy reached him and made a theatrical bow. "Much good you've been! We had to do the whole business ourselves; you might as well have stayed at the airstrip."

"It really wasn't our fault," apologised the gipsy, in highly ungipsylike and unexpectedly familiar accents. "We met a helicopter parked up above, so we stopped to interrogate the crew and tie them up. Then a man came pelting up from here, so we thought we'd better make a parcel of him too. We have them all up at the top; Ahmed is keeping an eye on them."

"Oh yes, you did right," Capranis said. "That will have been Mixie's Albanian friends. I'm obliged to you. Now, as you *have* come, you can do some more tidying up. There are three people in the valley below, two hurt, one dead; you can collect them and bring them round to Aghios Georgios. By sea would be easiest. Tie them up if they give trouble; there's a man and a woman."

"And Captain Cruikshank," I reminded him.

"Oh yes. A sick man on the motor launch. Bring them all. And some of you help us get all these children and the professor home."

The chief gipsy gave orders to three others, who climbed off down the gulley. Then he addressed the kids:

"Come on! Who wants a piggyback? You'll have to take it in turns because there are only eight of us."

"I thought you were going to dance," Dino objected.

"Oh, we'll do that back at the castle. Better give the butterflies a chance to go to sleep."

So, in a straggling procession we started off up the steep path, some children carried, others led. Everybody was rather silent until we reached the top of the valley. There, as we came out of the trees onto the bare hillside we walked into hot sun, and had a refreshing view of the sea. Ahead of us lay Aghios Georgios on its crag. Half a mile to the right, a helicopter perched glumly on the hillside with a dejected-looking crew sitting by it, guarded by three more gipsies.

The children, recovering their spirits, began to chatter like starlings.

"So we meet again, Miss Georgia, how delightful," said the head gipsy, swinging easily along beside me on his red espadrilles. He carried little Persephone. One end of his corsairlike moustache had come loose, which made it even more dashing.

"What happened? Didn't you care for the Jordan desert after all?"

"It was embarrassing! They didn't want us. They said they had more than enough planes already and too many mouths to feed. So there was nothing for it but to take ourselves back to Dendros. There we happened to run into your friend Mr. Capranis, who said he could do with a hired army. The police kindly agreed to postpone prosecuting us for borrowing the aircraft—I think the airline belongs to Mr. Capranis anyway—"

"Very likely—"

"Until we had flown him back here and helped him with his troubles. So now I hope I shall have sufficient time to convince you about the doctrines of Pythagoras."

Capranis drew alongside. He was carrying Paul. He looked battered but cheerful.

I said, "That was a brave thing you did down there, Paul, leaving your father and going to the other children."

"Thank you," Paul answered gravely. He had grown up a bit, I thought, in the course of this day. So had we all.

"Papa," Paul asked presently, "What did Suzanne's mother mean when she said that I wasn't your son?"

"She meant what wasn't true, Paul. You are my son, as much as you can possibly be. I'll explain the whole thing to you when you are older."

Firgaard would disapprove, I thought; he would feel that the bare truth should be unfolded at once. But Paul seemed satisfied with this reply. After a while he said that he wanted to get down and walk with Suzanne. Capranis followed him with a careful eye, saw him skip up to her, and, reassured, turned to me. I forestalled him.

"How long ago did you know about Mixie?"

"I'd had my doubts for some weeks. But the other day

when she went into Dendros she met a contact there, this man Gionaj. Plastiras had been having Gionaj followed for other reasons; he suspected him of dope running to Albania, using Dendros as a stopover; what they heard was him giving Mixie a rocket for not getting on with the job faster. They also gathered that there was another agent at Aghios Georgios keeping a tag and reporting on her."

"Do you know who that was?"

"Now I do," he said grimly. "It was Newhouse. He's up there at the helicopter. Didn't you notice?"

"So it might have been Newhouse who lured the bees to your bathroom? To stop Mixie getting led away on matrimonial red-herring trails?"

"Possibly," he said dryly.

"Would you have married her?"

"He who owns a black swan is the best judge of soap," Capranis replied with an enigmatic grin.

I heard Firgaard talking to Suzanne, who held his hand on one side, Paul's on the other.

"I am afraid your mother is dead," he said, evidently answering her question. "She must have thought—wrongly—that the butterflies would do her some harm. She panicked and fell and broke her neck."

"Oh, well," Suzanne said. She bit her lip and blinked fiercely. "I guess she didn't really love me much at all; see, she was about to shoot me along with the others. And she used to get into awful, awful tempers sometimes."

"She was in a muddle," Firgaard said with more gentleness than usual.

"*I'll* say she was, Professor! Why, she even shot *you!*"

"So don't grieve too much, Suzanne. Her soul structure was not strong enough. I'm sure Mr. Capranis will look after you."

"Maybe," Suzanne said rather dubiously. "I'd rather Miss Georgia did. I sure hope she stays at the castle." Then, catching sight of Gregorious, she dragged Paul along to him, crying, "Gee, Greg! Wait till we tell you about how Lady Lurgashall kidnapped us. It was real, real cool, wasn't it, Paulie!"

She'll be all right, I thought. She'll get over it. Strong soul structure.

Firgaard turned to me with a cough of contrition.

"I feel I must apologise for the incident in the organ, Miss Marsh. It would not have done you any great harm, but I regret it. I was overtaken by an impulse of the Muddle Principle; I wished to discourage you, to make you decide to leave Aghios Georghios, but I should not have done it. I feel that now, strongly."

"Discourage me? You didn't think I'd been sufficiently discouraged by falling down the oubliette and being baked in the oven?"

"Na? Baked in the oven?" He was puzzled. His Scandinavian accent intensified.

"Forget it; it was nothing. In fact I could do with some of that insecticidal smoke right now." The local midges had discovered my honey-soaked skin and concluded that I was a kind of walking delicatessen.

"And then I lost my temper terribly just now," Firgaard lamented. "Indeed, I have succumbed to muddle over and over."

"Haven't we all? Between you and me, all the time I've been at Aghios Georgios I've never been *out* of a muddle."

I was delighted that the funny old bird seemed willing to bury the hatchet; maybe the children's bullfight act had also shown him that a little muddle can sometimes be a useful element.

It was a long, slow trail over the scrubby hillside which was baking hot, even at that early hour. But when we were halfway home, Sandstrom and Phyllora rolled up in a minibus. Apparently Yussuf had reached Aghios Georgios ahead of us, in the launch.

The whole party were packed into the bus like pilchards and Sandstrom zipped us with nonchalant skill along the bumpy track, across the olive-silvered plain, and through the streets of Imandra, where, as we waited for a donkey to make up its mind at an intersection, old Mrs. Panas waved to me and called, "Is it true that you were abducted by Albanians? Mind you come home this evening and tell us all about it!"

We entered an electronic door in the hillside and were decanted into a huge vault, where about twenty cars stood. A lift took us up to the Canaletto-hung main hall.

"Bed for some, breakfast for others," Phyllora said.

Capranis hurried off to phone the police. He was on the telephone for about half an hour; soon after, they arrived in force to take charge of the helicopter and its crew. But the *Moskva Rika,* scenting trouble, had long ago steamed out of territorial waters and was, they told us, heading home to the Black Sea.

I went to Phyllora's room to wash off the honey and put some of her embrocations on my wounds; then, seeing from the window that all the children were gathered under the fig tree, I went down to join them. They were telling Phyllora and Poppy their adventures. Ali and his gipsies were there too.

Suzanne ran to me and hugged me.

"Hi, Miss Georgia! You all okay now? Gee, listen, Mr. Capranis says Mr. Suleiman and the other gipsies can stay on here and be teachers if they like, isn't that *cool?*"

"Stunning," I said. "What a versatile lot you are. Hi-jackers one day, teachers the next—"

"Well, in fact we really *are* teachers," Ali explained modestly. "We got, you know, carried away by the urge to hijack a plane—"

"I told them they could stay so long as they would promise not to engage in any further political activities," Capranis said, strolling up, "since we are now rather short of staff. And it might be useful to have some teachers who are also trained guerrillas—"

"Just wait till Firgaard gets to work on you," I warned Ali. "He can out-hypotenuse Pythagoras any day."

"Breakfast is waiting for you in the study," Capranis told me.

Breakfast turned out to be orange juice and champagne.

"You may have coffee too if you wish."

"No, no! Firgaard says it shortens one's life by fifteen years. Just now I feel so pleased to be alive at all that I'm prepared to settle for the maximum sentence. So many people have tried to do me in during the last few days that I've given up even trying to get them sorted."

Capranis beamed.

"Mike Plastiras asks to be remembered to you and thanks you for saving his life. He is making a good recovery. I told him that you had saved *my* life, also, several times, and he sends you his felicitations."

"Parakaló! Think nothing of it. Who did lambast Plastiras in the cellar?"

"It was Newhouse, who had gone down to replace the safety net which Mixie had removed. He wanted you alive; she, for some reason, wanted you dead."

"The dear creature. But tell me, is Paul safe now? Have all the people who were after him been rounded up?"

"Yes," he said, more soberly. "And it seems most improbable that anyone will try again, now all is exposed. Though of course the family of someone in my position must always be on their guard. That is why I hesitate—"

"*Why* were they all after him? The East Germans? The *Chinese?* Surely not just as a swap for Lady Lurgashall's boring old brother? The Chinese can't have wanted *him?*"

"No, that was entirely a pretext. They wanted Paul for genetic reasons."

"I wondered if that was it," I said slowly. "It only occurred to me last night. It was because of Martin's memory, wasn't it?"

"Yes, he was a psychological phenomenon, a mnemonist."

"Total recall. He hated it. He could never forget anything. Of course it was useful for his work. But in other ways, dreadful. But were they all hoping that Paul had it too? They *couldn't,* surely, think that he would remember anything about his father's work? After all he was only two when Martin died."

"Who knows what they hoped? Perhaps, by digging everything possible out of his mind, stripping out every seed of memory, they thought to find some clue to the plan on which his father was working. Perhaps they merely wished to experiment on Paul—to lay the foundation for a race of totally retentive memories."

I shivered. "Anyway, they were wrong, weren't they—about Paul? His memory is no better than anyone else's. Thank goodness."

"Thank goodness," Capranis agreed seriously. "He remembers nothing, nothing at all, of that bad time."

"You'd think Mixie would have realised," I said.

"She was not very bright. And she didn't know which child was Martin's."

"How did she find out, incidentally? What brought her along the valley?"

"The boys told her—remember? Also she and New-house were monitoring the signals that Smith was sending and receiving from the *Moskva Rika.*"

"You'd think she'd have noticed that no child here had a special memory, and told her bosses that it wasn't worth the search. Oh, but of course she had her own reasons for wanting to stay on here."

"Yes." Capranis looked demure. "Miss Georgia—"

"What about Suzanne? Has she relations in the U.S. or shall you keep her?"

"Mixie was Chinese. I think I shall keep her. You are right, I believe she has a good *fonds,* that child, and Paul certainly seems fond of her. Miss Georgia—"

"What about Captain Cruikshank? Is he all right?"

He became grave. "No. I am sorry. Well, for his sake I am glad, because his life was no life at all, but I am sorry if this gives you pain. He must have had another heart attack on the boat. He was dead when Yussuf found him."

Capranis turned and called through the french window to the group under the fig tree. "Mark!"

Mark came bounding up and gave me his teasing, friendly grin.

"Herete, Miss Georgia. How are you, how is your arm? Uncle Dion says you are very good at throwing stones!"

"Don't let me catch you coaching Mark, that's all," said his uncle. "Mark, you said that Captain Cruikshank gave you a message for Miss Georgia."

"I think it was for you, Miss Georgia," Mark said slowly and carefully. "He was getting a bit queer and muddly in the boat; we thought he was drunk. He talked about you, saying you had a good heart, not like your cousin. Then he said something about a pontius pilot; we thought that meant him, lying in the boat, telling us how to steer. Then he said, 'Give her my love.' I said, 'Who, Georgia?' and he said, 'Georgia. Esther Summerson. Tell her Patrice sends love to Esther Summerson.' Is that right? Do you know what he meant?"

"Yes. Thank you, Mark," I said. He grinned at me again and raced back to the others. The gipsies were beginning to dance.

Capranis kindly passed me a handkerchief and filled my champagne glass.

"Now—Miss Georgia," he said, "for the last ten minutes I have been trying to say something and you have kept interrupting and it is making me nervous, so will you please listen?"

"Yes, all right. Oh, but what about *L'Aiglon?* Who took her round to the anchorage? And what happened to Sweden's body? And *who killed Sweden?*"

He sighed. "Patrice killed her—in the hope of preventing you coming here and identifying Martin's son."

"He *did?* But I thought he said he didn't!"

"If so he lied to you—doubtless he wished to retain your goodwill. After killing her, he took the boat out to sea and sank her body, weighted with the anchor. Then he left the boat in the commercial harbour, in the boatshed of a friend of his who was away cruising. Later he brought her round to the anchorage, intending to scuttle her, but was taken ill and had to delay the job. He told me all this when he was in the sick bay after his heart attack. Does that satisfy you?"

"I'll have to think about it and work out how often you have been lying to me. What about Mixie? Had you really promised to marry her?"

He looked scandalised.

"Good heavens, no! A brief passage—purely for the sake of discovering her purpose here—"

"I know, I know. Just like Patrice and Sweden. What a businesslike lot you are round here. So you didn't offer her your heart, your mango, and your prayer mat?"

"By no means. *Now* are you content?"

"I daresay I'll think of some more questions in a minute."

"Well, please contain them. Miss Georgia! In the past my manner of life may not always have been such—been such as to—"

"Did your wife really run away with the prime minister of England?"

"Who has been filling you up with such tales?" he said crossly. "No, it was the chairman of I. G. Farbenindustrie. She did very well for herself. I divorced her fifteen years ago. *Will you please listen?* You keep chattering idly while

I am trying to say something important. I know our habits of life are rather dissimilar—and there is an age gap, but what is sixteen years? A mere grape pip—somehow, in spite of these things, I do not know how it has come about, perhaps it is because we have saved each other from death so many times in the last few days—"

"*I've* saved you more than you have saved me—"

"Be quiet! Somehow I have acquired a strong feeling for you, my dear Georgia, and wish to ask you if you will be my wife. I am sure—I hope, rather—that you will want to help me with these children. So, what do you say? Do, please consent to this request!"

Well, what else could I do?

Besides, I was fond of the wicked little fellow.

So I said yes.